About Roland Cheek
and *Lincoln County Crucible*

Great fiction doesn't merely parallel past events but meshes with them so inseparably that readers must pinch themselves as reminders that characters used weren't always *real.* Or were they? Solid historical novels weave real figures from the past into scenes, adding authenticity and style to the page. There's only one way authenticity can be consistently created and that is through meticulous research and recording. It also helps, when writing about the West, to be cut from the same fabric—one that, in my case, allowed me to roam wild and free for upwards of 35,000 horseback miles throughout the Rocky Mountain West.

The truth is, I've "been there and done that" when I write about the West that was—and still is—in the kinds of places I call home. Maybe my heroes are not the giants created by others, but they're *authentic.* They rise to occasions not necessarily because they're smarter or braver, but because there's no one else to do it. They're not stronger or more fleet of foot or maybe not as fast on the draw as the gunslinger on the next bookshelf. But when push comes to shove, my books are peopled by folks you can trust to do— if not the *right* thing—the thing they think they'd ought to do at that time and in that place. If the thing they must do means facing up to a kill-crazed gun-slick, or outsmarting a mob, or falling in love, or trying over and over again to ride the meanest bronc in the corral, or even dying with grace and verve ... well, they do it.

To be perfectly honest, my characters and the places they inhabit and the things they accomplish aren't my creations at all. Sure, I've placed them in the story and they do things I tell them to do. But Somebody Upstairs that's bigger and better actually created Western people, Western times, and Western action.

I'm just proud to be their stenographer.

Other Books by Roland Cheek

(non-fiction)

Learning to Talk Bear

Phantom Ghost of Harriet Lou

Dance on the Wild Side

My Best Work is Done at the Office

Chocolate Legs

Montana's Bob Marshall Wilderness

(fiction)

Echoes of Vengeance

Bloody Merchants' War

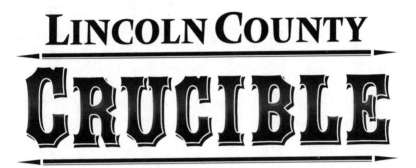

LINCOLN COUNTY CRUCIBLE

LINCOLN COUNTY
CRUCIBLE

ROLAND CHEEK

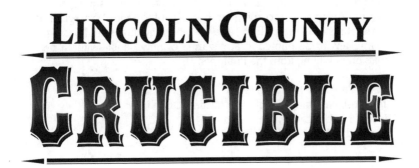

a Skyline Publishing Book

Cover design by Laura Donavan
Text designed and formatted by Michael Dougherty
Edited by Tom Lawrence
Copy edited by Jennifer Williams

Publisher's Cataloging in Publication

Cheek, Roland.
    Lincoln county crucible / Roland Cheek: author ; Tom
Lawrence, Jennifer Williams: editors. — 1st ed.
    p. cm. — (Valediction for revenge ; 3)
    ISBN: 0-918981-10-7

      1. Frontier and pioneer life—West (U.S.)—Fiction.
    2. Ranchers—West (U.S.) 3. Farmers—West (U.S.)
    4. Lincoln County (N.M.)—Fiction. 5. Western stories.
    I. Title.

    2003

ISBN: 0-918981-10-7
LCCN: 2003090801

Published by   Skyline Publishing
                P.O. Box 1118
                Columbia Falls, Montana 59912

Printed in Canada

Dedication

To Mark, who saw the muse in a storyteller
years before I first glimpsed it myself.

⇒ PROLOGUE ⇐

New Mexico's Lincoln County War was one of the bloodiest chapters in western history; a power struggle between two factions contending for economic control of southeastern New Mexico. The war's foundations were laid during a time of ruthless exploitation of Anglo and Mexican/American farmers, small ranchers, and business people by Lincoln County's dominant merchant enterprise, the J.J. Dolan & Company, commonly known as Dolan-Riley.

Through a combination of adroit business dealings, political control of Lincoln County government, and their association with a close-knit cadre of territorial officials and military officers—known as "the Santa Fe Ring" (who exercised real power in New Mexico Territory), Dolan-Riley held the southeastern region's people in desperate servitude. Their corrupt sore of exploitation festered for several years until, at last, a leadership triumvirate rose to challenge Dolan-Riley's economic collar.

The triumvirate was an unlikely combination: John Tunstall, rancher and son of a wealthy English merchant, conceived the idea of directly confronting Dolan-Riley with an honest competitive merchant enterprise; Alexander McSween, an articulate Lincoln attorney who recognized Dolan-Riley's graft, but sought to replace it with a trading monopoly under his own control; John Chisum, a wealthy Pecos cattleman who saw an opportunity to encourage others to fight an exhaustive war with Dolan-Riley, then pick up the monopoly's rich military and Indian reservation beef contracts for himself.

When its doors opened in mid-1877, J.H. Tunstall & Company proved effectively competitive. Tunstall's success provided encouragement for Chisum's ranching enterprise to raise the pressure ante through low bid rates for government beef contracts. Dolan-Riley struck back against Chisum's and Tunstall's herds, utilizing outlaws and thieves operating under the pseudo-protection of the ring's political influence.

Then John Tunstall was brutally murdered by a sheriff's posse composed of known outlaws and Dolan-Riley partisans acting without warrants. The murder outraged the ordinary people of Lincoln County and a band of hard and ruthless men formed for revenge.

Leadership of the reform group passed to Alexander McSween. Lawlessness, gunfights, and pillage became the order of the day, culminating in a five-day siege and gun battle where Alexander McSween and four of his partisans were shot down and the McSween home destroyed.

Other McSween defenders made a daring escape from the burning home, shooting their way to freedom, led by a young daredevil named William Bonney, who was rising to notoriety as "Billy the Kid."

A crucial factor in the epic mid-July battle in Lincoln was the intervention by United States Army troops from nearby Fort Stanton on behalf of Dolan-Riley.

With destruction of their opposition, local law enforcement in their hands, support from federal troops, and high-level territorial influence, Dolan-Riley should have reigned supreme. However, the company was physically and financially hemorrhaging at the same time the last vestiges of law and order disappeared from southeastern New Mexico. No courts functioned, no law enforcement was recognized or accepted, respect for the U.S. Army was absent. A state of anarchy existed.

Into the void crept the worst forms of human life to prey upon the innocent. From throughout New Mexico, they congregated; from Arizona Territory and Indian Territory; from Colorado and Mexico, but especially from Texas they came. With no restraining authority, they ran roughshod throughout southeastern New Mexico, pillaging and raping and murdering as they moved.

Thus begins *Lincoln County Crucible*.

CHAPTER ONE

When Jethro Spring's eyes fluttered open, the Indian was sitting cross-legged by the long-dead campfire, apparently dozing. From the distance of fifty feet, he could make out the raised welts of long-ago knife and bullet scars peeking from beneath folded arms and resting chin. Even the jagged white line on one cheek caught the early morning sun. The Indian was, Jethro thought, the meanest-looking human on earth.

Jethro had known he could not remain long among these high mountains without being discovered by the Mescaleros. So the gray-eyed man made a game of it, moving by night, carefully wiping out tracks, using seldom-traveled trails, building a fire only when necessary. Each time he'd set up his meager camp in a defensible place, then retreat to sleep in a commanding niche where he could survey the camp and its approaches. This time, he'd even taken time to place tiny warning devices upon those approaches— trip ropes, a bent sapling, a balanced rock or pebble. Apparently none had worked.

Jethro glanced at his two peacefully grazing horses, content on their picket ropes. He slowly swung his head to gaze up at the cloudless sky and saw it would be another scorcher of a day, even in these high forested mountains. Sunlight kissed the highest Sacramentos to the west. It also kissed his perch and the slumbering Apache.

As if on cue, the Indian also raised his head and gazed at the sunlit peaks. Then he swiveled it to stare at the sprawled figure on the ledge above.

"Welcome, Malvado," Jethro called. "Welcome to my camp."

The Indian said nothing, continuing to sit with arms folded and legs crossed, transfixing the visitor to the Mescalero reservation with unblinking black eyes. He was growing long in the tooth, this Indian; his once raven hair was salt-and-pepper flecked and stagged unevenly to hang tangled to his cheekbones. The Apache wore nothing but a breechclout, a sash, leggings, and moccasins. A butcherknife and a revolver were thrust into the sash, and a glistening, newly oiled Winchester lay across his knees.

The gray-eyed man sat up, stretched, then scrambled down from his perch to take a seat by his visitor. "What can I do for you, Malvado?"

"I have once again come to talk to the man-called-the-season-of-the-hunger-moon."

Jethro smiled. "The man called Winter would look upon it as an honor if Malvado would eat with him."

"Malvado waits."

Later, with both men sated via venison steaks, bannack bread, and innumerable cups of coffee, Jethro leaned back against his saddle to wait for Malvado to speak. But the Apache patted his stomach and merely grunted unintelligibly in his native language, then curled into a ball and fell asleep. There was nothing for Jethro Spring to do except wait.

Malvado awoke at mid-morning and he was again hungry. After washing down more steaks with another pot of coffee, the Indian said, "The young-one-who-shoots-as-a-striking-snake would speak with you."

Billy? Jethro wondered. "Do you mean Billy the Kid?"

Malvado stared without replying.

"Does he have blue eyes?"

Malvado said, "And they are as cold as the snow that lays through the seasons."

"Did he say why he would speak with me, Malvado?"

"Because he and the-man-called-the-season-of-the-hunger moon are old friends."

"That is true, Malvado," Jethro said. "But that is no reason for him to wish to speak with me."

"It is enough for Malvado to leave his wickiup and search for you," he held up eight fingers, "for this many days. It is enough that I asked other warriors to search for the-man-called-the-season-of-the-hunger-moon for he moves like a shadow through our land."

Jethro dipped his head at Malvado's compliment. But he said, "Tell Billy the Kid that Winter has nothing left to say to him. Whatever friendship we had is now gone. Tell him Winter is no longer in Lincoln County, or the Rio Ruidoso, or the Sacramento Mountains. Tell him I have no interest in either the people of this territory, or what is in it. Tell him to find other friends who care about him and the things he does."

When he finished, the Apache said, "It will be done." Then he was gone.

They found Jethro's camp at Elk Springs, on a headwater fork of the Rio Penasco. The youth, Billy Bonney, rode into the firelight accompanied by Ruidoso farmer Doc Scurlock and Malvado, the Apache. The men reined their horses to a halt and Billy, blinking against the campfire's flickering light, called to Jethro, the man they knew as Jack Winter: "All right, Jack, we rode in fair and square. You know who we are and you know we're showing our hands. You got us covered, but you know well enough you needn't bother."

Jethro materialized out of the darkness. "Where's Bowdre?" he asked.

"We left him behind. We know you and him rub each other."

"Being as you're here, you may as well step down and sit. I'll see if I can rustle up something to eat. Not for you two, of course. But I know Malvado is hungry."

The trio dismounted while Jethro Spring busied himself with venison chops and coffee. After their saddles were stripped and their mounts staked out to graze, Bonney, Scurlock, and Malvado returned to the fire. Jethro shook hands with Scurlock and Bonney, then handed a half-cooked steak and a cup of sugar-sweetened coffee to the Apache.

"Miz Susan asked about you, Jack," Bonney said as he took a plate and stabbed a steak with his belt knife. "We heard you was up here some place and I promised her I'd look you up."

Jethro busied himself with the cooking, pointedly turning his back.

"Kinney and Andy Boyle both threatened her life, Jack. She says, by God, she's not leaving until she brings her husband's murderers to justice."

Jethro handed a plate to Scurlock, then held the coffee pot, pouring for the farmer and Bonney.

"She's got grit, Jack," Bonney continued. "She's ever' bit as game now as she was when they burned her house in Lincoln. But she can't fight the bastards without help. French and Bowdre was in town a week ago to look in on her. Doc and me came from there just a couple of nights ago. She's been asking about you right reg'lar."

Jethro forked up another steak for Malvado, then smiled at the ruddy-faced farmer he knew was fearless and capable. "Doc," he said, "seems like every time something is going on, you're in on it. How do you ever get any farming done?"

Scurlock grinned—his two front teeth were missing—

and pointed at his mouth with his knife point. Then he swallowed, swallowed again, and said, "Don't get near enough farmin' time, that's for shore. But whenever I jumped in this thing to whup Dolan's outfit, I planned to stay 'til the job's done."

Scurlock's words brought a blush to Jethro Spring's dark face, but the farmer was too busy with his knife and steak to notice. Scurlock continued, "It's like the Englishman allus said: 'In for a penny, in for a pound.' But hell, you remember that, Jack; you and Billy both worked for him."

Jethro's mouth pinched at mention of Tunstall. "So you two are here to talk me into getting back into the fight?"

"Could be," Bonney said.

"It's over, Billy."

"Who said it's over?"

"McSween is dead. So is Tunstall. Chisum won't help. The army and the law both belong to Dolan's outfit. He's got the judges in his hind pocket and the governor making new laws for him. Don't tell me it's not over."

Bonney spread his hands, plate in one, knife in the other. "What do we have to lose from here on out? The old bunch is still pretty much together. We've got some good fighting men. And Dolan is cutting his outfit down now that he thinks he don't need 'em no more."

"For one thing," Jethro replied, "a whole bunch of good men can still lose their lives. So far, besides Tunstall and McSween, we've lost Brewer, McNab, Morris, Romera, Zamora, and Salazar. How many more will it be before enough is enough?"

"Salazar ain't dead," Bonney said. "They got him when he came out of the house with McSween, but he didn't die."

Jethro blinked. "Eugenio's all right?"

Scurlock nodded, "He crawled away while the bastards celebrated getting McSween. It's the truth that he's on the mend."

Jethro spat into the fire. "What the hell does that change? It won't bring John Tunstall or Dick Brewer back.

And both of them were among the world's finest."

"McSween, too," Bonney muttered.

Jethro shook his head, "McSween wasn't half the man either Tunstall or Brewer was."

"Tunstall wasn't no fighting man either," Billy said, mistaking Jethro's meaning.

Another steak went to Malvado, then Bonney said, "We need you, pard."

Jethro sighed and sprawled upon the ground, leaning his head against his saddle. "I'm happy the way I am. I eat when I want, sleep when I want, ride when I want, where I want. I don't sleep with one eye open and a gun in my hand. Why should I go back?"

"We need you, pard," Bonney repeated.

Jethro tucked his hands behind his head and stared into the night sky. "You know, people's been saying that ever since I came to this country a year ago. Chisum, McSween, Dolan, Riley, Salazar. They all said I was needed. Now you say it. Dick Brewer and John Tunstall were the only two who didn't say they just had to have me on their side. And they didn't drool for want of my gun." He stopped as suddenly as he'd begun; the fire popped in the stillness. At last, he continued, "And you know what? They were the only two I really wanted to side with."

Doc Scurlock seemed mesmerized by the fire. He said, "Jack, you wonderin' why we need you?"

"Nope. I really don't give a good goddamn. You see, whether I'm needed or not makes no difference to whether I'll go or won't."

"Don't forget Sue McSween," Bonney said. "I don't see how a body could walk away and leave her holding the sack."

Jethro's grim smile never reached his gray eyes. He pushed to his feet. "I'm going to bed, boys. We'll finish this in the morning, while reason shines on it."

Jethro Spring was first up. It was shortly after daylight when he carried a bucket of water from where water bubbled from the ground. The Apache lay near the still-smoldering fire, but Doc Scurlock and Billy the Kid had, with Jethro's same wary cunning, slept away from the camp. Bonney and Scurlock came in a few moments later and all three visitors watched Jethro as he worked to prepare breakfast.

At last, Scurlock said, "Billy, you reckon we'd ought to shift the picket pins?"

Jethro straightened from his pots and watched them head for the horses. He glanced at the Indian, who also watched the others move horses. "Why are you in this, Malvado? What do you hope to gain by bringing Billy and Doc to me?"

"What can a Mescalero do these days?" the Apache asked. "There are always men who steal from other men. These, my people can still fight. But we cannot fight the big store who cheats us of our allotments; who steals from us with the help of our agent and of the army. Should not Malvado help any who fight the big store?"

Jethro returned to his chore.

Malvado continued speaking as if the listener still faced him: "The-man-called-the-season-of-the-hunger-moon is but half-Indian and if he wishes, he can leave to go to the setting sun, or to the land of the big water. But that is a thing the Mescalero cannot do. We are told we must stay on our reservation where our old people sicken and die because they give their food to hungry children. There are not enough of us to fight the soldiers who are so many they are like stars in the sky. Our young men even now steal away to join Victorio, or the Chiricahua called Geronimo who, it is said, fights the Mejicanos. But they leave our women and children and our weak. Those of us left must decide. Will we fight and die? Will we stay and watch our people hunger and become begging dogs? Or will we try to do as I do, by helping any who may in turn help the Mescalero?"

Jethro thought of the Apache's scarred torso, cruel face,

and clenched fists. "You are a strong and brave man, Malvado," he said. "You have more courage than those who steal away to fight because you stay to help your people."

Bonney and Scurlock returned from the meadow. After breakfast the men sprawled against their saddles. Bonney asked, "Have you give it any more thought, Jack, about coming back with us?"

"No. You don't need me and neither does Susan McSween."

"The way I see it, we do," Scurlock said. "Billy and me, we talked on it some after you bedded down. You been thinking right most-near all along. Trouble is, them who made the final choices wasn't listenin'. Hell, we know you didn't think we shoulda come back to Lincoln to fight it out, and you was right. We know you was the one who figured the army would step in and back Dolan."

"Don't forget the fight at South Springs, too," Bonney chimed in. "You got us out of that one when Chisum would've throwed us to the wolves."

"You're the best leader we got, boy," Scurlock said, then grinned and added, "Truth tell, we ain't got nobody else."

Bonney said, "Damn it, Jack, you're respected by most everybody. And the Mexicans—they'll answer your call."

"They did," Jethro said. "That's when I led them into that trap at Lincoln, where Zamora, Romero, and Salazar got …"

"Salazar's alive."

The men fell silent, each lost in his own thoughts. Jethro broke the silence. "Besides, Dolan-Riley's sheriff probably has warrants out for my arrest."

Bonney hooted. "Hell, Peppin's got warrants for everybody's arrest. Yeah, including yours. But he ain't got guts enough to serve none of 'em. Your warrants are minor, Jack, and they'll be dismissed as soon as the court gets out a grand jury again. What you got? Assault against two sergeants at Fort Stanton when you got away from them for trying to arrest you without no charge; the other is resisting arrest from that Seven Rivers mob at Chisum's. Hell, you're as clear as a man could be and still be on Dolan's shit list."

"Billy's right, Jack," Scurlock said. "Dolan's bunch is pretty well broke up now that they're back on top. Peppin hasn't got enough backing to arrest anybody that don't want arrested. If Billy and me can come and go with murder warrants over our heads, you sure as hell won't have no trouble in Lincoln town."

"Especially as scared as them bastards are of you," Bonney added.

The group fell silent again. Jethro wondered if a more disparate and desperate group could gather. *Malvado means evil or wicked in Spanish*, he thought. *I don't know much about his early days, but I'd bet a lot of money he's one tough, mean, sonofabitch if he's backed into a corner. He might be along toward the tail of his prime, but that only means he can use his head now, too.*

And Billy. He looks as innocent as a new babe, but he may well be the deadliest one here. He's got his whole life ahead of him, but he's off to a bad start. He kills too easy. This Lincoln County thing was a poor place for a young man to begin. John Tunstall's was an unlucky place for Billy to work, and to get to like and trust the owner.

Me, too, for that matter. Hell, I didn't want into this, but when they killed John, one of the finest, most honest men I ever knew, I ...

"Word is out Frank Wheeler has got some of the stock belonging to Tunstall's estate, down at San Nicholas Spring," Billy said. "Me'n the boys are gathering to go after 'em. We'd be obliged if you'd join up."

"We'd like to have you *head* us up, Jack," Doc Scurlock corrected.

Scurlock's an earnest man, Jethro thought. *Tough as whang leather and mostly honest, with a wife and kids back on his ranch. He's fighting for his home and family. What do I have in this fight, anyway? How do I tell him he's got more in it than me? Do I tell him I'm a half-breed drifter with a fed-*

eral murder warrant hanging over my head? Do I tell him I killed an army major up in Dakota Territory? Never mind that the sonofabitch killed my ma and pa. What's it been— seven years? But it's still a damned good reason for me to drift away from here before somebody adds my numbers.

"We just don't think the bastards ought to get away with stealing John's life and then stealing his ranch blind before the estate's settled," Scurlock said.

If they hadn't shot Tunstall down like a dirty cur, I'd be gone by now. He was a good man, John Tunstall. A friend. I stuck around because of that. And I got in deeper and deeper with people I couldn't believe in. Yeah, John, it was because of you. And because of another man's wife. Damn you to hell, Susan McSween!

"Miz Susan is trying real hard to hold both her husband's and Tunstall's estate together 'til settle-up time. We can't run out on her, Jack. Not when she needs all the help she can get."

You stupid bastards! Jethro thought. *How can I get across to you that I believe Susan McSween drove her husband's wild plan to overthrow Dolan-Riley in an all-out gun battle? How can I tell you, Billy, that I think she led us all into that trap in Lincoln in a crazy gamble that she planned right from the beginning? How can I tell ...*

"What about Sue, Jack?" Billy asked. "I mean, me'n the boys ain't so blind that we don't know you two looked at each other with calf-eyes."

Jethro's head flipped around and he glared at Billy.

The Kid held out a hand. "Now hold on, Jack. Don't get riled. I know damn well there wasn't nothin' to it and so did her husband. All's I'm saying, though, is that you do think an awful lot of her as a woman. And no wonder, the spunk she's got. But now she's alone and in trouble. If I was you, I wouldn't be squatting on some way-off mountain peak talkin' to gophers or rock chucks. Hell no, I'd be cozyin' up, offering to help any way I could."

Billy, Billy. How can I love a woman I suspect deliberately led her husband to his death, knowing I was there waiting in the wings if he failed? She sent me away on a wild goose chase before that last battle, don't you see? She knew it was a senseless ride because she knew Chisum would never help. She sent me away to keep me safe for her future plans. Yet she was perfectly willing to throw your life and others away.

"She told us you might be peeved because you missed out on the Lincoln fight," Scurlock said. "She figured you thought everybody made you out as a coward because of it."

Jethro swung his head to glare at the farmer.

"Well, it ain't so. Them as counts knows you was riding for help. Besides, the rest of us left the boys in McSween's house a-hangin' when the army showed and set their cannon lookin' down our throats. We ran off, sure enough. And nobody holds us at fault because of it."

Jethro leaped to his feet. "No," he said. "No, no, no! I'm not going and that's final!"

CHAPTER TWO

On August 5, 1878, near two o'clock in the afternoon, twenty men—all former McSween partisans—rode from the forests surrounding Blazer's Mill and the Mescalero Indian Agency headquartered there. The men told the agency clerk they were bound for Tulerosa to search out stock belonging to the estate of the late John Tunstall.

Though it was generally known that some of the cattle delivered to the Mescalero agency by Dolan-Riley carried Tunstall's brand, no one can guess why the clerk, Morris Bernstein, chose that moment to turn stupid. Perhaps emboldened by a squad of Fort Stanton cavalry that was camped nearby, the clerk accused the riders of being on their way to steal Mescalero cattle. Bernstein died with four bullets in him. His pockets were rifled and left turned inside out, his weapons stolen. What had been a grim factional dispute was now descended to pure pillage and murder.

A week after Bernstein's killing, a body of riders raided the old Fritz Ranch, long a Dolan-Riley stronghold, and made off with one hundred and fifty head of cattle and fifteen head of horses. Two nights later, an arson attempt was made on the J.J. Dolan & Co. store in Lincoln.

Lincoln County Sheriff George Peppin could secure no willing deputies to assist him in enforcing unequal laws. Neither could the military make headway in solving Bernstein's murder in the face of general public apathy and hostility.

Gradually hostility became so general that Sheriff Peppin sought refuge at the military post. The Dolan-Riley store became a barricaded fortress. Away from Fort Stanton, federal troops were reviled and insulted. Safety could only be found in numbers and few soldiers dared leave the post for anything but duty. Two Dolan-Riley supply wagons, traveling the short distance between their Lincoln store and Fort Stanton, were waylaid and burned, their drivers shot to death and left to lay.

In a virtual state of siege, Colonel N.A.M. Dudley ordered escorts out for needed supply contractors for both Fort Stanton and the Indian agency at Blazer's Mill. His command was stretched thin.

Amid the spreading anarchy, Victorio, the deadly Mescalero chief, struck north from Mexico, leading a lightning raid up the Mesilla Valley and across the Organ Mountains into the Tulerosa Valley. Dudley called off pursuit of Bernstein's killers and recalled his contractor escorts to march against the marauding Apaches.

Alexander McSween's death and the military's involvement in it caused a storm of outrage that reached Washington. Just as he'd earlier been assigned to investigate the death of British national, John Tunstall, and the reports of mismanagement of the Mescalero Apache Agency, Judge Frank Warner Angel was once again dispatched as a special investigator for the United States Justice Department. Susan McSween made it known she planned to assist Judge Angel in his gathering of affidavits. More threats were issued against her life. Again, with the threat of open warfare, the J.J. Dolan & Company employed outlaws and mercenaries for defense.

After night fell on September 16, 1878, Jethro Spring knocked on the door of a small frame bungalow in Lincoln.

"Who is it?" came a muffled voice from within.

"Open up, Susan. It's Jack Winter. I must talk with you."

He heard a gasp, then the door was thrown open and he stared into the over-and-under barrels of a twin .25-caliber Derringer. "It is you!" she exclaimed.

Jethro shoved the Derringer aside with an index finger. "Maybe for security's sake, you should invite me in."

"Yes! Yes, of course!" She began to cry.

He nudged the door closed with his heel. She'd lost weight, her cheeks were sallow, eyes sunken, and hair disheveled. Tears coursed freely down the wan face. At last, she shook her head, then dabbed at her eyes, unmindful that she still clutched the Derringer. "I forgot," she mumbled. "Tears doesn't help with you." And her eyes welled afresh.

He said, "I'll make some coffee," and started around her.

Susan stopped him. "Please let me make the coffee. It will give me time to regain control."

He nodded and made for a chair. She was a long time returning. When she did, her face was scrubbed, color in the cheeks, and hair brushed until it shone. She'd also changed her dress and now wore a dark green percale wrapper with a neatly trimmed braid on the collar and a ruffle in front forming a bolero effect.

Susan handed him a small cup of coffee resting in a saucer, then sat down a decorous distance away and asked, "Why did you wish to see me?"

"For the best possible reason, ma'am. Your life is in danger."

"Oh? How droll."

He lowered his cup. "I came to help you get away."

"Strange," she murmured. "The last time I saw you, you wondered why I wasn't like my husband—dead."

When he made no reply, she tried again. "I'm sorry my present quarters do not allow me to entertain in the manner to which you've become accustomed at the McSween home. You see, there's no sideboard for liquor and no maid to serve."

He held the saucer on his knee and waited. She dabbed at her eyes with a linen handkerchief and said, "Please forgive me. What was it again that brought you here?"

"I believe your life is in danger."

"Sooner or later, everyone must die."

"Susan, your life is in immediate danger."

"Is that too different from yours? Or Billy's? Or Jim French? In truth, everyone who fought on my late husband's side? Once, we argued because I did not share equally in the dangers of those around me."

He leaped to his feet and the empty cup tipped from its saucer and dashed to pieces on the floor. She stared at the broken cup and tears once again flowed. "It ... it was the last piece of china. I saved it from the ashes."

Jethro stared down at the saucer still in his hand. He laid it gently upon a cloth-covered packing crate used as a serving table. "Good night, Susan. I'll return at a better time."

She sighed and yet another tear trickled down. "Sit down, please, Jack. I don't know what's come over me. Perhaps the pressure of the last two months...." She buried her face in trembling hands. Finally she took a deep breath and looked up. "I know you too well, Jack Winter, not to believe you have a good reason to think my life in danger." He settled back into his chair as she continued, "And you have a terribly annoying habit of being right." Susan's hazel eyes drifted away, then swept defiantly back. One brow arched the question.

"I've heard that Dolan ordered your execution. There's supposed to be men headed this way from Seven Rivers who have orders to attack this house."

"And you believe it to be true."

"Susan, I know it's true."

"How?"

When he failed to reply, she bit her lip and said, "I should have known better than to ask that, too. It did sound as though I distrusted you, didn't it?" When he still made no comment, she continued, "As a matter of fact, Mr. Winter, you are rare—one whose word another can always take at face value. With you, one always knows exactly where one stands. And why." Her eyes misted again.

Jethro gently said, "They plan to arrive in Lincoln tomorrow afternoon and hit this place just after dark. I thought about trying to get in touch with Billy's bunch for a guard around the house, but that would only give away the fact we've got inside knowledge about what they do. Besides, it could lead to a showdown and maybe another big gunfight. We still can't win one of those as long as the army sides with Dolan-Riley."

"So you are suggesting I leave?"

"Yes."

"Tonight? Right now?"

"Before Dolan's gang gets here."

"What if I say no?"

His sardonic cackle was worse than a physical blow. "That would be in character, Susan. But this time you don't have but one knight in shining armor and I won't stay to die for you."

"Do you hate me so?"

"Don't be stupid." Then he added, "'Cause I won't."

She squeezed her eyes, but a tear trickled out. "Where should I go?"

"That's up to you. It should be some place near enough Lincoln that you could return when it's safe."

"You think I should return?" she asked. "You approve of my struggle to bring my husband's murderers to justice?"

"Certainly."

"So you approve of my continuing Alex's and John's efforts to rid this country of corruption and outlawry?"

"Well, that's a taller order. But, yes. It's noble."

"But you won't help?"

"I'm here, am I not?"

Her heart fluttered! She lowered her eyes and asked, "Does that mean I can count on you?"

He was so long in replying that she went to the kitchen for more coffee. When she returned with two pewter mugs, he stared into one and said, "Somewhere in a book I once read, a famous man—Ben Franklin, I think—said, 'Nothing will make certain the triumph of evil as much as good men doing nothing.'" He paused and looked up to see if she was amused. "I may not have that quite right, but that's the way I remember it."

She nodded. "Please go on."

"I feel sorry for Doc Scurlock and George Coe—the struggling farmers and ranchers who've barely survived in this country while Dolan-Riley grew fat cheating them." He was grateful she had the presence of mind to let his tongue wag. "Do you remember Antanasio Salazar?"

"The little old Mexican who always sits on the porch of Tunstall's store? Yes."

"Well, I feel damned sorry for all his people, too."

She felt she was expected to say something. She chose, "All right." It triggered more from her visitor:

"Did I tell you I met this Apache?"

Susan McSween shook her head.

"Well, all of a sudden he showed up at my camp. He told me about Jesse Evans and Tom Hill and when I trailed them they were robbing that sheep camp."

She leaned forward. This was the first time he'd ever spoken of his exploits.

"Well, Malvado—I think he's some sort of chief—he told me how their agent and Dolan-Riley are in cahoots to steal from his people. That was why he wanted to help any who fight against that evil. I've talked to Malvado twice more. Each time he's told me more about their troubles. The telling isn't pretty and Dolan-Riley is at the bottom of most of it."

She sipped coffee. So did her visitor.

"Yeah, I feel sorry for the Indians, too."

He was quiet for so long she feared he'd quit. She allowed him all the time he wished.

"John Tunstall," he muttered, "was motivated by the right reasons. He really did want to bust up Dolan-Riley and the 'Santa Fe ring'. He wanted to do it because it was the right thing to do, to set himself against rotten thievery and stinking corruption...." His voice trailed off as he groped for his next words. She supplied them:

"But my husband was not impelled by such altruistic motives?"

He took out a small writing pad and pencil from his shirtpocket. "How do you spell that?"

She smiled for the first time since he'd knocked on her door. "You mean altruistic? So you're still trying to improve your mind?"

He waited, focusing on the notepad.

"A-L-T-R-U-I-S-T-I-C. It means noble, unselfish."

He added that information to his notepad.

When he'd finished writing, Susan asked, "What makes you feel Alex McSween was not cut from the same cloth as John Tunstall?"

He glanced up at her and their eyes locked. "Are you sure we should be talking about this?"

She nodded. "For two months—ever since Alex was killed and you rode from my life—I've prayed for another chance to talk to you. This is the answer to my prayers. Please, Jack, let's talk about whatever stands between us."

He nodded. "The question was, why do I think Alex wasn't the man Tunstall was?"

She averted her gaze.

"Do you?" he asked.

"What? Do I what?"

"Do you think Alex could throw the same shadow?"

"I should think that question unfair. I believe I had asked you. Not the other way around."

"All right," he replied. "What would you say if I told you I overheard you and your husband discussing his planned trading empire?"

"That, perhaps, would explain a lot. Although I can't for the life of me recall when it could have been, I can't deny that Alex had dreams."

"It was just after Dolan and I had words over you. I was walking along the riverbank, going to tell you and Alex that I would work for you after all. Your voices came through an open window. You wanted him to remain a lawyer. His vision was more grand. I wasn't trying to eavesdrop. It just happened."

"You make his dreams sound dirty."

"I'm trying to point out the difference between Alexander McSween and John Tunstall, as I see it. More than that, I'm trying to show you how much easier it was for me to support a man like Tunstall."

"Why? Each seemed to have destruction of evil as a common goal."

He carefully placed both hands flat on the packing crate table. "Look, do you want to continue this?"

She nodded, not meeting his questioning gaze.

"Okay, their difference was in their methods. And in their desired ends."

"How did those differ?"

"Aside from their goals—which we both know were different—Alex winked at illegal things done in his name. Our methods became no better ..." He paused, thinking, then continued: "Our methods became no more altruistic than Dolan-Riley's. Then there's the matter of the Fritz inheritance money."

"Will you never forget that!" she flared.

He shook his head. "No, I won't. You're the one who asked why I thought John Tunstall was a cut over Alex

McSween. Dammit, woman, did Alex embezzle the money he used to buy into Tunstall's store?"

She again buried her face into her hands. "I don't know," she sobbed. "Please, Jack, I don't know. The grand jury found him innocent. Can't you leave it at that?"

"They found him not guilty. But I question if anybody will ever find him innocent."

She took a deep breath and dropped her hands. "Will you believe me when I say I've been able to find nothing? I don't know what happened to the Fritz estate money. All the records burned in our home. I just don't know!"

"Even his desk?"

She nodded, sobbing again.

He sighed. Besides the Fritz estate records, that meant the **JETHRO SPRING—DEAD OR ALIVE!** wanted poster Alexander McSween had held over his head was gone, too.

"I'll get more coffee," he said.

After he'd poured and returned the coffee pot to the kitchen, she asked, "Have we cleared up anything between us, Jack?"

"What do you think?"

"Must you always answer a question with a question?"

He smiled, but before he could speak, she said, "No, there are still things between us that need to be discussed: Like what you consider my willingness to sacrifice men's lives for foolish, selfish gambles; like my supposed sending you to safety because of our love for each other; like what you think of as my sacrificing my husband to make way for you."

This time it was he who looked away.

"That's a huge order, Jack. But it is necessary that we talk about those things, isn't it? I made up my mind several weeks ago that if the opportunity ever presented itself, I would steel myself to do so."

He chewed thoughtfully on the inside of his cheek while studying her. Finally he said, "More than likely you're right,

Susan. Feeling as we do, it's something that has to be laid
bare. But not now. It's getting late, and we'd better work on
getting you out before Dolan's men get here."

The following morning, a woman dressed as a Mexican
laborer's wife, wearing a red shawl and a coarse print dress,
slipped out of Lincoln on the mail hack. Three days later,
Susan McSween stepped off the stage in Las Vegas. She went
immediately to the office of U.S. Justice Department Special
Investigator, Judge Frank Warner Angel, where she handed
over a baker's dozen sworn affidavits from credible Lincoln
County residents. The affidavits all pertained to circumstances surrounding the death of her husband, the burning
of her home, and events leading to both. Charges of criminality against Lincoln County Sheriff George Peppin and
Colonel N.A.M. Dudley, commanding officer at Fort
Stanton, were prominent in most of the affidavits.

Later, in the seclusion of her hotel room, Susan
McSween thought once again of the man she knew as Jack
Winter and their last parting. She'd asked, "Won't you come
with me, Jack?"

He shook his head.

"Well, when will I see you again?"

He shrugged.

"Well, then, *will* I see you again?"

He nodded. "Yes, I think so. Tonight cleared enough air
so I'll want to talk again.

Susan stretched languidly in her Las Vegas hotel bed and
smiled at the thought.

"Selman's Scouts" was an organized band of Texas and
New Mexico desperadoes commanded by a man who'd
recently fled Texas with a vigilante posse hard on his heels.

The man entered into relations with James Dolan and Lincoln County Sheriff George Peppin in late summer of 1878, at the very time the Santa Fe ring's southeastern New Mexico power was ebbing. Selman formed his gang of rustlers and murderers under pseudo-authority from Sheriff Peppin, ostensibly to guard the Seven Rivers section from Billy the Kid's band who, it was feared, might try to retaliate for the part the Seven Rivers people took in earlier Lincoln fighting.

Two hours after dark on the evening of September 17, Selman and his men struck the home formerly occupied by Susan McSween. They first riddled it with bullets, then set it afire. Then they returned to Wortley's saloon to drink off their disappointment at finding no one home. Just as the Scouts' revelry was at its peak, Jethro Spring crept into Wortley's corral. Working with his pocketknife, he weakened the cinch on every saddle thrown carelessly over the top corral rail.

Selman's hung-over riders provided considerable amusement to discreet observers as, the following morning, one after another of the celebrated Scouts hit the ground when their saddle cinches parted.

CHAPTER THREE

"**D**olan and Riley are in a terrible dither, Jack. Leastways that's what we hear."

Billy Bonney tilted the bottle, then handed it on to Charlie Bowdre. The Kid's eyes danced in excitement. "They're getting a taste of their own medicine and it sure as hell is pinching 'em."

Jethro Spring surveyed the motley group. Bowdre's hat fell to the ground as he tilted the bottle. His Adam's apple bobbed once, then again. At last the man lowered the bottle and swiped the back of his hand across his lips, sneering up at the newcomer. Jim French sprawled against a tree trunk, hands behind his head, seemingly lost in his own thoughts. George Coe cleaned his rifle with an oily cloth and his cousin Frank poked absently at the ashes of a long-dead campfire.

"You're outside the law, Billy," Jethro said, turning his back to the group. "Now they got a legal reason to bring the hounds down on you."

"We fight fire with fire," Billy replied. "They steal, we

steal. They kill, we kill. They had things their own way long enough."

"We don't see we got any choice, Jack," Doc Scurlock said. "Hell, Dolan-Riley had open-pickin's on us for more'n a year. They rustled our stock and shot us down without so much as a by-your-leave from their law. Billy's right. We're down to where we got to fight the bastards usin' their tools."

Jethro faced them. "Even if you win, even if you beat Dolan-Riley, you lose. You'll all be branded as outlaws. Even a sympathetic court and jury would have to find against you."

Bowdre took another pull, then handed the bottle to Tom O'Folliard. "We tried you peacemakers' way," Bowdre snarled, "and all that come of it was that we lost good men. Now we're doin' things the way they should've been handled from the start. Kick Dolan where it hurts, then we'll get our farms back and drive the bastards out of the country."

"It's going to be hard driving the army out, too," Jethro argued. "Look boys, I know it hasn't been easy. But before now, folks in this country could count on at least one side trying to do the right thing. Now?"

"We still are, Jack." It was Doc Scurlock again.

Jethro pointed at the man and said softly, "I don't feel too good about Morris Bernstein, Doc. Nor about turning his pockets out and stealing his guns."

Scurlock's eyes strayed to Bonney and Bowdre, then fell to the ground.

"Bernstein claimed we was on the reservation to steal from the Injuns," Jim French said. "It was an accident that can happen when mean words are mixed up, one with another."

"Mistakes sometimes happens," George Coe said.

Jethro returned to Bonney. "That's just what I'm talking about—mistakes. Honest people getting trampled. Who'll be the next innocent cut down by us?"

Billy the Kid said, "We stung Dolan and Riley when we

hit their cow herd at the Fritz place. We hurt 'em when we stopped their delivery wagons to Stanton and the reservation. And if I could burn 'em down tomorrow, it'd be all right with me. Like Jim said, Bernstein was an accident."

Jethro knew his arguments were falling on deaf ears. Most of these men belonged to the old "regulators" who existed to get even with Dolan-Riley. They were honest farmers and small ranchers exploited by the big store too long; who'd seen friends and neighbors robbed and cheated and killed. They pursued in desperation what they thought was the last course open to them. But it was a wrong course—one that would make outlaws of them all, hunted to their dying days; a course gradually evolving into one where thievery and murder became less discriminating. Could he stop them? Even slow them?

It'd taken much soul-searching, but after visiting with Susan McSween and pondering the plight of Malvado's Mescaleros and of Antanasio Salazar's down-trodden people, Jethro Spring decided to rejoin his old band to fight Dolan-Riley and the Sante Fe ring. He'd worked out the regulator's cold trail into the foothills of the Rio Ruidoso and had ridden into their camp unannounced. He'd been welcomed as a long-lost comrade only minutes before....

Jethro studied Billy Bonney and the Kid stared back in a contest of wills. "No more Bernsteins or Bradys," he said at last. "We're in deep enough already."

"Brady got what he deserved," the Kid said. "I get a chance and Peppin will get the same. So will that shit-assed colonel. They both bought and paid for their funerals a dozen times over."

For Jethro, it was as if the two men existed alone. "A little while ago, Billy, you asked me to come back. Then you thought I might make a leader."

"Still do," Scurlock interrupted.

"We could use you," the Kid admitted. Then he shook his head. "We want you, dammit. You need more?"

There was a murmur of agreement.

"I don't," Charlie Bowdre said. "I don't like you and I don't think you're God Almighty."

Tom O'Folliard laid a restraining hand on Bowdre's shoulder as Jethro said, "If you think I'm worth something, Billy, then I'm worth listening to. I say no more Bernsteins or Bradys."

The Kid visibly relaxed, his buck-teeth flashing. "No more Bernsteins for sure. No more Bradys, either—he's dead. But if you're asking us not to give tit for tat to Dolan and his bunch, then we'll all tell you to go to hell. It was agreed we hit their herd, stop their supply wagons and burn their store. Far as I know, we all agreed to hit them any way we could. It was also agreed amongst us all that that sono-fabitchin' sheriff and his watch-dog colonel will die. I didn't pass the death sentence on 'em alone. Change that if you can."

Jethro asked, "Will you agree to what the group decides?"

The Kid unhitched his thumbs from his belt and fluttered his palms upward. "Sure, if everybody else agrees."

Bowdre chuckled aloud. "I can tell you right now, ever'-body ain't gonna agree with that sanctimonious half-breed."

"Shut up, Charlie," the Kid said. Bowdre stopped in mid-cackle.

"Okay, Jack," Scurlock said, "have you got some plan?"

"No. But I ..."

Bowdre began cackling again. Jethro lunged. Before anyone else could move, he gathered the front of Bowdre's shirt in his fist and hauled the smaller man thrashing to his feet. Bowdre snarled and twisted and clawed for his gun. Jethro slammed the heel of his free hand on Bowdre's wrist and the gunman's hand fell away. Jethro pulled him forward until their noses were only inches apart, with Bowdre hanging unmoving, toes an inch from the ground. Hate twisted his face.

Jethro heard the click of a revolver hammer behind him. He flung Bowdre to the ground. Without turning, he said into the unnatural hush, "Whoever pulled the gun best put it away, else I'll kill him sure as God made little angels." It took seconds for him to complete his turn. They all shifted uncomfortably as he stared at each man in turn. Tom O'Folliard's face was beet-red, but no gun except the rifle being cleaned by George Coe was in sight. Jethro took a deep breath as another hammer clicked behind.

This time it was Billy the Kid who held the muzzle of his Colt against Bowdre's curly hair. "Charlie, now dammit, you ain't thinkin' too clear."

Bowdre's hand fell away from his own half-drawn weapon. He, too, took a deep breath, then said, "That's the second time you laid a hand on me, Winter. There'll not be a third."

Jethro ignored him. A second deep silence fell as he sought, found, and locked on the eyes of each man in turn. When he came to Scurlock, Doc said, "Charlie didn't mean nothin', Jack. We still need you. Most of us know you'd be best for heading us up."

George Coe shifted his position on the ground, shook out his cleaning rag and spat a big stream of tobacco juice to the side. "That don't mean the whole bunch of us don't get a chance to decide what way we're goin', though."

"It does mean we'll listen," Cousin Frank said. "And give a good plan a chance."

"But if you ain't got no plan, then you can't hardly knock ours," Jim French said.

Jethro's voice was measured as he told them he shared their anger and their frustration at a corrupt legal process that was in the pockets of their enemies. He explained that, though they all had warrants out on them, they'd largely gone free because anyone could swear a warrant. "But," he said, "it's another thing to convict a man against an honest jury when the man had done no wrong."

He saw them listening, even though George Coe still wiped his rifle and Tom O'Folliard stirred the fire with a stick and Billy Bonney leaned indolently against a live oak tree.

"But now you're all headed to become wanted outlaws!"

Doc Scurlock drifted back into the firelight as Jethro said, "Dammit, this war is going to end someday. When it does, it seems to me like it'd be nice if we could all go back home knowing there's no posters for our arrest hanging on Post Office walls."

The gray-eyed man paused, remembering his own WANTED - JETHRO SPRING posters. Then he continued: "Bernstein's killing may have already changed that—I don't know."

He explained how an honest jury might look at the entire Lincoln County thing and conclude that one side did less wrong than the other. Then he asked who was hurt the worst when they stopped the supply wagons from getting through to the reservation, Dolan-Riley or the Apaches? He asked them if they'd thought what it might mean to their families and farms if the Mescaleros broke from their reservation in starving desperation?

"Who are you after?" Jethro asked. "The big store or the Apaches or the common soldiers at Fort Stanton? Is it worth getting Dolan and Riley at the expense of hurting a lot of innocent people. Goddammit, that's what happened with Bernstein and the wagon drivers, wasn't it? Sure, maybe it was a mistake. But innocent men are dead and we likely lost support because of it.

"Who will be next? Are you smart enough to sort it out? I'm not. Do it legal and there can be no mistakes." He fell silent.

Someone coughed. Another shuffled his feet.

The lengthy quiet was broken by George Coe. "Trouble is, Winter, me and Frank swore we ain't runnin' from them murderin' scum again. Like Billy said, we decided on tit for tat and I still favor it some. I guess I ain't real comfortable with what happened to that young agency fool what tried to stop us, and I never thought about what stoppin' the supply wagons might mean to the Injuns. But ..." Coe spat another brown stream. "... what about hittin' Fritz's place? Tell me what innocent folks got hurt there? That was a Dolan herd pure and simple, and some of it was rustled first from us. I don't see where we done wrong there. You tell me where we did, huh?"

"Maybe you didn't," Jethro conceded, "if you don't care about being marked outlaws with a price on your head. Maybe that's a price you're willing to pay. Are you?"

"All of us want to see them bastards suffer," Frank Coe said. "They burned me out and shot me out of the saddle for no reason except they happened to be killing McSween men that day. Yeah, I guess what George is saying is that if we're branded owlhoots anyway, let it be for something that takes them down a peg."

There was a murmur of agreement. Scurlock asked, "Will you come in with us—lead us—if we decide to go on with our plans to hit Dolan's outfit before they hit us?"

Jethro started to shake his head, then suggested a compromise. "I'm out," he said, "if another Bernstein or the supply wagons happens again. But I won't stand in your way if the group decides on tit for tat with Dolan-Riley."

Scurlock and Bonney smiled, but the smiles turned to frowns when Jethro said, "There's more. Don't plan any strikes for thirty days. That's not too much to ask." He was stalling for time and knew it. But what he was really after was a pause—however brief—in the incessant warfare and killing.

When Bonney asked what thirty days would bring, he explained that he needed time to talk to their neighbors of Mexican extract, to see where they stood if it came to another fight. He also told them about the special investigator who was even then checking into McSween's death and the army's role in the Lincoln fight.

Hoots of derision met him, but Jethro waved them down.

"I know how you feel. I know how we all think he whitewashed Tunstall's death and the agency's cheating the Apaches when he was here on the first investigation. But dammit, men, he's got mud on his face from that one. And they don't send a man like Judge Angel out here, get him home, then send him out a couple of months later without somebody getting pissed off about it. His first report proved there was smoke where we knew a fire burned. I'm betting the second one will roll some heads. At least while he's here, we've got to keep a damper on."

He told them how the judge was conducting his investigation from Las Vegas because he'd received death threats from Lincoln; how Susan McSween had collected affidavits and delivered them to Las Vegas. "You have to know these things will work in our favor if we help him and the other side tries to block him. All we need is time. Like thirty days."

Doc Scurlock said, "I reckon I could mind my manners for thirty more days, provided Dolan-Riley minded theirs." The broad-shouldered, ruddy-faced farmer eyed the circle around. "How about the rest of you?"

There was general assent from the group. Charlie Bowdre stalked away, his face tight and angry.

"What's the date now?" Bonney asked.

"September twenty-first, I think," Jethro said.

"Well, Winter"—the use of his surname did not go unnoticed by Jethro—"if there ain't no change come October twenty-one, I'm going back to war. And I don't give a big goddamn about the rest of this outfit."

George Coe unwound his big frame from the ground and stood, rifle and rag in hand. "I reckon that's how the rest of us feel, too, Winter. One month you asked for. Now you got it. See what you can do with it."

The gray-eyed man nodded. "Does that mean I lead?"

"Best figure on the rest of us as your board of directors," Coe said.

"For one month," French added.

"All right," Jethro said, "I'm withdrawing the death sentence you boys passed on Peppin and Dudley."

Another hush fell. Most eyes turned to Bonney. The Kid's face held a tight smile.

"Well?" Jethro asked.

"For one month," Bonney said.

"And nobody goes out on his own to break the peace?"

"For one month."

"What about Bowdre?"

"Charlie'll do what we decide," Billy said. "He'll keep the peace—until we say."

"Just what, exactly, do you want us to do for the next month?" Doc Scurlock asked.

———•••———

Later that evening, Jethro checked on their grazing horses. The night was cool. Billy the Kid found him perched on a flat rock, staring into the moonlight. The two sat side by side in companionable silence.

Jethro was perplexed about the unpredictable youth. Billy could be so polite and engaging one minute, and so deadly the next. He thought of the men Billy had killed, or was rumored to have killed: Morton and Baker and McCloskey, Sheriff Brady, Dolan-Riley store clerk Burns, maybe Morris Bernstein and the two wagon drivers—God!

And how about me? Is there a difference between me and Billy? Jethro thought of the three men he'd killed: the U.S. Army major who'd been responsible for the brutal murder of his parents; Frank Freeman, who'd tried to ambush and kill him; Tom Hill, who he'd surprised robbing a sheep camp and preparing to kill the Indian camp-tender. With Hill and Freeman it was kill or be killed. Jethro knew he was deadly with his gun—perhaps faster than this youth whose name was beginning to strike terror in people's minds all over southeastern New Mexico. What made one man become so casual with other men's lives? It was rumored Billy had killed ten or twelve men. Was this slender youth truly a product of his environment—this so-called Lincoln County War? Or would he have developed into a deadly killer in any event? Jethro thought about himself. Was he traveling Billy's path? Was human life becoming cheap to him, too? He tried to shake the thought from his mind.

Billy said. "You look like you seen a ghost."

Jethro tried to laugh, but couldn't.

"Jack, we hurt Dolan-Riley," Bonney said. "I just want it clear that your way could be wrong for us. It could give 'em breathing room and breathing time. Maybe they'll get the money together to bring Kinney back, or them boys at Seven Rivers might join up again."

"They already have."

"What do you mean?"

Jethro sighed. "It looks like Dolan hired himself a wild bunch from Texas. They call themselves 'Selman's Scouts'. You ever hear of 'em?"

"I've heard of John Selman. They say he's hell-for-leather."

"That's the one. They're from the Big Bend country and the Texas Pecos. They're a mean bunch. Jesse Evans is with them."

"What about 'em?"

"They went to Lincoln to kill Susan McSween. Probably on Dolan's orders. That's why I went there: to get her out."

"You said she was okay."

"She is. She's in Las Vegas with those affidavits. But the point is Dolan-Riley is coming to strength again. This time they're hiring cheaper help than Kinney's mercenaries. They're still working out of Seven Rivers, but this is a bunch of rif-raff border poppers. From what I can see of the cut of 'em, Selman's bunch will run wild on their own."

"And we sit back and let 'em?"

"For one month. Dolan might be cutting his own throat this time."

Billy's sudden humorless laugh startled Jethro. "You know," the youth said, "I've known you for a year now, and seen you in action a bunch o' times. And I still don't know if you've got any guts."

"You won't find out, either. Not for a month."

⇒ CHAPTER FOUR ⇐

Despite minor warrants for his arrest, Jethro Spring rode openly into Lincoln, New Mexico, at high noon, September 23rd. He came up the road from San Patricio, riding the same fast-walking sorrel mare he'd first ridden into Lincoln a year before. He passed the homes of Isaac Ellis, Esequio Sanchez and Juan Patron; passed Lincoln's jail, Jose Montano's store, the Lincoln County Courthouse, the home of Santurnino Baca. The sorrel's hooves kicked up puffs of reddish dust. Jethro tried to recall how long it'd been since it rained.

The old man, hat tilted down over his eyes, was sitting in his usual place beneath the shading roof of the wrecked and looted Tunstall store. Jethro reined his horse to the hitchrail. He involuntarily glanced at the burned-out remains of the McSween home and his lips pinched.

The old man stirred and tilted back his big sombrero. "Buenos dias, Senor Jock."

Jethro stomped upon the board porch. "Hola, Antanasio. But maybe I should tell you you've slept too long. It's not morning now, but afternoon."

The old man chuckled and glanced at the shadows thrown by porch posts. "So! You are right, mi compadre. But sleep is easy to the old, eh?"

Jethro squatted on his heels near Antanasio's rickety chair. He leaned with his back to the wall while his keen eyes ceaselessly roamed the street.

The old man pulled off his huge sombrero and laid it aside. Then he tilted his chair back against the wall. Conversationally, he said, "There is little for you to fear in Lincoln, mi compadre. The sheriff, he fears for his life and spends most of his time at his old work, which is *carnicero* at the Fort of Stanton."

"Carnicero? Post butcher?"

"Si. You learn *Mejicano muy rapidomente*, senor." Neither man spoke for several minutes, then Antanasio added, "Senor Dolan, he is not favored in this village for *mucho* weeks and he stays within his store."

Jethro nodded. "I think I understand. I have little to worry about from anyone in Lincoln just now."

"Mmm. It is *posiblemente*. Unless one sees a large posse of men ride in. Then, who knows?"

"I've not been here for a long time, Antanasio. I cannot know how things are in Lincoln these days."

The old man continued as if he'd not heard Jethro. "Such a body of men would be as the ones calling themselves 'Scouts of Senor Selman'. Have you heard of this Senor Selman, *mi compadre?*"

Jethro looked quickly at the old man; his eyes were closed. "Seems like Selman is a name I should know," he said.

"*Malo hombres,*" the old man murmured. "Just a few days ago, these Scouts, they came to our miserable village to shoot and burn and loot."

Jethro said nothing.

"By the good grace of the Virgin Mary, the house these bad men choose to loot and burn was vacated earlier that ver' same morning by the poor widowed Senora McSween."

Jethro smiled to himself as the old man paused to allow him to speak. "It is indeed fortunate the widow McSween left when she did," he muttered.

"Si. The Gods favor her, senor. Yet it was strange. She left dressed as a poor village woman riding only to San Patricio. And can one believe she left on the old mail coach?"

"Don't sound logical, if you ask me."

"That ver' evening, these *malo* Selman *hombres*, they come to her casa and they are drunk with mescal. They build a fire against her casa, which is but a little way down the street from where we sit. And they watch it burn, as if they made no mistake."

"Then what happened?"

"These *hombres*, they ver' drunk. They shout and drink and shoot throughout the village. All the little children, they hide from them. And the women are frightened. At last, these *malo hombres*, they go to sleep with their bottles and our poor village people breathe freely again until the day begins anew. Then we expect these Selman *hombres* will awaken with aching heads and bodies that are sick with evil."

Antanasio glanced at Jethro to see if he appreciated the story. The listener solemnly nodded.

"But will wonders never cease? These men who are so sick—one's heart goes out to them. *Comprende?*"

"Yes, I understand."

"These men, they saddle their horses to ride from our miserable village—this is where the wonder comes in, senor."

"I can hardly wait to hear the rest, my friend."

"Si. The great God in Heaven chose that very moment to strike the saddles upon each horse, senor. Though one can hardly believe it, every saddle cinch was made to break and those *malo hombres* who had caused so much worry among we of this miserable village, they fell from their horses—much to the excitement to those ver' same horses."

Antanasio Salazar turned in his chair to better see his friend.

"And?" Jethro asked.

Solemnly, Antanasio said, "One shuddered to see it. These *hombres*, some of them fell, oh so hard. I even saw one who fell upon his head, may the saints preserve him. And another two who landed upon their poor sick stomachs."

Jethro shook his head, as solemn as Antanasio. "How can a man not pity the poor bastards—and curse their luck?"

"Can you believe there are those in our village who do not easily forgive when bad things are done to them? These villagers, they do not so easily understand that all men sometimes do bad things. These villagers have hearts that are like stones to these poor Selman *hombres*. Some even laughed."

"No!"

"Si, senor. Some of them laugh even when these poor men are hurt."

"Damn poor manners."

"*Muy malo* manners, indeed, senor. Of course it was forgivable because they at least had the kindness to hide while they laughed."

Both men were silent, staring up the street to the big Dolan-Riley store. Antanasio chuckled. "It was something to see, senor. None in our village, even though they were in hiding, could miss these men when they fell or were bucked from their horses. A pity you could not watch such a tragic thing happen."

"One might learn from such a lesson."

"Si. It was so easy to see from our poor village." Again Antanasio glanced at Jethro. "The only place better to have watched, perhaps, would have been from the *tierra montanosa del sur....*"

Jack glanced at the hilltop where he'd watched through his spyglass.

"Of course, one would have needed a *telescopio* to watch from such a distance."

Jethro wagged his head in silent admiration of the old man.

"It would be much better, senor, for one to watch with a telescopio from that southern hill, however, than to cross the Rio Bonito and view such an event from the north. From those *montoncillo de tierra del norte*, the sun, she might glisten on the glass, eh? And show where one sits while watching."

Jethro chuckled. "Is there anything you do not learn, just by sitting on this porch?"

"Oh yes, Senor Jock," the old man said. "For instance, I do not know how you knew these *malo hombres* of Senor Selman were planning to kill the Senora McSween."

Jethro's smile faded, but his eyes mirrored merriment. "There was this note tied in this special place, but to mention it might compromise its future effectiveness."

Antanasio nodded. "Have no fear, my friend. I will not ask. Of course, such information is too valuable to intrust to another."

The gray-eyed man stared into the distance. Antanasio watched him for a moment, then turned to also focus where the other stared. The two men were silent for at least a half-hour as travelers passed by. At last, the sorrel mare shook herself, the saddle stirrups rattling in the stillness. Jethro broke from his musing and the old man said, "You have been gone from our life for too long, Senor Jock."

"I was too ashamed to return, Antanasio."

"So! It was as I thought. You blame yourself. No?"

"I blame myself for not preventing their deaths, Antanasio."

The old man sighed and shifted uncomfortably in his chair. "Eugenio tells us how it was. There is no blame for you, Senor Jock."

"I'm glad Eugenio survived, my friend."

"The will of God."

"I'd like to see him, someday. If it would be permitted."

"*Por cierto*, Senor Jock. Whenever you wish."

When the younger man ventured nothing immediately, the old one gently said, "Even if it had been the will of God that my son and all others within Senor McSween's home died that evil night, we still would know you should bear no blame, Senor Jock."

"Thank you, my friend."

Antanasio fell silent. All preliminaries had been observed. Now he waited for the young man to tell why he had come.

Jethro shifted, stood quickly to stretch, then settled again to squat against a post, facing the old man. "There are some who say the war is not yet over, my friend. They say they will make war upon the big store as long as it is here."

"And you wish to know what I think of such a plan?"

Jethro nodded.

"Evil still stalks the land, *mi compadre*. How can any with goodness within their heart not resist?"

"I didn't say 'resist', Antanasio. I said war."

Antanasio Salazar's eyes veiled. He shrugged. "We who are friends, one with the other, should speak the truth, Senor Jock. We should not be as coyotes skirting a campfire in the darkness of night."

Jethro nodded.

"There are many different ways to fight a war, Senor Jock," Antanasio continued. "Perhaps one can learn from experience."

"Perhaps."

"The big store, they are strong, while we are weak. To stand in one place and try to match our strength with theirs would be foolish. But to bite and snap from many directions can sometimes wound and bleed a stronger opponent until he is the weaker."

"Yes, Antanasio, that is what I think, too. But if such a war becomes a reality, then it is important to have many coyotes biting and snapping and bleeding the stronger opponent. Will your people join the Ruidoso farmers in such a fight?"

The fire in the old man's eyes flared anew, but he shrugged. "Perhaps some would, Senor. But many would not. Others have already fled. Such a leader as Juan Patron, he has gone to Fort Sumner, along with many of his followers."

"So have many of our people, Antanasio. Bob Widenmann for one. John Middleton for another."

"So! Only you and Senor Bonney are left to fight, of poor Senor Tunstall and all his men."

"So it would seem."

Antanasio thought for a moment, then said, "My people always hope, Senor Jock. It is the only bread upon which many of them think they have to live. These times are now so hard, but the great Dolan-Riley store, she has been weakened by the past year of war. Its grip falls away. Most of my people pray their hand will continue to relax and all will be well. Therefore, they will only watch and wait."

Jethro shifted on his heels to stare again at the southern hills. It was as he expected. The regulators could not expect help from this quarter.

"It will not always be so, Senor Jock," Antanasio softly said.

Jethro glanced at the ancient one.

"My people who wish for only good to come without themselves making an effort to bring it to pass will bite the bitter fruit of their own weakness."

Jethro shook his head. "It seems to me like you're speaking in riddles, Antanasio. Yet I know you too well for that."

"The sheriff, he is not in Placito—in Lincoln. He fears to return. The *soldados* are not welcomed here. Even they retain so little respect among the people that they cannot keep order except in their very own presence. There is no law, Senor Jock. No order. In such a terrible times, this big store, she has nothing to protect it from the outrage of people they have robbed and cheated for many years. The big store is now weak from the battles of the past and the losses they have suffered from thieves more recently. They can no longer afford to pay their own private *soldados* for protection, so they do what they must—they invite the worst kind of *bandidos* into this poor country to protect them from their enemies. They say to these *bandidos* there is much to pillage in the homes and farms of the big store's enemies. They promise these terrible *hombres* protection from the law, so they come. From all Texas and New Mexico, they come. The worst men of a worse land come to prey upon the innocent. My people will suffer from the evil men of Senor Selman. When they do—when they have suffered enough—they will bark and snarl and tear at Senores Dolan and Riley."

"And when will that be, Antanasio?" Jethro murmured, certain now of the old man's wisdom.

"*Quien saber?* Soon."

Jethro said, "I have a month, Antanasio. There will be no war from my men for a month. They have agreed not to make war while I see if victory is possible without war."

"Ahh." Antanasio Salazar's eyes lit up. "You are their leader, *mi compadre?*"

"For now, at least. I have thirty days. I don't know if I will lead them if we go to war. But I came here to find out where your people stand, just in case."

"If you truly lead the people of the Rio Ruidoso, Senor Jock, you will find more of my people will join you."

"But most will still try to avoid a fight?"

Antanasio wagged his head and sighed. "You have a month before the fighting begins? Then no, senor. There will be little chance for anyone to avoid the next war. By the time a month has gone, Senor Selman will have so pillaged this country that all my people who are left will join you."

Jethro shifted to watch a burro laden with two huge bundles of dried branches plod past. The burro was led by a stripling of a lad no more than ten. He returned his attention to Antanasio. "There must be a way to stop Selman and his men."

"No senor. Even if there was a way, we should not do so. As terrible as it will be, it will lead to a fierceness from my people like none have known before. And it may lead to the undoing of Senor Dolan and Senor Riley; so much so that their hands will loose from our throats."

"Part of the responsibility of leadership, Antan ..." Jethro broke off in mid-sentence as a ball of light skipped across his feet. He glanced across the street and when the light flashed again, saw that it came from metal or a mirror on the southern ridge. Antanasio saw it, too. It flashed twice more.

The old man's chair thumped the floor. "I must go, *mi compadre*. It is best if you do likewise."

Jethro leaped to his feet. "What is it, Antanasio?"

The old Mexican jammed his sombrero on his head and shuffled from the porch. "There is a big body of riders, Senor Jack. They come to our poor village from the east. They will be here in but a few minutes. You should depart Lincoln this very moment, perhaps by riding west."

Jethro jerked his mare's halter rope loose from the rail, gathered up the reins and swung into the saddle. Antanasio hurried to the lad leading the laden burro, took his halter rope and rattled something in rapid Spanish. The boy darted down the road.

Jethro waved to a stranger leaning against a porch post of J.J. Dolan & Company's big brick store. The mare walked steadily past the western outskirts of Lincoln until the road wound around the edge of a redrock cliff. Once out of sight from town, Jethro pushed the willing horse into a rocking-chair canter until she rounded two more bends. Then he turned the mare toward the Rio Bonito and its thick sheltering willow brush.

Two hours later, satisfied there was no pursuit, Jethro Spring's sorrel horse again waded the Rio Bonito, this time far to the east, skirting Lincoln via the Capitan foothills.

They came upon the first evidence of carnage as they climbed from the river to the Lincoln Road. Six goats lay where they'd fallen. Since the dead animals were in group, it was obvious they were in a band, probably being herded along this road. Each animal had so many holes punched into it that entrails oozed and flies droned. Turkey buzzards circled overhead. Three of the goats had swollen udders. Since no kids lay among the dead, Jethro knew these were milk goats. He muttered a curse.

Nearby was a tiny hovel with doors ajar. Brightly colored clothing was scattered about, some on nearby bushes. He ground-hitched the mare and stepped inside. Cheap pottery dishes lay smashed upon the floor of the single room. Corn flour was strewn about. Everything breakable had been broken. Everything scatterable or tearable was torn or scattered to the winds in what had certainly been an orgy of senselessness.

There was no blood, however. At least none seeped into the dirt floor of the hovel's interior. Jack left through the rear door, his soft boots making only the faintest whisper. In the hardpacked dirt of the backyard, he saw tracks where the family had fled. No boot tracks overlayed them, so there'd been no pursuit.

Jethro encountered many similar scenes all the way to San Patricio. Chickens, goats, and sheep senselessly slaughtered, the poorest homes ransacked, their contents destroyed. Two sheds had been burned. So was the roof of one tiny hovel. Yet the Fritz Ranch had been spared destruction from Selman's men, as had a few other farms and ranches of Dolan-Riley partisans.

San Patricio stood silent, the few windows boarded, doors closed and locked, the tiny community apparently lifeless. Yet Jethro could feel dozens of eyes upon him as he paused to survey the hamlet. He cursed again, as he had a dozen times after coming onto the Lincoln Road. Then he reined his mare up the valley of the Rio Ruidoso, thinking all the while of the uncanny predictions of Antanasio Salazar. He wondered if the wily old patriarch had expected them to come to pass so soon?

Dwellings along the Ruidoso had been spared. But it was apparent news had already traveled throughout the valley. Most of the farms appeared vacant. No one tended the fields. There were few livestock in sight—no horses or mules or cattle, few goats and fewer sheep. Chickens had all been loosed from their coops. People were only spotted at a distance. All appeared armed and wary. The lone rider wondered if some of their eyes squinted at him down rifle barrels.

Jethro Spring turned into the foothills at the first chance, riding south, ever deeper into the mountains, toward Alamo Canyon where his men awaited. He pondered how he could brace himself for their fury when he told them of the ravages of Selman's Scouts. Could he hold that fury in check while the devils James Dolan had unleased upon Lincoln County destroyed J.J. Dolan and Company, along with their evil Santa Fe protectors and military supporters? Antanasio Salazar was right—this time Dolan had gone too far. Or had he? The man expected his enemies to match atrocity with atrocity, destruction with destruction, until the web of violence was so tightly woven no one could trace it back to its origin. Amid the violence, James Dolan expected to right his waning fortune.

But even Dolan could not have guessed the destructive rampage of these new outlaws he'd set loose in the county. If Antanasio kept his people in check and Jethro could sufficiently control his regulators until the revulsion against Dolan's and Selman's carnage manifested itself in high places....

CHAPTER FIVE

When Jethro Spring pressed the point of his knife against the sentry's throat, the man's eyes flipped open, their whites gleaming in the moonlight. A tiny trickle of blood ran along the knife blade. Then Jethro sheathed the knife, lifted O'Folliard, spun him around and kicked him to the ground. "You idiot!" he snarled. "You could get everybody killed."

"Good God! Jack, is that you?" O'Folliard scrambled to his feet.

Jethro pounced upon the sentry again. This time, O'Folliard swung in self-defense, but Jethro easily batted the flailing arms aside and snapped the side of his hand against the base of O'Folliard's neck. The sentry sagged and Jethro buried a fist into his opponent's mid-section and another hand-edge to the neck. As O'Folliard's lamp flickered out, Jethro dipped a shoulder beneath the guard and carried him into camp.

Jethro dumped O'Folliard near the fire, then turned a three-sixty about the circle of lounging men. "This is a bunch of bullshit!"

George Coe squatted nearby, honing a knife. He eyed the unconscious sentry and said, "Goodness, but you're on the peck tonight."

Before Coe could move, Jethro kicked the man's knife from his hand. Coe's mouth fell open. "What the hell ..."

"Shut up, George! I'm doing the talking."

Coe fell silent.

Jethro spun again. He noted Billy Bonney leaning indolently against a spreading pine. Jethro thought about challenging him, then Doc Scurlock strode into the firelight. "What the hell is going on here?"

"That's what I want to know, Scurlock," Jethro snarled. "I leave you in charge. Then when I come back and take out your goddamned sentry I could've killed the lot of you. And you all talk about trotting off to war! What the hell is wrong with you? This is the second time I came into your camp unannounced. Well, I'll guarantee you it'll be the last!"

Scurlock's anger faded. He glanced at George Coe, then back at Jethro. "Winter," he said, "you been a-drinkin'?"

"The whole world's crashing down around you bastards," Jethro said, his voice ringing like steel upon steel, "and you wonder if I've been drinking!"

"What you talking about?" Scurlock asked. Other men crowded into the firelight from the sheltering darkness.

Jethro shook his head in disgust. "Doesn't it mean anything to you, for Christ's sake, that you don't have a sentry out there?"

"Aw, dang it, Jack, what the hell's got into you?"

Jethro Spring saw Frank Coe holding a drawn revolver. He held out his hand for the gun and Frank sheepishly handed it to him saying, "I didn't mean nothin', Jack."

Jethro turned and hurled the weapon far out into the darkness. "All right, you bastards," he said, "you elected me as your leader and from now on, you're stuck with me."

Scurlock began, "We didn't say ..."

"Shut up, Doc!"

Scurlock frowned. Obviously puzzled, he looked down at the still-seated George Coe, then turned and stared at Jim French and Billy the Kid. He shrugged and wheeled back to Jethro. There was no apparent fear in the man. "Then, Winter, you'd best tell us what you're driving at."

Jethro saw Charlie Bowdre edging away, into the darkness. "Bowdre!"

The small man paused, then turned. "You call me?"

"Yeah. I want you here. I'm talking to you."

Bowdre tensed, hand falling near his gunbelt. "Make me stay."

Jethro's hands were clammy. A trickle of sweat ran down the small of his back. His plan to take the offensive against these fiery independent farmers had thus far succeeded. But here was his greatest test. He'd cowed or bewildered most other members of the band. Naturally it had to be Bowdre.

"Bonney," Jethro called. "Calm that snaky-mean Frenchman down and bring him back into the light." Another bead of sweat squeezed from beneath his hatbrim and rolled down his cheek, but Billy the Kid detached himself from his tree and tapped Bowdre on the shoulder. The two younger men whispered together for a moment and Bowdre's hand fell away from his gunbutt. Then he and Bonney moved into the circle of flickering firelight.

Tom O'Folliard stirred and Jethro said, "Somebody help him to his feet."

George Coe jumped up and he and his cousin lifted the dazed sentry.

Scurlock hooked his thumbs behind his gunbelt. Here was a man uncowed and growing angry. "I asked you once what's goin' on, Winter. I ain't askin' again."

"You're fired, Scurlock," Jethro said. "You run a camp with security as loose as this, you're not second in command."

Scurlock shrugged. "Suits me. I don't remember wantin' the job in the first place. What I do remember was wantin' you to head us up. Now I ain't so sure."

Jethro whirled from Scurlock. He glared at Billy the Kid. "As of now, Bonney, you're second in command. And as of now, this outfit is on a war footing."

A surprised murmur ran through the group. Even O'Folliard stared open mouthed, eyes slowly focusing. Scurlock's scowl softened and his brow wrinkled. "What is it you know that the rest us of don't?"

Jethro told them of Selman and his so-called "scouts." A stunned silence met him. Jethro's description of the Selman ravages sank slowly in and an angry murmur started around him. Jethro let it go for a while, then snarled, "Okay, shut up! All of you!" He held his breath, but the murmurs ebbed and died as each man turned attentively to their accepted leader. Even Charlie Bowdre and Tom O'Folliard gave him their undivided attention.

"All right," Jethro said. "they haven't hit the Ruidoso yet. But it's next. The thing for us to do is protect our women and kids. Like I said, this outfit is on a war footing. That means sentries"—he looked squarely at O'Folliard—"stay awake. None of you better forget it, or I'll personally kick the shit out of you each time. And you'll be damned lucky if I find you before a kind-hearted Selman savage does."

He glared. No one met his eye. The tension he'd held in check since he'd carried O'Folliard into camp began to ebb. At last, he said, "We're at war, but we're not shooting, dammit, until I say so."

Another murmur made the rounds, but Jethro knew it was not a challenge.

"What we're going to do is get our women and kids out of the Ruidoso. Yours, Doc, and yours, George, and yours, Jim. Charlie, your wife goes and so does yours, Tom. We're packing them up and taking them up to Fort Sumner for the duration. We're going to ride shotgun, boys, all up and down the Ruidoso while we get the women and kids loaded up. We'll move 'em in one bunch and we'll ride herd until we get to Sumner."

"When do we leave, Jack?" Scurlock asked in a subdued tone.

"The sooner, the better. We'll break camp in the morning. All of you'd better turn in—we'll be busy the next few days. I'll take the first watch." Jethro glanced up at the moon. "Billy, you relieve me when it's high-moon. Doc will take your place when the moon's a hand-span from the horizon."

----·+·----

Billy the Kid came quietly to the rock outcropping where Jethro Spring sat his sentry post. "You know your hat gives you away?" Billy chuckled. "It sticks up above the rocks and ..." The young man stiffened, then reached over and pulled the hat from the stick that held it. A throaty chuckle came from behind. The Kid turned, saying, "You are plumb full of surprises tonight, ain'tcha?"

Jethro took his hat from Billy. "Surprises?"

"That was some show you put on back at camp."

Jethro's teeth gleamed in the moonlight. "Show?"

"Show," Billy reiterated. "I gotta hand it to you, though. You pulled it off neat. You plumb took the play away from 'em and none of them knowing it. A body's got to admire class when he sees it."

Jethro jammed his hat in place. "It's all yours, Billy. Doc'll replace you before morning."

Bonney nodded, then shook his head. "I just want you to know you didn't fool everybody."

"I still got twenty-six days to see what I can do. I was just trying to be sure I get 'em."

"Twenty-five," Billy replied. "It's after midnight now. This is September twenty-six. You only got twenty-five days left. Then we go to war."

----·+·----

The Ruidoso "regulators" moved with military precision into their home country. Jethro posted men at each end of the twenty-mile-long valley and along the trails leading to Lincoln and the Rio Penasco. Billy the Kid was placed in charge of preparation and moving. Frank Coe was dispatched the hundred and twenty-five miles to Fort Sumner, charged with the responsibility to prepare that tiny community for the influx of Ruidoso refugees.

For three long days, heavy farm wagons loaded with meager household furnishings, food, and families rolled down the valley of the Rio Ruidoso. It was a somber gathering of tough, hard-bitten men and armed, hard-eyed women at the unkempt land of Dick Brewer, their dead former leader. It was during the evening of September 28. Each farm had been hastily boarded and such equipment and furnishings of value not already loaded upon the wagons were stashed or hidden. The livestock, a large band of mixed horses and cattle, were driven together to the staging area. Guards posted at the valley's perimeters were recalled. All was ready for tomorrow's march down the Ruidoso and the valley of the Rio Hondo, awaiting only daylight and their leader's order to begin their week-long trek.

Even before the Ruidoso people prepared for their move, John Selman had led his Scouts into Lincoln. On the afternoon of September 25, after an orgy of drunken looting and destruction in the Rio Hondo and Rio Bonito valleys, it became Lincoln's turn to host terror. For the next three days, the townspeople of Lincoln dwelled in a virtual state of siege as Selman's outlaws continued looting and destroying. Only determined resistance saved Jose Montano's store and the home of Isaac Ellis. Gun battles were frequent, but losses few as the outlaws seemed unwilling to force their attentions on those willing and able to resist. The big store was untouched, of course, as was Sam Wortley's hotel and the

Cisneros, Mills, and Stanley homes. Others were ransacked. Day and night the revelry, destruction, and erratic gunfire continued until, by late afternoon of the 27th, Selman and his men ran low on ammunition. Since they'd already exhausted the ready supply of J.J. Dolan and Company, and the remainder of the community's ammo supply was likely to be in the hands of their enemies at Montano's store, Selman and company reasoned their best source might be at the military reservation at Fort Stanton.

Selman's Scouts found Hudgens' saloon, just off the post, to their liking. While there, they tried to persuade Hudgens to act as their agent in purchasing ammunition at the post sutler's store. When Hudgens refused, Selman dispatched four of his best men into the post with orders to buy several thousand rounds of cartridges.

Colonel Nathan A. Dudley, who'd refused several appeals for help from the Lincoln community to combat Selman and his men, found this latest effrontery by the border-jumping outlaws to be too much. He ordered Selman's men stopped before they'd left the post, then marched them back to the military store and made them return the ammunition.

When Selman's indignant men returned to Hudgens' saloon, the crowd went on a rampage, wrecking the saloon and insulting and mishandling Hudgens' wife and sister. When local men present tried to stop the women's mistreatment, a general melee developed and innocent men were pistol-whipped by Selman's Scouts.

Hudgens and his family, along with other frightened settlers in the vicinity, fled to the sanctuary of Fort Stanton. More embarrassing to Colonel Dudley, Hudgens and other refugees reported they'd recognized several Dolan-Riley men among those who terrorized innocent people in Fort Stanton's very shadow! Sheriff Peppin was called from his job as post butcher and asked to perform his duties as sheriff. Peppin, no hero, refused.

While Dudley chewed his lip and evaluated options, the

Selman mob decided discretion the better part of valor and started home for the protective confines of the Seven Rivers region.

While on their way, they made another abortive attempt to attack the Lincoln home of Isaac Ellis before daylight on the 28th, but were driven away by the Ellis family. By mid-morning, Selman's men were below San Patricio, heading to the Rio Penasco road.

Two young boys, Cleto and Desidero Chavez y Sanchez, worked in a hayfield. Several of their father's horses grazed nearby. Those horses attracted the attention of John Selman. When Selman's men began rounding up the horses, Cleto ran forward shouting that they must first talk to his father before taking the horses. Cleto died for his bravery. So did Desidero who, at twelve, was two years younger than his brother.

Selman and his men did take the boy's advice, however, pausing long enough to talk to the elder Chavez y Sanchez, leaving the Mexican citizen, held in high local esteem, lying sprawled in his own blood across his doorstep. Gregorio Sanchez and Lorenzo Lucero died as they ran to the wounded Jose's defense.

"But it don't make no sense, Jack. Jose Chavez y Sanchez—he never even took sides in this here Lincoln County War." Doc Scurlock, like all the rest of the Ruidoso people, milled in stunned confusion as Jethro told of the latest ravages of Selman's Scouts.

Charlie Bowdre pushed through the crowd surrounding Jethro. He stopped inches away from the gray-eyed man, a pained expression on his usually sullen face. "Look, Winter, are we runnin' out?" he asked.

"No, Charlie," Jethro said softly through the sudden hush. "What we're trying to do is get your families to some safe place. We'll be back in a couple of weeks."

"What's these other people gonna do while we're gone?"

"Same thing we'd do if we stayed. Defend ourselves. Same thing we'll do if they try to hit us on the road to Fort Sumner."

Scurlock said, "It goes against the grain, Jack. Damned if it don't. We been the only ones standin' against Dolan and his bastard outfit so long, maybe I come to think of it as a duty."

There was a low growl of assent through the crowd. Jethro took a deep breath. "Think of it this way, Doc, Charlie: Dolan wants us to strike back. He wants us to bust loose—expects us to. He wants us to do it so it'll confuse things in everybody's minds about who's at fault. I know it hurts to let Selman and his damned mob get away with what they're doing. But we've got a plan. That plan is to get our women and kids to safety, then come back and play their game. If we don't fight back for another week or two, nobody in the world could blame us for what Selman and Dolan has done."

Charlie Bowdre scuffed his boot into the dust and Doc Scurlock coughed. Both, as if on cue, pushed their hats back with a thumb at the same time.

"Remember, Doc, Charlie, your families come first. Before, women and kids were safe. Now, with this Selman riff-raff, they're abusing women and girls and shooting boys. We've got to get our people to hell out of the Ruidoso."

Honest emotion twisted Bowdre's face. When he finally nodded, it was at precisely the same moment the thoughtful Scurlock reached down and picked up one of his children— a girl of three. "No doubt about it, Jack, it's best to get the families out. After that, though, there'll be hell for them to pay."

———•─•———

The migration of the Ruidoso regulators to Fort Sumner began early in the morning of September 29. Most of their trip took place without Jethro Spring, who stayed behind to monitor developments in southern Lincoln County. Billy Bonney was in overall charge of the wagon caravan. It moved briskly, flanked by hard-eyed riders who, no one doubted, would shoot first and ask questions last. The departure of the Ruidoso people—the only effective counterbalance to Dolan-Riley lawlessness—left a void. Into that void quickly moved the outlaw gang of John Selman and the worst elements from Seven Rivers. Unhindered, these outlaws vented their spleens upon the farms of the regulators they'd feared, rampaging throughout the valley of the Rio Ruidoso in a debauchery of destruction. Finding little to loot in the abandoned farms of their enemies, the outlaws burned and wrecked what they could, then turned their attention once more to the usually subservient Mexican-Americans still dwelling on their farms.

At last the docile Mexicans had had enough! They organized and resisted from San Patricio to the upper Ruidoso, and all along the Rio Hondo and Rio Bonito. Though at first it appeared spontaneous and erratic, rifles barked from hiding places or shotguns roared from the darkness. Saddles emptied of Selman's scouts. It swiftly became dangerous to travel the roads of southeastern New Mexico in anything but the largest parties. Mail contracts were delayed. Traffic ground to a near-standstill.

The outlaws reacted even more viciously. On the evening of October 2, Selman's men raided and burned Bartlett's Mill, located midway between Lincoln and San Patricio. There, they repeatedly raped, then killed the wives of two of Bartlett's employees before moving upriver toward Lincoln.

But Lincoln, too, had had enough! A band of thirty-six men met the Selman gang just outside the village and drove them away in a running gun battle, toward the Rio Penasco. Led by Anglos Isaac and Ben Ellis and former Dolan-Riley partisan Ham Mills, and accompanied by such formidable Mexican fighting men as Eugenio Salazar, Gregorio Sanchez, and Ramon Montoya, the Lincoln men gave much better than they received in an inconclusive two-day battle. Amid it all came the stunning news that Governor Samuel B. Axtell had been removed from office by the President of the United States. All New Mexico was agog that their new governor, former Civil War General Lew Wallace, in a move apparently designed and implemented in secrecy, had already taken office. Rumors were also rampant that Wallace and President Rutherford B. Hayes were also about to remove the suspected head of the Santa Fe ring, Territorial Attorney General Thomas B. Catron.

Three days later, notice trickled down from the Bureau of Indian Affairs that Frederick C. Godfroy had been removed as agent for the Mescalero Indian Reservation. Godroy's temporary replacement was an unknown Washington paper shuffler named Fairfax Wheeler.

———•◦•———

"Well, Antanasio, your predictions came true."

"Alas, it is so, *mi compadre.*" The old man leaned in his old chair, tilted in its usual manner against the wall of the abandoned Tunstall store. But somehow Jethro felt things were different for his friend. His eyes were closed as a slanting October sun beat upon the lined and weatherbeaten face. Tiredness? Old age? Sorrow?

Jethro shifted on his heels. Out in the street, dust devils played where wind whipped. A page from an old Mesilla newspaper blew past, gusting from side to side with the vagaries of an erratic wind. People walked the street—more people were visible from the empty store porch than Jethro had seen in Lincoln for some time. Up the street, workmen were busy boarding up the front windows of J.J. Dolan and Company. *Fortunes of war,* he thought.

"Your people will soon return?" the old man asked without opening his eyes.

"Yes. I had word they'd arrived at Fort Sumner and were busy settling in their families. I'd guess they'll be back in three or four days."

Antanasio Salazar nodded. He opened his eyes to the sun, blinked and turned his head to peer kindly at his friend. "I, for one, will be glad when they return, Senor Jock. I fear these bandidos of Senores Dolan and Riley will soon visit us once more."

"With your people and mine together, we can drive the bastards from New Mexico."

"That would be *magnifico*. However, one must not expect so much so soon."

"What will happen now, Antanasio? With this new governor? A new attorney general? Does it mean the break-up of the Santa Fe ring?"

"Again, Senor Jock, one must not expect so much so soon."

"Why not? It will happen, won't it?"

"*Quien saber*, my friend? Senor Dolan, tomorrow he leaves for Santa Fe."

"To see the new governor?"

"I would not rule it out, *si*."

Jethro stared up the street at the big store. "My God, they're like one of them many-headed snakes I read about. Chop one head off and it grows another. What does it take to beat them?"

Antanasio murmured, "The big store, she is already beaten."

Jethro shook his head, puzzled. "If you say they're beaten already, why is Dolan going to see the new governor?"

Antanasio again closed his eyes. "The struggle now becomes one to see who replaces the big store, Senor Jock. Wherever men dwell, there will be those to serve them. But there are also those who try to bleed them. There is much dinero to be made by men who trade in Lincoln County. Should not we who are either to be bled or served, concern ourselves with which it is to be?"

Jethro plumbed the depth of Antanasio Salazar's sunken eye sockets. "I wish I had half your wisdom, my friend."

The eyes opened and a fleeting smile flashed across the old face, then was instantly replaced by an infinite sadness. "Senor Selman is, I fear, not yet driven from New Mexico. And the Rio Penasco still harbors evil men who prey upon the simple. Senor Jock, believe me when I say there is still much time of sadness before us."

"I believe whatever you say will come true."

"We must yet prepare to defend ourselves from this evil. Even while we await a sign from this new governor, we must be ready to drive the *bandidos* away."

"Why don't we carry the war to them, Antanasio?"

Antanasio's eyes wandered to the southern hills where the sun was sinking slowly beyond the horizon and shadow stole silently across the land. "This new governor, he must have time to think and learn, Senor Jock. It would be better, would it not, if we were not—how you say—too quick to fight? No, better that we defend ourselves and plead for the protection of this new governor. Then he mus' wonder why we need his protection. Perhaps he will look for the truth, eh?"

Even as Jethro weighed Antanasio's words, the old man gently asked, "Can you hold your men when they return, senor?"

He shook his head, visualizing what would happen when the Ruidoso men returned to find their homes destroyed. "I don't know, Antanasio. Perhaps. It depends on how active Selman and the Seven Rivers bunch are. My regulators are itching for war."

"Tell me, my friend, do you not think I am right? Is it not better to continue as before? Let the devils of Dolan loot and kill and steal while we defend ourselves. Is not that the best way to prove that it is we who are wronged?"

The terrible burden that Antanasio carried suddenly dawned upon Jethro; the agony of indecision he faced while his people were butchered and robbed and turned from their homes. "Again, my friend," Jethro murmured, "I wish I had half your wisdom."

Relief spread across the lined face, then as quickly disappeared. The chair thumped to the porch floor and the old man said, "It is a great pleasure to visit with you, *mi compadre,* but now I mus' leave. There is soon to be a meeting where my people consider marching against the *bandidos* of Seven Rivers. I mus' try to prevent this from happening. No?"

Jethro stood. "Perhaps not becoming the avenger will be the most difficult thing we have left to do, Antanasio."

CHAPTER SIX

J ethro Spring's regulators returned to Lincoln on the tenth day of October, 1878. They were grimy and unshaven, slumped in their saddles, grim of face; a meaner-looking contingent of hardcase men might be hard to imagine—even in Lincoln County, New Mexico.

The regulators were accompanied by Susan McSween. She rode side-saddle, as becomes a woman of culture, and her attire, though also dusty, was impeccable in its modesty despite the fact she was surrounded by a motley crew of hard-bitten men. But the way her eyes lit up at sight of Jethro, the way she leaped unattended from her side-saddle, the way she dashed across the dusty road, and the familiar way she threw her arms around the red-faced regulator leader, laughing and crying all the while, belied any image of demureness.

"Jack! Oh, Jack! I've missed you so. I was afraid I'd never see you again. Then when I ... oh! The new governor. Have you heard of our new governor? Isn't it exciting? He's a military veteran, you know. Served in Mexico. Will that make him unpopular here? Oh yes, and the Civil War. A general. I haven't met him as yet, but I've written asking for an audience. Isn't it wonderful? That horrid Governor Axtell removed and his being replaced by a genuine *hero!* I can't wait to meet him. Dolan-Riley is beaten, Jack. Isn't it wonderful? Now we can reopen Tunstall's store!"

Jethro freed an arm from her grip and placed a finger on the woman's lips. "It's nice to see you, Susan. This is, uh, Antanasio Salazar. Do you remember him?"

Antanasio held his big sombrero across his chest and bowed.

"Oh, of course I remember Mr. Salazar. When we reopen Mr. Tunstall's store, he can continue to sit on our porch, can't he Jack?"

Jethro's eyes rolled as Susan continued her excited chatter. He thought for a moment that Antanasio winked, but a moment later the Ruidoso men crowded near and Jethro could never be sure.

"...and it's so horrible, the news coming from here, Jack. Those beasts of Dolan's must be punished. Just as soon as we explain it to Governor Wallace, I'm sure he'll order the army out after them. No doubt he'll jail that terrible Sheriff Peppin, too. And court-martial Colonel Dudley, don't you ..."

Jethro gently removed Susan's other hand from his arm and stepped around her. "Hello, Doc. Billy. How'd it go?"

"Our families are safe," Doc said. Lines of exhaustion creased his face. "But we don't like what we're hearin' from down here."

"It's not good. But the worst is behind. Selman's bunch has run their course and the Seven Rivers boys got a taste of the same. Just as soon as we get some law and order re-established in this county, we'll be moving your families back."

"What's our farms look like?" Frank Coe asked, crowding nearer.

"They took some licks. Nothing that can't be fixed. We

knew it'd happen, though, when we figured the families came first."

"Yeah, we did," George Coe growled. "And we figgered to get our pound of flesh when we got back."

"Tell you what let's do, boys," Jethro said, raising his voice to the farthest member of the group. "Let's go on down to Wortley's saloon and I'll stand you all to a drink."

"Wortley's?" chorused several voices. "Sam Wortley is on Dolan's side."

Jethro nodded grimly. "Yeah, he is. Can you think of a better place for us to start throwing our weight around?"

Doc Scurlock grinned. "No, by God!"

"Yippie!" yelled Tom O'Folliard. Even Charlie Bowdre laughed.

"Can I go?" Susan McSween asked.

"A saloon is no place for a lady," Jethro said.

"I know. But can I go?"

"Let her," Billy the Kid cut in. "She's got more invested in this than the rest of us—her husband, her home, her husband's business. What the hell."

Sam Wortley fled the room when the regulators trooped into his emporium. But Sam's thirst for profit overcame fear and when he heard few sounds of violence, the man poked his head around a doorjamb to see what was going on. Liquor already flowed and he'd collected nothing for it, so the proprietor ventured back inside. At best, he collected only ten cents on the dollar for all the whiskey and beer consumed by the regulators that evening. But considering the temperament of these patrons and the tenuous nature of his current lease on life, Sam Wortley later decided he'd done very well, indeed.

And Jethro Spring had averted yet another crisis to his leadership....

———·•·———

Susan McSween bumped Jethro, even though she held

his right elbow with both hands. "Oh!" she giggled. "Bless me, I'm sorry."

"Where will you stay?" he asked as the laughing, shouting, milling, backslapping regulators trooped from Wortley's saloon. The time was well past midnight.

"With you," she replied, smiling crookedly up at him.

"C'mon," Tom O'Folliard said, throwing an arm around Jethro's shoulders and pulling him along. "If we gotta go, so do you."

"I asked where you intend to stay?" he whispered fiercely to the woman at his side.

She tried to focus up at him, failed and said, "I told you. With you."

"Dammit, Susan, this is no time for games." He tried to stop but O'Folliard jerked him along anyway.

"Some games are all right," she giggled. "Since ladies aren't allowed to drink in saloons, I must not be a lady any more."

He glanced quickly around, but the shouting, drink-filled men were making so much noise no others heard. "Okay, I'm taking you to Salazar's. Or Isaac Ellis. They'll take you in for a night. We'll wake 'em up."

Susan gripped his elbow harder and wagged her head. "No, don't wake ... please. Juan Patron said I ... I could use his house as long...." She hiccuped.

"No, you can't do that. Selman's men wrecked it. It'll need to be cleaned. We'll go to the Ellis place."

"No. Patron's is good enough. Please Jack." They'd stopped in front of Tunstall's store. Most of the men were untying saddlehorses to lead them to the adjacent corral. The crowd was splitting up. Susan's hazel eyes were wide and pretty, her face framed by long, wavy hair.

"We'll walk down and take a look," he said. "Maybe we can put things in order enough so you can get by tonight. If not, then by God, you're going to Ellis's."

She nodded and tugged at him.

The door of the Patron home stood open a crack. They

pushed it further and stepped inside. He scratched a sulphur match on the doorjamb; in its sudden flame, they saw broken dishes, torn window curtains and ripped clothing scattered at random across the front room floor. Susan nudged the door closed with her foot and blew out his match. Then she was in his arms, mouth seeking his.

Numbly, his arms went around her and she melted to him. Then she arched her back and they both stumbled. He threw out an arm and his hand struck the wall. He caught his balance and managed to hold her on her feet. She wriggled nearer and he retreated until his back was against the wall. Throughout, her lips had never left his and their teeth ground together. She wriggled nearer and he groaned. Slowly his back slipped down the wall....

"Me'n some of the boys been a-talkin', Jack. We want to make a social call down to Seven Rivers."

Jethro studied Doc Scurlock, the two Coe cousins, and Jim French. He leaned against the Tunstall store's hitchrail. Billy Bonney leaned by his side, chewing a dead grass stem. It was two days since the Ruidoso regulators had arrived back in Lincoln after moving their families to Fort Sumner. "Billy and me was just talking about what we should do, Doc."

Scurlock waited, saying nothing, the blocky man's legs spread, arms folded. French and the Coes flanked him, waiting for Jethro to continue.

"We've got to be careful now, boys. There's a chance things might go our way."

"We got some licks to get in, Jack, for what they did to our farms. We're owed that. We want to collect."

"I can't argue that," Jethro conceded. "I know, and you know our cause is right and just. What I'm arguing right now is timing. It's the end result we've got to look at. And while revenge might be satisfying, it could hurt us."

"I don't get your drift."

Jethro took a deep breath. "We've got a new governor, right?"

George and Frank Coe both nodded. Scurlock and French were still.

"We don't know about him," Jethro continued. "He may be a good governor, or a bad governor, but he's a change. And from the governor we had, you'll have to admit it's an improvement."

"We ain't arguing that," Scurlock said.

"Likely this new governor was sent here to help clean up a mess, otherwise the change would never have been made."

"High time, too," Jim French muttered.

"Right," Jethro quickly agreed. "But just now this new governor is being fed the story of both sides of this Lincoln County War."

"Ain't but one side," George Coe growled.

"That's true, dammit. But this new governor don't know that. He's hearing both sides, and lately he's only heard about how one side—our side—has had our homes destroyed, our stock run off and stolen or butchered, our men and boys slaughtered while tending their fields, our women raped and killed. Right now, this new governor can't come to but one conclusion. But now you boys want to make a raid on Seven Rivers to pay back our enemies. You'll burn and loot and kill and it won't bring back the Chaves kids or restore your homes. The sacrifices we've already made will be useless because all of a sudden our side won't look no different from the other one. Dammit, boys, that's my drift. We shouldn't do anything that could turn this new governor against us until we know which way his wind is blowing. Defend ourselves? You're damned right! But I'm dead-sure against giving the other side any reason they can use to excuse what they've done in the past."

Scurlock and his companions exchanged glances, then Doc said, "You make a pretty good case, Jack. I ain't real sure you're right and there ain't none of us been over to the

Ruidoso yet to see our farms. When we do go, likely it'll cause some of us to say to hell with your notions on peace. But maybe we can put a damper on our tempers for a while longer."

Bonney cleared his throat. "Besides, boys, we promised Jack thirty days before we went to shootin' again. There's still eight days to go."

"Eight days it is," Doc Scurlock said. Then he turned on his heel and marched away. French and the Coe cousins followed.

As Jethro watched them, he said to Billy the Kid, "I asked for thirty days to see if we could make any progress toward a lasting peace, Billy. Don't you think that's what's happening, with a new governor and all?"

"Could be," Billy agreed.

"Then don't you think there might be some value in not continuing the war after the thirty days are up if there's reason to believe progress is still being made in that direction?"

"Could be."

Jethro studied the younger man. "Billy, is it that you want war?"

Billy pursed his lips and stared at the mail hack as it rolled in from Roswell. "You or me neither one has got no farm. It ain't our places that Selman and Dolan ruined. But tell you the truth, Jack, I'm getting damned tired of this war."

Jethro impulsively reached out and gripped the young man's shoulder. "It'll be hard to hold 'em back once they get over to the Ruidoso and see their homes, Billy."

Bonney nodded. "Especially if they run into any of them bastards from Seven Rivers while they're over there."

The mail pouch was thrown off at the Wortley Hotel and the hack rolled away to Fort Stanton and the brand-new mining town of White Oaks. Jethro stared after it, lost in thought. Directly, he said, "Tell you what, Billy. Let's you and me take a little ride over to the Ruidoso tomorrow. We'll scout out the lay of the land and see if we cut any sign of

Selman's bunch. If it looks clear, we'll take the regulators in the next day."

Bonney shrugged and Jethro added, "It'll give us a chance to talk, Billy. I'd like to set up some sort of defense line, say a band around the Ruidoso and Bonito and upper Hondo. We'd need to do it with our boys and Antanasio's people. Run regular patrols. Maybe have a flying squad to hit our enemies when they get into our territory. That sort of thing."

Billy the Kid pushed away from the rail. "Sounds like an idea worth talking about."

———•◦•———

The screams came from the scrub oak above the Ruidoso Road. Jethro Spring and Billy Bonney both reined in their horses at the first piercing shriek. The screams continued, one after another, then was joined by a higher-pitched shriek. Jethro buried his spurs into the flanks of the sorrel mare, followed a split-second later by Billy the Kid.

The mare dashed uphill, tearing through branches, dodging pinon pine and oak scrub as Jethro yanked his hat lower to shield his eyes. Just seconds later, man and horse thundered into a clearing. A small naked child ran screaming through the clearing. Behind her stumbled a bearded man, laughing wildly and clutching at a pair of unbuttoned breeches hanging to his thighs. Another man swung a big lazy lariat loop above his head as he galloped a bay horse to cut off the girl's flight. All this Jethro saw in an instant. He saw also that the hysterically screaming child could not be more than seven or eight years old. And he saw the bright red blood streaming down the inside of her thigh....

The sorrel mare had burst from the thicket only twenty feet from the man holding his trousers. The man skidded to a stop, his face suddenly blank. He carried no gun—apparently gun and belt were cast aside at the first assault of the child. At the range, Jethro couldn't miss—and didn't—

shooting the bearded rapist between the eyes.

The rider dropped his lariat and clawed for his gun just as Billy the Kid burst from the trees. Billy's first slug slammed the man from the saddle, but three more ripped into him before his body hit the ground.

The wailing child disappeared into the shrub, but other screams came from beyond the clearing. Again, Jethro and Billy spurred their horses. Only seconds had gone by since they'd burst upon the scene and shot down the rapists. A few more seconds of pell-mell crashing and their horses bolted into yet another tiny clearing. There was little time to think as a man fired at Jethro from behind a pinon pine. He returned fire, even while rolling from his plunging mount. Subconsciously, he saw the spread-eagled woman and another man clawing frantically at his trousers, reaching futilely beyond for a holstered sixgun.

Jethro drew the sheltered man's repeated fire as he hit the ground rolling. Once, twice, bullets kicked up dirt and turf alongside. Jethro snapped a shot that took bark from the man's cover tree. Then Billy the Kid thundered in from the side and gunned the man down with his Colt's last two shells. Jethro dimly heard Billy's revolver hammer click twice before the Kid realized he held an empty gun.

The fourth man ceased scrambling to reach his belted gun and threw up his hands. "Don't! For God's sake. Please. We didn't mean nothin'."

Jethro pushed to his feet, holding his gun on the pleading man. He heard hoofbeats pounding away, then he looked to the woman. She'd stopped screaming; now there were only low moans. She was spread-eagled, her wrists and ankles bound to small trees with bits of rope. Her dress had been pulled over her head and tied at the top, exposing her completely from feet to armpits. Jethro whirled back to the man, earing back his Colt's hammer.

Please, mister. I don't know who you are," the man bubbled, "but we didn't mean no harm. They're just greasers, for Christ's sake. Gimme a chance."

Billy the Kid, still mounted, rode up alongside Jethro. Wild lights danced in the youth's eyes. He holstered his empty revolver and slid out his Winchester. The polished rifle whispered on the leather as the muzzle cleared. "Ridiculous sight, don'tcha think, Jack," he said in a high-pitched, stilted voice. "His pecker draws up any farther and it'll come out his ears."

Jethro nodded. The man presented a ludicrous figure, standing with hands above his head, while his trousers hung about his knees, the body unnaturally white where clothing normally covered, his genitals shrunken and ...

Billy's Winchester roared and the genitals disappeared. The man screamed and doubled over, hands clawing at his crotch, bright red blood pumping through the fingers. Billy's second bullet smashed into the top of the man's bent-over head, splitting it like a ripe melon.

Billy swung down from his horse, walked to the sprawled figure of the man who'd first shot at them and put yet another bullet into the man's head. "Still breathing," he said as Jethro cut the ropes holding the woman.

She rolled into a fetal position, sobbing wildly. Billy gently pulled her dress down and began speaking to her in pidgin Spanish. Jethro glanced around. He walked to the line of scrub, eyes methodically studying the ground before him.

Ten minutes later, he strode back into the clearing. The woman sat propped against a tree. She turned a fearful, tear-streaked face his way, body still jerking as spasms overcame her.

Billy walked toward his friend. "She says there was five."

"I know," Jethro said. "One of 'em got away up the hill. I think I can recognize his horse's prints."

"So what do you think?"

"I'm going after him," Jethro growled.

"Yesterday you told us there wasn't going to be no war. Today you aim to start one?"

Jethro's face was set. "No. Today, I'm going to end it. Yesterday I hadn't seen any raped children. Have you found the girl?"

"Haven't looked. But I'd better come with you."

Jethro shook his head. "These people need help. You speak the language. I can handle it."

"Where'll we meet?"

"Back at Lincoln. Try to hold the regulators from going to war until I get back. Tell 'em about the defense plan we talked about. Tell 'em anything. If I can bring back that other bastard's scalp, maybe we can still keep the lid on."

Billy glanced at the still-sobbing woman. "Okay, pard. Luck to you."

As Jethro swung into the saddle, Billy smiled his buck-toothed grin and said, "Still seven more days of peace left."

The dark-faced man touched his hatbrim and clucked at the mare. He turned her onto the Ruidoso Road and then began studying the road, thinking about where his quarry might have gone.

If the fugitive was from Seven Rivers, there were several ways to get there. First of all, Jethro concluded, the trail past Pajarito Spring is most direct. But he could either travel up or down the Ruidoso. If he went upriver into the Sacramento Mountains, he could then work down the head-waters of the Rio Penasco, then to Seven Rivers. On the other hand, if he went down the Ruidoso Road, he would join the Rio Hondo Road and then to the cut-across road to the Penasco.

Downriver, however, would mean running a gauntlet of angry Mexican farmers. And sometimes they're shooting anglos these days, not a good risk for a lone rider. Upriver, similarly, meant traveling through the Mescalero reserve—also distasteful for a lone white man, especially given the fact that Victorio made a raid north of the border only a few weeks ago. No, it had to be Pajarito Spring. Jethro rode directly for the trail.

He was disappointed in not finding the tracks he sought embedded in the dust of the Pajarito Trail—the worn caulk of the right hind and the poorly shaped left front.

Shrugging, determined now to waylay the man somewhere along the Rio Penasco, he put the mare into a steady jog trot. He'd passed the spot where his friend John Tunstall was so brutally murdered some eight months before and was just passing up and out of the foothills of the Ruidoso when the thought suddenly struck that he could be *ahead* of the man he sought.

After all, the fugitive had cut and run to the north, into the foothills between Ruidoso and Bonito Rivers. In order to swing out and hit the Pajarito Trail, he'd have to make a half-circle. And in order to do it safely, he'd have to move cautiously. While Jethro had spent fifteen or twenty minutes tracking the fleeing man and etching his horse's tracks into his brain, he and his sorrel mare had ridden directly to the trail.

He decided to wait for an hour or two at Pajarito Spring....

———————

The man rode cautiously to the spring at midnight. He swung wearily from his saddle and knelt to drink while his horse sucked thirstily beside him. The horse sensed danger, snorting and pulling away just as Jethro's boot smashed the man's face into the mud at the bottom of the spring. The outlaw spluttered and thrashed away, clawing for his gun. Jethro kicked it out into the water. The man dived at Jethro's legs, but received a kick to the side of his head for the effort. He rolled away into deeper water, splashing out on the other side. Jethro leaped after him and threw him back. The outlaw, desperate now, staggered Jethro with a crazed swing, then jerked a knife from his belt. The blade flashed twice in the uncertain light, then the man was driven back into the water with a heel to the pit of his stomach. He charged back immediately, slashing and slashing again, only to be driven into the spring once more.

"Who are you?" the man cried, gulping for air.

"I'm God. And I'm sitting in judgment on those who rape and maim women and little children."

With an oath, the man charged again. This time, the knife was slapped aside and a hand-edge slammed into the outlaw's throat, knocking him into the water. He was trying to rise when a boot thudded down on the same throat and its already shattered larynx, driving the outlaw's head beneath the water. He gurgled and thrashed a little more, jerked violently, then lay still.

Jethro Spring waded away from the man he'd just killed. He saw the knife laying in the grass, picked it up, then dragged the dead man from the water by his hair. After resting a moment, he cut the man's gunbelt and the belt holding his trousers, then slit down an outside seam and pulled the trousers down....

Jethro Spring rode into Lincoln at daybreak on the morning after Billy the Kid had brought the news of what happened on the Rio Ruidoso. The regulators' horses were saddled and the men were tying on bedrolls and saddlebags and checking rifles and revolvers, preparing to ride. Their weary leader reined the sorrel mare to a halt and gazed silently at the motley group. Then Jethro swung from the saddle and said, "There'll be no war."

"Now see here, Winter ..." Jim French began.

George Coe cut him off. "The rest of us got a vote on that, Winter. And whether you like it or not, we vote war."

"I said there'll be no war," Jethro growled, turning from his saddlebags, clutching a handful of leaves and dried grass. The dark face was twisted with a craziness that caused the others to fall silent. Then he threw the handful of leaves and grass at George Coe's feet. The leaves fluttered away, along with most of the grass. Lying among the remnants was a man's bloody genitals.

"Like I said, there will be no war. They're avenged.

73

Anybody wants to ride out of here headed for Seven Rivers until I say so will do it over my dead body. What we're going to do is organize a defense line with our friends. Billy can tell you about the plan. Right now I'm going to get some sleep. Any objections?"

Every man's eyes were on the bloody bits of skin and muscle lying in the dirt. George Coe muttered, "I say you're the boss!"

CHAPTER SEVEN

Governor Lewis Wallace made his first move to quell the anarchy spreading across southeastern New Mexico by publishing a proclamation from the President of the United States of America. The proclamation primarily consisted of presidential authorization for the new governor to declare Lincoln County in a state of insurrection and declare martial law—if he deemed it necessary in order to control turmoil and achieve peace in the country.

Though a military veteran, General Wallace had been a practicing attorney in his home state of Ohio. He was also an amateur artist and had literary pretensions, even working on a novel he preliminary titled, *Ben Hur: A Tale of the Christ*. As result of his legal background working in tandem with the man's artistic sensitivity, Wallace was reluctant to utilize the extreme measure of martial law. He, therefore, sought to bring an end to the Lincoln County troubles via a seven-point plan. The plan's features were:

I. To dispatch all available troops from other posts in the Territory to Fort Stanton and distribute them in temporary camps in Lincoln and Dona Ana counties.

II. To have these soldiers scout thoroughly in these counties to break up all camps and corrals of outlaws.

III. To arrest without fear or favor all persons or bands of persons found in such camps or on the highways in possession of stolen property, or property for the possession of which they could not account satisfactorily.

IV. To hold all such persons until the proper court of the county met and took action according to legal procedures.

V. To have the property taken from such persons placed, if stolen, in safe keeping for identification and reclamation.

VI. If officers were satisfied that any one arrested by them was not deserving of arrest, they might at once release such persons.

VII. Army officers were to be especially careful not to interfere with good citizens going peaceably about their own business, since the object of this whole plan was to secure protection for all.

The president's proclamation and Governor Wallace's seven-point plan was issued October 14. Word reached Lincoln with arrival of the mail hack on the 16th. The presidential proclamation and its accompanying governor's plan made the front page of both the *Santa Fe New Mexican* and the *Las Vegas Gazette*.

When Jethro Spring awakened from an exhausted sleep after returning from the Ruidoso and Pajarito Spring, he found several knots of men gathered along Lincoln's dusty street. Henry Brown thrust a newspaper at him.

"What do you think?" Brown demanded when Jethro had finished reading.

"Well, I ..."

"Sounds to me like he's going all out with soldiers."

"Yes," Jethro said, "but he's stopping short of martial law."

"Still, it sounds like the soldiers got a free hand. That means that sonofabitch, Dudley."

Jethro chewed his lip, wondering himself what the proclamation and its accompanying plan really meant. Billy Bonney and Doc Scurlock wandered over to listen. At last, Jethro said, "I'm not sure it means Dudley at all, Henry. Look at the first step in Wallace's plan. It says, 'To dispatch troops from *other* posts in the territory to Lincoln County.' Then it says in step two, 'To have these troops scout and break up camps of outlaws.' Sounds to me like Wallace might not be planning to use Dudley or the Fort Stanton command at all."

Brown took back his newspaper to read again, mouth moving as he silently struggled with the words. Then he handed the paper back to Jethro and said, "Maybe. But I still don't trust soldiers."

"You think maybe this Wallace is okay?" Scurlock asked.

The longer Jethro thought about it, the more confident he became. "Hell, boys, I don't see a thing in that proclamation, or in the governor's plan, for us to worry about. We all know there's got to be law and order some day. For all practical purposes, this county has no sheriff. Such as we've got is on the side of the outlaws. The army is the only tool Wallace has. If I was him, I'd plan to use it, too. What I like about it is that it sounds like he plans to bring in outside troops, ones that aren't tied to Dolan-Riley and the Santa Fe ring."

"Does this change things about what we plan to do?" Scurlock asked.

"I don't see why it should, Doc. We'll still go ahead with our defense plan for our valleys. I'll see Antanasio right away—him and Ellis. I'll see if we can get together for a war council later today and plan our strategy; you know, the patrols, placement of our men, that kind of stuff. We'll get a defense plan underway, no matter what the new governor does."

Scurlock thrust his hands into his rear pockets and nodded. "I hope to God you and this new governor are right, Jack. Surely we all do."

Antanasio Salazar wasn't sitting at his favorite spot, but his big sombrero lay by his chair. The door to Tunstall's store was open, so Jethro walked in. He paused in the semi-gloom for his eyes to adjust. Susan came forward, broom in one hand and a broad smile on her face. Antanasio stood behind, also carrying a broom.

"Jack! It's about time I saw you again. I should say you've been neglecting me."

Jethro wondered if Antanasio saw his face burning amid the gloom. Then he recalled there was little the old man didn't know that went on in the village. "It's nice to see you again, Susan."

"Nice! Is that all you can say, you big oaf? This is the first time I've seen you since the night of my return from Las Vegas. Don't you know I've missed you?"

He said nothing, embarrassed by the implications of what she said—and by Antanasio's presence.

"That was a brave and wonderful thing you and Billy did to those awful Selman ruffians, Jack. I'm so proud. They deserved to die horribly. That poor woman and child. So terrible."

Susan wore a red bandanna around her luxuriant hair and a simple blue print gingham dress gathered at her waist and hanging modestly to the floor. He looked around at the big room. "Doing some swamping out, I see."

She smiled. A tuft of unruly, sun-bleached brown hair hung from beneath the bandanna over her forehead. She chided him, "You didn't come to see me, did you?"

He shook his head, hardly able to keep his eyes from her. "Antanasio."

"Did you see the governor's proclamation? What do you think?"

"That's what I'd like to talk to Antanasio about, Susan."
He glanced at the old man, "Can I bother you, Antanasio?"

"But of course, Senor Jock." The old man leaned his
broom against a broken counter. "Would it be *convenido* to
talk upon the porch, *mi compadre?* An old man's bones perhaps would not cry out so loudly if they were permitted to
rest in the sun."

"The porch it is. Will you excuse us, Susan?"

"I will. But only on the condition you return to talk with
me."

Outside, Jethro squatted on his heels, leaning against a
post. "You've seen the paper, Antanasio—the president's
proclamation and the governor's plan to restore peace?"

"It was read to me, si."

"I wish to know what you think of it, my friend."

The old man's forehead crinkled. He deliberately tilted
his rickety chair against the wall and closed his eyes to consider. "I think, Senor Jock," he began, "this new governor,
he may be a ver' wise man, no?"

Jethro nodded. "My thinking, too. If he goes about his
plan right, it could bring peace and justice to Lincoln
County."

"There is but one flaw."

"Oh? And what is that, Antanasio?"

"To bring *soldados* to Lincoln County from other forts
within the territory, to find them and give them orders, pro-
vision them and march them here, will take mucho time."

"No doubt."

"And during all this time, one wonders what Senor
Dolan and the *bandidos* from Seven Rivers will be doing."

Jethro nodded again. Directly, he said, "Which brings us
to one of the points I wished to discuss with you—my regulators would like to develop a defense plan for the Ruidoso,
Hondo, and Bonito, Antanasio. We'd like it to include your
people as well as ours."

"Si. A plan for defense would be a good thing to have,
Senor Jock. My people, they are ready to do as you wish."

"Do you suppose we could get together with some of your key men and work out the details?"

"Without question."

"Such a plan should include patrols, outposts, development of defense squads, dispensation of our forces, points of supply—what do you think?"

"Me, Senor Jock? How would I, a useless old man, know of such things? But what you suggest, ahh; that it is a most necessary thing I do not question. When would you wish such a meeting?"

"As soon as possible."

Antanasio's chair thumped down and he reached for his sombrero. "Then I will go and make the arrangements muy pronto. Where will I find you?"

"I'll be around somewhere." Jethro watched Antanasio Salazar until he disappeared down the street. Then he stood and leaned against the post, thinking. At last, he walked into the store.

Susan McSween smiled. "I hoped you'd come back, Jack. I do so want to talk to you."

He hung his head. "I guess we do have to talk. That's for sure."

She moved closer. "Why do you avoid me?"

He swallowed. "Well, for one thing, Susan, I'm not real proud of myself."

"Why, for heaven's sake? You have much to be proud of. I'm proud of you."

"For what happened the other night, I mean. How can you be proud of me. I don't know what came over me. Too much to drink, I guess. Both of us. I shouldn't have let you go to Wortley's. I blame myself."

She shook her head in disbelief. Then she smiled. "You really are sincere, aren't you. You really believe you've disgraced me."

He looked away, unable to meet her eyes.

"Listen, Jack, would it help if I said I was proud of you for what happened the other night?"

"You can't mean that. You're a decent woman."

"Of course I'm a decent woman. And I also happen to be in love with one of the most decent men I've ever known. Don't you suppose decent men and decent women have natural impulses, too?"

"Yeah, but they don't give in to them."

"Jack, Jack—don't be so naive. You are thinking only of what those beasts on the Ruidoso did to that poor woman and her child. And I'm thinking about the most beautiful, wonderful experience that can ever happen between two loving people. You do love me, don't you?"

The question caught him off guard. "Yeah, sure, I ..."

"I mean really?"

She stiffened when seconds elapsed while he considered. Finally he said, "Yes, I guess I do, Susan. Otherwise maybe I wouldn't feel so rotten about what happened the other night."

"And you're worried about how the thing that happened the other night will affect me, right?"

He nodded.

She reached up with both hands and unknotted the bandanna holding her tawny hair. When she pulled it loose, the locks cascaded down her neck, framing her face. Then she smiled up at him and asked, "Want to do it again?"

"*Wha-a-t?*"

"You ninny. You didn't seduce me. What happened between us is as natural as day and night. We love each other. I wanted it to happen and if you'll be honest with yourself, so did you."

His face actually paled. "You don't know what you're saying. We ... we haven't even talked about getting married, or anything."

Her smile broadened. "Is that a proposal, Jack? If so, it's a strange one." Then she sobered and laid a hand on his arm. Jethro winced as though her fingers burned. "There may come a time when we talk of marriage, my love. Certainly we cannot do so with my late husband so recently in his grave.

Indeed, he must first be avenged before I would consider remarriage. Then there's our age differential. How old are you?"

"Twenty-six," he mumbled.

"Seven years, you see. Not insurmountable. But certainly something to be considered."

"But we can't just ..."

"Who's to say not?" she demanded. "Despite our not being formally married, we love each other. We have natural desires, exactly as other people. If we love each other and mutually agree to share our physical love with one another, and if we enjoy doing so, why shouldn't we allow nature to take its course?"

He shook his head. "Susan, it's ... it's just not done."

She giggled. "I can't believe how naive you are."

"But your reputation. What if you had a child?"

"Jack, I'm thirty-three years old. I've been married before. Don't you think I would already have children if I could conceive?"

Jethro shook his head in bewilderment. "I can't believe we're even talking about this kind of thing."

She sighed. "Jack, please understand that I love you. What we are talking about is love as natural as breathing. It's natural that I'd want you and want you to make love to me. It hurts neither of us. I'm not a virgin and you are a virile, healthy man who loves a woman. As long as we are discreet in our love, no one else will be hurt. Nor will they even know.

"Please don't think of something as beautiful as our love for one another as something dirty. It's not. And please don't think of me as a harlot. I'm not. No more than you are a rapist. I'm merely a woman who knows exactly what she wants and goes after it." She moved closer. "*And I want you.*"

His arms went around her and he mumbled into her hair, "Damned if you don't make it sound kinda right."

She lifted her face to his and whispered, "Kiss me."

He did as she asked—hungrily. At last she gasped and moved back in his arms. "What I really wanted to talk to you about is to ask you to supper tonight. Will you come?"

"I reckon. Sure."

She flashed her most coquettish smile. "Wonderful! However, I'll probably work here late, and won't be prepared for you until, oh, say an hour after dark."

Lines crinkled at the corners of his mouth and eyes. "I think I'll be free about then."

A discreet cough came from the doorway. Susan slipped from his arms. Antanasio stood with his big sombrero in his hands. "My people, they are ready to meet with your people, Senor Jock."

It was a little after seven when Susan McSween let the man she knew as Jack Winter in the back door of Juan Patron's home. As soon as she'd closed the door behind him, Susan stood on tiptoe to place a light kiss on his cheek. He pulled her into his arms and sought her lips eagerly. She yielded for a moment, then pushed him away, gasping for breath. "Goodness, such enthusiasm! But don't you think we should have supper first?"

"Supper?" he said. "You mean you really did invite me for supper."

She frowned. "Of course." Then she understood. "Jack Winter, you don't mean to tell me …"

He nodded miserably. "I … I misunderstood. Susan, dammit, I'm no good at this sort of thing. I already ate."

It struck her as funny and soon he, too, laughed. When they'd subsided, she said, "Well, sir, you will just have to eat again. I shouldn't care to simply discard the results of my kitchen drudgery. Besides, I'll have to eat in order to keep up my own strength for what is to follow." She held out a hand. "Come along now."

She'd cleaned the house thoroughly. The curtains that

had lain on the floor were washed and hung at the windows. The broken dishes and pottery and scattered clothing were picked up or swept away. Usable remnant dishes were set at a small, intimate table where two candles flickered in their holders. Full wine goblets stood at each setting. "Please sit down," she said, "I'll join you in a moment."

She dimmed the room's two oil lamps, then brought a pot from the stove to the table. "It's just as well you ate before coming, Jack," she said. "I only had time for something simple—a Mexican dish: frijoles and chili. I hope it's all right."

"I feel so stupid," he said.

"Oh, don't be a boor. It's wonderful you could even come." She sat down, picked up her goblet and extended it to his. "To us," she said. "May there be many, many years ahead for our love."

"To our love," he murmured, touching goblets.

"It's good," he said minutes later, though already stuffed.

She laughed. "How was your meeting with Antanasio's people?"

"Good. I think we've got the basis for a good patrol system. We might be pretty effective at protecting this section of the county."

"How large an area will you attempt to defend?"

He told her.

"Doesn't that seem like quite a lot? Shouldn't you just try to protect Lincoln, itself?"

His brow wrinkled. "Susan, Selman hasn't hit Lincoln as hard as the Hondo and Ruidoso. It's the outlying areas that need help."

"Of course." But the way she said it meant she was unconvinced.

"It looks like we might be able to recruit upwards of a hundred men. If we can get it going, Selman's Scouts and the Seven Rivers bunch will maybe get a surprise or two."

"That's wonderful." Her eyes wandered to a spot over

Jethro's head and she mused, "If only we'd had such a force when Alex was killed...." She saw him stiffen and quickly said, "But let's not talk of the past, shall we."

"A hundred men. A thousand. It wouldn't have made any difference against the United States Army, Susan."

"Jack, let's not ..."

"And it won't now if the army steps in. We're betting they won't. Not for the likes of Selman; not for the likes of outlaws and thieves and murderers and rapists. Dudley wouldn't dare, especially with a new governor."

"Jack, I'm sorry ..."

"Then, they at least had the pretense of siding with the law. Now it's different, there's no question about that—if we can only keep our own men from going on a rampage on their ..."

"Jack! Stop it! I said I'm sorry I brought it up!"

He stopped abruptly, his face red. He didn't apologize and she knew he didn't intend to do so. She knew positively that he was still sensitive about the past, and suspicious of her role in the death of Alexander McSween. She wondered if this strange man still thought she deliberately sent him from the final battle in order to keep him as her hedge in case her husband and his men met defeat. Would even marriage bring his fierceness to heel?

She smiled her prettiest and said, "This night is ours, Jack. So is whatever life we have ahead of us. Let's live it that way. Let's put the past behind us."

He nodded, his mouth tight. Finally he reached for his wine and emptied the goblet.

She refilled it.

CHAPTER EIGHT

Selman's Scouts made their next raid on October 20. They came up the Hondo twenty-seven strong. Bound where, no one ever learned. The newly organized "Lincoln County Mounted Rifles" met them below San Patricio, in the vicinity of Joe Storm's farm.

The first of the "Mounted Rifles" to come to the battle site was a small contingent from San Patricio composed of Ignacio de Govera, Jerry Hockradle, and Trinidad Virgil. They arrived at their pre-planned position, hurriedly taking to the rocks above the road. They were in place when the other eight members of the San Patricio detachment arrived to a face-to-face encounter with Selman and his men.

Led by angry and indomitable Martin Chavez, the San Patricio men were first to unlimber their weapons in the dusty collision of whirling, rearing, surging horses and their riders.

Caught by surprise at a withering fusillade coming from hillside rocks and the audacity of this handful of Mexican and Anglo peons, Selman's men momentarily fell back, only to mount a charge as the San Patricio men scrambled from their horses and dashed uphill to shelter. In moments, telling rifle fire spat from those same rocks, driving Selman's men back out of range.

Time was wasted in consultation and lost in argument. At last, John Selman outshouted his loudest Scout and it was decided they must destroy this hillside nest of viperous settlers. The Scouts dismounted and split into two groups. One advanced cautiously, firing at targets of opportunity. Other in the second group climbed and circled in an attempt to get above and behind the defenders.

A little more than an hour passed before the circling men ran into an ambush and were beaten back. Then Mike Cosgrove and John Newcomb arrived from the Ruidoso, followed shortly by Crescencio Gallegos and Francisco Pacheco from the lower Bonito.

Selman decided a determined charge would rout their enemies, but his men had little taste for battle with an enemy who had both the firepower and the determination to shoot back. Thus the battle raged inconclusively for three hours more before a larger force of mounted riflemen arrived from Lincoln to rout the outlaws.

The Scouts broke and ran. But unlike before, these victors didn't immediately return to their homes to boast and celebrate. Instead, they pursued the outlaws down the Rio Hondo, across the Penasco Road, clear to the Rio Feliz, emptying saddles of laggard outlaws along the way. Finally at the Rio Feliz, choosing defense of their homes and families over vengeance, the Lincoln County Mounted Rifles turned back. As they jogged homeward, Billy Bonney trotted his horse alongside the weary sorrel mare of Jethro Spring.

"Only one day to go," Billy shouted, over the clip-clop of dozens of horses, the creaking of saddles, and jangling of bits.

"One day to go?" Jethro asked.

"Your thirty days are up tomorrow," Billy the Kid grinned. "After tomorrow, we can go to war."

Jethro's taut face relaxed. "Sounds good. I'm getting tired of all this peace anyway."

———•◦•———

It had been a long time since the residents of the village of Lincoln had something to celebrate. But when the Lincoln County Mounted Rifles trooped wearily into town early on the morning of October 21, virtually all Lincoln turned out to rejoice in their delivery from the outlaws. Shouting, laughing, singing, and dancing was the order of the day and well into the night.

Accolades came freely to the architect of their defense. The Mexicans were ecstatic in their appreciation, their Anglo compadres mollified in their desire for vengeance. Even Antanasio Salazar was uncharacteristically enthusiastic.

"It is a grand day, Senor Jock, that our very own people could so destroy such a powerful and evil enemy. It is to you we owe victory." The old man teetered on his chair, his toothless grin spread wide in the day's fading light. Children shouted up and down Lincoln's single street, while men and women gathered in little groups to laugh together. Antanasio surveyed each activity like a benevolent parent, proud of his progeny.

Jethro sat on the porch steps staring glumly out into the street. "I don't like it, Antanasio."

"Is this so? Why is it you do not like this thing, mi compadre?"

"They're acting as if the war is over. All we won is a battle. Don't you suppose Selman might be figuring how to even things up right now?"

"Si. But do you not think these poor people learned from their victory? Have they not learned they can fight and win? Besides, Senor Jock, do not deny them a few moments of happiness. They have had so little."

Jethro stared at his feet, lost in thought.

The old man said, "You have out the patrols, yes? Is this

not done?"

Jethro nodded, then looked back at the wrinkled, happy face.

"Then what more is to be done? Your men are here and ready. This is a thing that is true also at San Patricio. You trouble yourself for nothing."

Susan McSween stepped from the door of Patron's home and walked toward them. She paused to pat a young lad on the head, then picked up a small girl and swung her around, both of them laughing. As Susan set the child down, guitar music wafted up the street in the dim light.

"I knew you'd be here," Susan said as she neared. "When will I have a chance to congratulate the conquering hero?"

Antanasio's chair thumped the porch floor and he stood to bow with a flourish. "Surely, senora, you mus' now take the time—if I would but be permitted to leave."

Susan curtsied to the old man. "Such gallantry, Antanasio! Rest assured I shall take good care of your friend in your absence."

Antanasio chuckled, then went tottering down the street.

"Jack, darling, you are positively wonderful! I've never seen these people like this in all the years I've lived here."

"How long has that been?" Jethro inquired, a euphoria settling over him with the woman's presence, the people's gaiety, and the strains of the far-off guitar.

"Oh dear—forever, it seems." She turned to gaze into the street, saying, "Three years. Perhaps more. We came in March, 1875."

"Three and a half. A lot has happened since then. Mostly all bad for these people. It's no wonder they haven't been merry when you get to thinking about it."

Susan spread her skirt and sat gingerly by his side, gazing at the darkened store building. "Just think, Jack, we'll soon be opening this store again."

"Is that wise, Susan?"

"Wise? What a strange thing to ask. With Dolan-Riley closing their doors there's a fortune to be made here with a properly run merchant enterprise."

"Maybe that's what bothers me, Susan. If there's a fortune to be made here, others might be thinking the same thing. You could be walking into a continuation of the trade war that's been going on here for years."

"And you think because I'm a woman, I can't compete."

He grimaced. "No. I said no such thing."

"But you thought it, did you not?"

Jethro pointed at the street filled with happy people. "Look at that. They've had enough of war and death. Peace, Susan. That's what they want more than anything. That's what I'm talking about."

"Still, someone will supply these people. Jose Montano cannot do it. You know that. Why can't that someone be me? Us?"

He shrugged. A muscle ticced in his cheek. "The wounds are too raw, Susan. I'm just afraid you'll be caught up in more war."

"I'm a capable woman."

"Dammit, I know that! But isn't there something else? Why does it have to be the very damned thing that brought the country to its knees to begin with?"

"Well, you're so positive. What else might a lady do to earn a livelihood? Start a bawdy house?"

He leaped to his feet, eyes flashing. She caught his arm. "I'm sorry, darling. I was only jesting. Here, I have a surprise." She held out a cigar.

He hesitated. "Please," she said. "I ordered them especially for you from Las Vegas. I know you smoke occasionally."

"It's been a while," he said, taking the cigar and studying it while fumbling for a match. She pulled one from a sleeve cuff, struck it, then held it to the cigar.

When he had it going well, she smiled sweetly and said, "I ordered an entire box, dear. But as you want more, you'll have to come to my house for them." He studied her through the smoke while she added, "After dark."

There was the faintest smile. "Do you think you could stand it? Sometimes I may want several smokes a day."

"I shall order another box at once."

Her hand stole into his and he squeezed gently. A bonfire was lit down the street and the night came alive with merriment. "How will you finance the store?" he suddenly asked.

She withdrew her hand. "Well, that's not exactly thoughts of love—not at all how I imagined your mind would be engaged."

"It takes money, Susan. How will you swing it?"

"I'm not destitute."

"Nobody said you were."

But she, too, could be given to fits of anger. "What will you do if I won't answer?"

"Same thing I've always done. Get up in the morning. Go to sleep at night. Put on my pants one leg at a time. Eat, sleep, ride. What else can a man do?"

Her anger melted. "John Tunstall's father has generously agreed to a favorable rental agreement. And I've also been in correspondence with several supply companies. Many will extend credit for a limited period. Other money as necessary will come from my own funds."

"Sounds to me like you'll be extended. You're taking a risk."

"Certainly there's some risk. But the profit potential is enormous. Believe me, Jack, it's a sound investment. Well worth the risk."

"I still don't like it."

Silence was like a curtain between them until she said, "Jack, you've never before mentioned your own situation. I know this is a difficult thing for people in love to discuss, but do you have any source of income?"

"No. Only what I can earn."

"And how much is that, dear? I know you worked for

John Tunstall before he died. But that only lasted, what, five or six months? Since then, I'm not aware that you've worked for anyone else. Have you?"

"No."

"I know you too well to believe you a thief. But, dear, how can you live?"

"I don't need much."

She again took his hand. "That is no answer."

He took a deep breath. "I had a little put away when I came here, Susan. Not much, and it's about gone. But my needs are simple."

"Mine are not," she said. "Jack, you once mentioned marriage. Do you think there's any hope for marriage on the basis of your finances?"

He shook his head. She was only dimly aware of it in the darkness.

"Then how in the world can you advise me against the store when it may well be the only way we can eventually wed?"

He was like a stone. Then he said, "Sure would make for an interesting marriage, wouldn't it? Dumb, penniless, cowboy yokel marries beautiful business-woman type who owns half of Lincoln County. Is that possible, either?"

"Must we continue this?"

"No, we don't, I guess. Not now, not then, not ever."

She gripped his hand in both of hers. "Jack, I'm planning the store for both of us. Please believe that. Of course we'll do it together. I simply couldn't operate the store without you and it would be ridiculous even to try. I've planned for you all along, you know that."

"Have you now?" he said, retrieving his hand. "Somehow I never figured me as a storekeeper."

"Oh Jack! You know there's more to operating a store than merely tending it. There are dozens of men we can hire for that. What I'm talking about goes beyond that. We'll need to bid on government beef contracts. And there's a distinct possibility we may acquire both of John's ranches on

the Rio Feliz and the Rio Penasco. Then there's the need for
..."

"What the hell did you say? The ranches? How could
you swing that?"

"Not for certain, mind you, Jack. The negotiations
aren't complete and I would appreciate your keeping it con-
fidential."

"But you're the administrator of the estate, since
Widenmann pulled out."

"Administratrix," she corrected. "Besides, what does
that have to do with it? Nothing in the law precludes an
administrator from making an honest acquisition during dis-
solution."

"But money! You're talking about one hell of a lot of
money. I thought you said you lost everything when Alex
was killed and your home destroyed."

"Jack Winter, it's beginning to sound as though you do
not trust me!"

To gain time, Jethro fumbled for a match of his own and
re-lit the cigar. "It's not a matter of trust, Susan. But the
dollars you're talking about! There are way too many zeroes
for a simple man like me. I guess maybe that points up the
fact that I'm no business head."

"Will you trust me, though?"

He patted her hand. "I guess I don't have any choice.
When a man ties to a woman, he's tied hard and fast."

She smiled into the darkness. "What is good for the gan-
der is also good for the goose."

The tip of his cigar glowed red. "What'll be the name of
your store, Susan?"

"I think we'll use the same name—J.H. Tunstall and
Company—at least for the time being."

"He'd like that. It's a good name. An honorable name
in Lincoln County. And that, in itself, is unusual."

———— ·•· ————

Selman's Scouts, augmented by some of the worst elements from the Seven Rivers outlaws, struck the Berrendo settlement four days after suffering their San Patricio defeat. The Berrendo settlement, located fifteen miles north of the Rio Hondo community of Roswell, was a remote, out-of-the-way hamlet of mild-mannered Mexican/American families who, thus far, had escaped the ravages of the Lincoln County War. Selman's men brought it home to them in a twenty-four hour orgy of murder, rape, and arson.

On their return to Seven Rivers, Selman's revenge carried over to an attack on the small Anglo community of Roswell. However, their robbery of the Roswell Post Office brought the wrath of the federal government upon them and a detachment of U.S. Army troops from Fort Stanton went into an encampment on the lower Rio Hondo, only three miles from Roswell. The troops began regular patrols along the lower Pecos, clashing from time to time with outlaw gangs.

Still unnerved at their losses to the Lincoln County Mounted Rifles and harried by federal troops from the Roswell encampment, Selman and his men again bypassed Lincoln and the Ruidoso to strike at the region of the upper Pecos. But there, taking a page from Lincoln's book, Juan Patron led a band of vengeance-seeking vigilantes from Fort Sumner to the attack. Once again the fighting became too hot for Selman's Scouts and they fled south to their Seven Rivers refuge. This time, however, they left not only empty saddles from gunfights, but two of their fellows swung from cottonwood limbs as a warning to others of their kind.

"Selman's taking some licks, Antanasio," Jethro Spring said, pulling the sheepskin-lined coat tighter around his neck. Out in the street, a brisk wind drove a cold misting rain with it.

Antanasio Salazar sat in his usual chair, tilted in its usual way. A heavy wool serape was pulled tight across his shoulders and another lay stretched across his knees. "Si, Senor Jock. It does one's heart good to know these Selman Scouts will soon be no more."

"I hear the Berrendo settlement is even taking up arms, despite federal troops camped in their backyard."

"To help one's self is best, *mi compadre.*"

Jethro shivered against the wind and wondered how the old man could sit so patiently immobile in such weather. "You think Selman is finished, then?"

The old man nodded. "For surely. But one mus' remember, he and his men still have fangs and claws and it is best not to let one's guard down until the beast is dead and buried."

"And Dolan-Riley is dead. Apparently it's true they've gone into receivership?"

"That is the story."

"But you don't believe it?"

"Si. I believe it, my friend. But one mus' wonder who will take the big store for money owed them."

"I don't understand. You see a threat there, Antanasio?"

"*Por favor? Mucho dinero* is still to be made in this land, Senor Jock. Surely there are those who lust after it."

➤ CHAPTER NINE ⬅

The news that the acknowledged leader of the Santa Fe ring, Attorney General Thomas B. Catron, was taking over the Dolan-Riley store hit the people of Lincoln County hard. Despite having resigned as New Mexico Attorney General, the administration sought to placate anti-administration Republicans in New Mexico by permitting Catron to retain his position until a successor was appointed. Catron, thought by many to be virtual dictator of New Mexico through his shrewd financial manipulations, moved swiftly to reinstate his store's influence by appointing his brother-in-law, Edgar Walz, to re-open and manage it for him. Then, using his political influence, Catron induced Lincoln County Sheriff George Peppin to again become active.

Peppin's November 11 move from Fort Stanton back to Lincoln was supported by a band of deputies recruited from the old anti-McSween faction, and augmented by a detachment of Fort Stanton troops commanded by Lieutenant J.H. French.

Resignedly, Jethro watched the troops march in and go into camp in the corral yard of the new Thomas B. Catron & Co. store. Most of the Ruidoso Anglos and any of the Mexican/Americans known to have outstanding warrants pending against them vanished overnight. Only the man known as Jack Winter and a "baker's dozen" of the more timid Mounted Rifles stayed behind.

On the afternoon of November 12, Jethro Spring entered Catron's store and asked to talk to Sheriff Peppin. He got an immediate audience.

"You're hell for guts, Winter," the stocky, mustachioed sheriff said as he came from his new office at the rear of the store. "I'll say that for you."

"As a resident of Lincoln County, sheriff, I think I have a right to know what you intend doing."

"You ain't no more resident than a turtle dove, Winter. You're a hired gun brought in here by that English jackass to cause trouble. It's trouble like you brung that I aim to stop."

A man wearing two low-slung guns moved to Peppin's side. Jethro saw two lounging soldiers come alert. He knew another man was somewhere behind. "Do you plan to stop Selman, too? He and his men have broken the law a little."

"I'll get to Selman all right. First off, though, I've got a bunch of old warrants that's been gathering dust. Your name is on one or two of 'em."

Jethro had known he risked arrest when he came to brace Peppin. But no one else seemed willing to present a backbone to this reincarnation of political evil and someone must at least offer a protest. At least he found out how it was to be. Jail or fight? he asked himself. *No dammit, you idiot, fight when you have a chance. Don't carry the protest too far.* "Tell me, Mr. Peppin, what kind of warrants? I wasn't aware...." His voice trailed away in apparent helplessness.

Peppin was disappointed that Winter chose not to fight, but he gloated to see the leader of his enemies grovel. "I've got 'em," Peppin growled. "I'll read 'em to you after you're behind bars. Right now, I'm putting you under arrest."

Jethro unbuckled his gunbelt. To Peppin, he said, "If it's old warrants you're wanting to serve, George, why don't you serve the murder warrant you hold on Jesse Evans? He's standing at your right elbow, you know. His warrant dates back to the murder of John Tunstall."

The blond outlaw grinned and his blue eyes gleamed. So did the deputy sheriff's badge pinned to his vest. "I was hoping you'd have guts enough to make a play," he said. "I owe you for a couple."

"Some day, Jesse. Don't get impatient."

They threw Jethro in the dug-out adobe jail and the trap door clanged shut overhead. It was cold. He sat stoically on the room's bare cot until his eyes became accustomed to the gloom. Then he stood and methodically began to pace, cursing under his breath that he'd foolishly put his life in jeopardy. *Some crazy notion of leadership responsibility,* he thought.

He thought about trying to break out. Simple, he knew, with outside help—it'd been done many times before. But who was left in the village to help? All the real fighting men had ridden out when the soldiers rode in. Damned good thing, too, or they'd be in here, too. I should've been smart enough to go with them.

Jethro heard voices beyond the trap door, probably in the outer office, but he couldn't make out who was speaking or what was being said. Soon it was quiet again and he resumed his pacing.

What will happen next? He supposed he would remain in jail until he stood trial. But the October District Court term was never held because of the state of anarchy within the county. When was the next term? April? Must he stay in jail until then? He quickened his pacing.

The door swung open to the dugout and Jesse Evans peered down at him. Evans was alone. "How do you like it, Winter?"

"Beats laying out overnight in the white sands," Jethro

replied, referring to his long chase of Evans, when the two had dueled for weeks after Jethro surprised Evans and Tom Hill during a sheep camp robbery.

"One thing about the sands, though, Winter—there, a man's got maneuvering room when somebody's chasing him. In a place like this, a man can't run far."

So they plan to kill me here in jail. "Some people don't have anything to run from, Jesse. Others have their whole life to look back on with nothing to be proud of. Which are you?"

The handsome outlaw grinned. "And others have only a little of their life ahead of 'em. Which are you?"

Just then, the jail's outside door opened and Jack heard Antanasio Salazar's humble voice. "Ah, there you are, Senor Deputy Evans. I now have the writ from the most honorable Justice of the Peace, Senor Wilson. Now will I be permitted to speak to Senor Winter?"

Evans snatched the paper the old man extended and quickly scanned it.

"It is—how you say—signed in counter by Senor Sheriff Peppin, no? Is that good, Senor Evans?" The old man stood with his head bowed, sombrero in hand, a serape over his shoulder and another under his arm.

Evans wadded the paper in his fist and threw it in a wastebasket. "All right," he growled. "Hurry it up, old man."

Antanasio pushed the ladder down and descended, smiling and bowing. When he reached the floor, he thrust both serapes toward Jethro.

"Hold on!" Evans rushed to the dugout with a drawn gun. He ordered Antanasio to hand him the blankets. When he was certain no weapon was concealed, he threw them to the floor below.

Ignoring Evans, Antanasio said, "Senor Jock, do not despair. Even as we speak, there is a guard going up around this building. The guard will see no bad thing happens to you while you are staying within. Do not fear."

Evans rushed to the front door and jerked it open. "Hey, you! What the hell are you doing here? Get away from this jail! You others, too."

Jethro heard Isaac Ellis say, "We got a right to be here, Evans. Here, this is a writ from Judge Wilson that says we can stand guard around this jail as long as Winter is cooped up inside. All fifteen of us have the same writ."

Evans slammed the door. "Your time is up, old man," he shouted to Antanasio. "Get the hell out."

"Oh no, senor. The good justice, Senor Wilson, wrote that I might stay for ten minutes."

"I didn't see where it said that." Evans turned the wastebasket over to retrieve the writ.

"Who's out there?" Jethro whispered.

Antanasio spread his palms. "Only old men, senor. They and some of our senoras. But they are your friends. And they" (Antanasio did the sign of the cross) "are made of such that the *soldados* dare not attack them. Neither will Senor Peppin drive such a group of old men and women away. They can shoot if there is such a need. And they will not be alone."

Jethro grinned.

"There will also be one sleeping in the jail, Senor Jock, along with …"

"Hey!" Evans yelled. "It don't say one damn thing in here about time. Now I'm tellin' you only one more time—get out of there!"

"Si, senor." The old man turned abjectly. Over his shoulder, he whispered, "Go with God, *mi compadre*."

Susan McSween came at dusk. To Evans, she sweetly but firmly said, "I have a writ from Judge Wilson allowing me to sleep in the jail tonight." She carried several blankets.

Evans had just ushered Susan to the ladder and returned to his outer office when yet another knock came at the jail's outside door. Evans jerked it open in exasperation. Sam Wortley stood outside, a towel-covered tray of food in his hand.

"Brung the prisoner some vittles," Sam said.

"Oh shit! Go on in. The rest of the town's been here already."

Wortley sidled in, tossing a tight little grin at Jethro after he, too, clambered down the ladder. "Peppin is a little put out," the ferret-faced hotelkeeper said, "but for a regulator and a troublemaker, you're an all-right sort."

Jethro smiled. "This isn't on the county, I take it?"

"Nope. It's on old Sam Wortley. Goin' soft, I reckon." Wortley turned to leave. "Jest set the tray up on the ledge when you're done. I'll get it when I bring breakfast in the morning. Sam eyed Susan, sitting demurely in a corner of the dugout, but said no more.

"It may be poisoned," Susan said after Wortley had gone.

Jethro chuckled and began eating. Around a mouthful of food, he said, "I'm well-protected, looks like."

"You're as safe as we can make it, Jack." She studied him as he ate. Finally she said, "I'm surprised at the depth of affection these people hold for you."

"Me too."

"One can't help but wonder why."

"I agree."

"One thing is abundantly clear—you'll be an asset to my merchant company."

He stopped chewing and she added, "*Our* company."

Still paused, he asked again, "I wonder if I'm cut out to be a storekeeper?"

After he'd set the tray upon the ledge, she said, "A letter of protest has been signed by thirty of Lincoln's most respected citizens and telegraphed from Fort Stanton to the governor. Judge Wilson, Jose Montano, Isaac Ellis—they've all signed it. They're protesting the use of military troops to enforce civil law, and they allude to the fact that Colonel Dudley is once again intervening, contrary to orders. I understand Dudley tried to stop the sending of it, but he changed his mind when he was told the message would be sent from Mesilla, along with an addition that he wouldn't allow it from the fort."

"But there *are* warrants for my arrest."

"Trumped up charges," she spat. "With rape and murder the order of the day in this county, resisting arrest and obstructing justice must look awfully ridiculous to our new governor."

"Sounds to me like Governor Wallace is being put to a test."

"Indeed? Do you suppose that decrepit old Mr. Salazar planned it that way when he suggested that you talk to Peppin?"

CHAPTER TEN

Governor Wallace's amnesty proclamation came in on the wires to Fort Stanton at four p.m. the following day. The man known as Jack Winter was released from custody within two hours. Sheriff Peppin again retreated to Fort Stanton, and another Lincoln celebration was soon in progress. Days later, when the full text of the amnesty proclamation became available, Jack read it carefully to Antanasio Salazar:

> For the information of people of the United States and of the citizens of New Mexico in especial, the undersigned announces that the disorders lately prevalent in Lincoln County in said territory have been happily brought to an end. Persons having business and property interests therein and who are themselves peaceably disposed may go to and from that county without hindrance or molestation. Individuals resident there but who have been driven away, or who from choice sought safety elsewhere, are invited to return under assurance that ample measures have been taken and now are and will be

continued in force to make them secure in person and property.

And that the people of Lincoln County may be helped more speedily to the management of their civil affairs as contemplated by law, and to induce them to lay aside forever the divisions and feuds, which by national notoriety have been so prejudicial to their locality and the whole territory, the undersigned by virtue of authority in him vested, further proclaims a general pardon for misdemeanors and offenses committed in said county of Lincoln against the said laws of the said territory in connection with the aforesaid disorders, between the first day of February, 1878, and the date of this proclamation.

And it is expressly understood that the foregoing pardon is upon the conditions and limitations following:

It shall not apply except to officers of the United States Army stationed in the said county during the said disorders and to persons who at the time of the commission of the offense or misdemeanor of which they may be accused were in good intent resident citizens of said territory, and who shall have hereafter kept the peace and conducted themselves in all respects as become good citizens.

Neither shall it be pleaded by any person in bar of conviction under indictments now found and returned for any such crimes and misdemeanors, nor operate the release of any party undergoing pains or penalties consequent upon sentence heretofore had for any crime or misdemeanor.

In witness whereof I have here unto set my hand and caused the seal of the territory of New Mexico to be affixed.

Done at the city of Santa Fe, this
13th day of November, A.D. 1878
Lewis Wallace
Governor of New Mexico

The old man sat throughout the reading, head bowed, lips moving as he silently repeated Jethro's words. When the gray-eyed man finished reading, he asked, "What do you think, old friend?"

Antanasio raised his head and stared unseeing at the southern ridge for a long time, lips still moving thoughtfully. When he spoke, it was to ask Jethro to read the section about pardon eligibility once more.

After the younger man had finished, Antanasio asked, "This pardon, it does not apply to the young Senor Bonney?"

"No, not the way I read it. He and Henry Brown are under indictment for Brady's killing. So is Fred Waite and John Middleton, but they've left the country."

"And is not Senor Bowdre under indictment for killing this Buckshot Roberts?"

Jethro nodded. "But Buckshot Roberts was himself indicted as an accessory in Tunstall's death, so a jury might overlook Bowdre because of that."

"Perhaps that would be so with Senores Bonney and Brown, no?"

"Could be."

"And is it not true, *mi compadre*, that Senor Evans, he is indicted for Senor Tunstall's murder?"

"Yes. And so is Dolan and Matthews."

The old man nodded. "I think, Senor Jock, this new governor is a very wise man. He rids himself of minor warrants that were sworn to by evil men trying to bend the law to their own ends. But he keeps the important indictments that were returned by an honest jury in an honest court of law. This Governor Wallace, he may some day be a great man, no?"

"Jack, I'd like to introduce you to Mr. Houston I. Chapman." Susan McSween stood between the two men in the partially stocked, but still unopened, J.H. Tunstall & Co. Mercantile. Jethro Spring surveyed the medium-sized stranger in the broadcloth suit. The man had one pinned-up sleeve. "Mr. Chapman is a Las Vegas attorney whom I've engaged to represent my interests."

Jethro extended a hand. "How do you do, sir. I'm Jack Winter."

"Quite well, I believe." Chapman took the hand. "Winter? Hmm. I believe I've heard the name. And just what is it you do, if I may ask?"

Jethro thought Chapman's question contained a touch of sarcasm and his first instinct was to dislike the man. And since the attorney still gripped his hand, so too, was his second instinct—sufficient reason why the reply was laconic. "Mostly I'm just a leach, Mr. Chapman. Living when I can off the handouts of friends, neighbors, and poor orphaned widows."

"Jack! That's terribly rude."

Chapman's eyes glinted behind wire-framed spectacles and he began squeezing Jethro's hand with his own powerful one-armed grip. The attorney's grin spread wider as he felt the satisfying relaxation of the gray-eyed man's hand. Then, however, the slack hand that had been schooled and exercised in Oriental fighting techniques, tightened and strengthened and squeezed until the Las Vegas man winced.

"Jack?" Susan said, not understanding what was happening between the two men.

Jethro released the attorney's hand and said to Susan, "No doubt you two have business to attend. So do I. I'll check by when I'm free."

After Jethro had left, she said to the attorney, "I would advise staying on the windward side of that man, Houston. He is much more than he appears."

Chapman rubbed his hand vigorously against a thigh. "He's the one you told me about?"

"He's the one."

"Perhaps you were not too far wrong."

"Others have come to that conclusion."

"And what role does he play in your affairs?"

Susan stiffened. "The mere fact that you are my legal counselor hardly gives you the right to pry into private matters."

"Not at all," Chapman said. "I just assumed Mr. Winter has a business role."

"He does. Jack Winter is rapidly becoming one of the more influential men in Lincoln County. He has a remarkable following among the county's poorer Anglo and Mexican elements."

"I see. And how does he sustain himself?"

"He will work for me."

"Oh?" Chapman said, rubbing his chin thoughtfully. The way he said it might have implied several things.

"Surely you did not journey all the way to Lincoln because of a concern over the staffing of my new store?"

"No. I came because I wanted to bring you up to date on my meetings with the new governor."

"I'd hoped as much. Shall we retire to my office?"

After they'd made their way through the dim store aisles to Susan's new and spacious office at the rear, Chapman said, "Yes, well I met with Governor Wallace twice ..."

"What kind of man is he?" she interrupted.

"Frankly, Susan, I don't trust him. He's somewhat gruff, but well-spoken. A big man. Bearded. I don't think he fully understands affairs here in the county, though I tried my best to explain them. He was entirely noncommittal about your own individual affair, even though he expressed his sympathy at your distress. He did seem disturbed about your letter accusing Colonel Dudley of responsibility for poor Alexander's death. He said he'd forwarded it on to General Hatch for investigation."

"You said you don't trust Governor Wallace?"

"I don't exactly mistrust him, either. But with all the information we've forwarded him, I should think he should be more openly supportive of our cause."

"Perhaps partisanship is too much to expect, Houston," Susan mused.

"It's our due. Especially after years of partisanship on the other side from the governor's office. At any rate, at the second meeting I tried as forcefully as possible to suggest to Governor Wallace that he should come to Lincoln for a first-hand view of the situation."

"And what did he say to that?"

Chapman laughed. "Aside from the fact he seemed to resent my insistence, he said he'd prefer to give people in responsible positions a chance to work out Lincoln County's problems. I chided him for such foolishness."

"Did you advise him that we intend to file civil suits against those responsible for Alex's death and my property's destruction, despite his amnesty proclamation?"

"I did. He agreed amnesty only extends to criminal matters and not civil liabilities. The man does have a reasonably sharp legal mind."

Susan McSween leaned back in her chair and tapped the ends of her fingers together while studying Chapman. "So what is your assessment, Houston?"

Chapman, too, leaned back in his overstuffed chair and gazed, as if in fascination, at Susan's tapping fingers. "I believe the plan is following our charted course, my dear. Despite the governor's pardon and despite his unwillingness to become our partisan, our position looks good. You and the senior Tunstall have excellent grounds for a civil suit. All we need do is to take the time for adequately preparing public sentiment in your favor. Financially, Dolan, Riley, and Peppin are all proper targets. Dudley is from a quite wealthy family, although we still need better proof of his role in the fateful July battle in order to get at his finances. However, Wallace may have unwittingly played into our hands when he included the officers of Fort Stanton in his pardon. I predict, milady, you'll be a wealthy woman out of all this."

"And you?"

Chapman smiled. "I'll get mine. That's what 'contingency' means."

Jethro Spring did not return to visit Susan McSween that day, nor the next. She found him idly braiding a horse-hair riata in Wortley's stable. "Antanasio said you might be here."

"His information is generally good. Trust him."

She wiped an accumulation of dust from an ancient three-legged milking stool and sat down near him. "You like him very much, don't you?"

"Yup."

"He thinks the same of you, you know."

Jethro continued braiding. Thus far he'd not looked at her.

"I brought you a cigar," she said, holding it out.

He took it and thrust it into a shirtpocket.

She smiled. They sat in uncomfortable silence for a long while. Then she said, "If the mountain won't come to Mohammed, Mohammed must go to the mountain."

"Huh?"

She laughed. "Just a saying, Jack. Why haven't you been to see me?"

"You're pretty busy with that lawyer fellow."

"Jack Winter, you're not jealous?"

"Nope. Leastways I don't think so. I always said you could do a lot better than me."

"That's ridiculous! Why I never ..."

"How long have you had him for a lawyer, Susan?"

"Since the middle of October. Why?"

"And you first told me about him two days ago."

"My Lord! Must I clear everything with you first?"

"No. But you have been making noises like I'm going to be more than just a clerk in your store. I'm not sure what you've got in mind, but it's pretty clear that being a con-sulting partner isn't included."

"I see," she said. "Now it's becoming clear why you

have your nose in the air."

He continued braiding the riata. She said, "Although I wonder why I must tell this kind of thing to the man I love, Houston Chapman is my *personal* attorney, retained by me to redress some longstanding *personal* grievances. The store has absolutely nothing to do with his employment by me. Therefore I felt in no way compelled to ask for your blessing."

Jethro laid down his riata, took out the cigar, and dug for a match while eyeing her. "This Chapman is pretty sharp-tongued, isn't he?"

"He's an intelligent man, if that's what you mean."

"That's not what I mean. What I mean is the way he's going around trying to fan the war's embers into flame."

"Houston's purpose is to redress my wrongs. I'm not entirely privy to his methods."

Jethro shook his head. "Not good enough, Susan. There's a lot of folks here in Lincoln who hope the embers just die out. Chapman seems to be singlehandedly trying to keep them burning. For God's sake, try to stop him before another war breaks out."

He picked up the riata. She watched him while he worked, placidly smoking his cigar. She said, "Now that Juan Patron has returned, I've moved to Santurnino Baca's home—should you wish to visit."

"I know. Antanasio told me."

Susan returned to her new home. Houston Chapman was there. The man handed her a copy of the *Santa Fe New Mexican*, datelined November 30, 1878. She opened it and read a paragraph Chapman had underlined. The underlined section was an open letter from Colonel Nathan A. Dudley to Governor Lewis Wallace.

When she'd finished reading, Susan McSween pitched the paper on a table and said, "It seems something pinched a raw Dudley nerve."

The attorney chortled. "That's what I call throwing down a gauntlet. Dudley couldn't possibly have better kicked the new governor into our camp than if he'd slapped him in the face. This is wonderful news!"

"What is our next move?" the woman asked.

Chapman slapped the table. "Why, we must fan the flames higher, my dear. What else? I should think a town meeting is in order."

Susan shook her head. "I certainly hope you know what you're doing, Houston. There are some in Lincoln who think you are pursuing a wrong course."

"Trust me, Susan. Becoming rich is well worth the gamble."

She smiled sweetly at the man, but a few moments later she caught herself biting a lip and studying her attorney through slitted eyes.

———•◆•———

The righteously indignant Colonel N.A.M. Dudley threw himself into his imagined role of law-and-order champion with a zeal. In his enthusiasm, the commandant released regular newspaper dispatches reporting his command's accomplishments in the field. One such dispatch told of a patrol by a unit under the command of lieutenant Milliard F. Goodwin to check on reports of widespread cattle stealing in the distant Tulerosa Valley. Unfortunately, Goodwin's investigation traced one herd to the Indian Agency and Dudley's ardor cooled.

The *Cimarron News and Press* did a follow-up story dateline December 5, 1878. The story proved highly embarrassing to the Colonel and his brand of law and order:

> "… it looks very much as if in certain official circles it is well considered no crime to steal in Lincoln County, provided it is done to aid the government contractors in filling their contracts.
>
> From such thefts as these the trouble in Lincoln County originated, and this singular action of Dudley

does not impress us with much confidence in the kind of peace he maintains. An impartial administration of military power there we believe would restore permanent peace. Governor Wallace's plan is all right, but we fear the military will render all his efforts unfruitful of lasting results."

⇒ CHAPTER ELEVEN ⇐

NOTICE

There will be a mass-meeting of the citizens of
Lincoln County, on Saturday, December 7th, 1878,
at 1 o'clock p.m. at the court house in Lincoln, for
the purpose of expressing their sentiments in regard
to the outrages committed in this county and to
denounce the manner in which the people have been
misrepresented and maligned; and also to adopt such
measures as will inform the President of the United
States as to the true state of affairs in Lincoln County.

All citizens are invited to attend.

Jose Montano, Judge Wilson, and Isaac Ellis tried to
persuade Houston Chapman not to hold his meeting:

"Dammit, Mr. Chapman," Ellis said, "there ain't been
nobody killed in Lincoln in a while. We'd like to see it stay
that way. This meeting of yours won't do no good and it
could do a lot of harm. Call it off."

"I'm afraid I can't do that, gentlemen," Chapman said.
"I should think you are all deluding yourselves if you think

the present calm will last. Unless someone takes firm action, I fear the next explosion will exceed the last in its intensity."

"That is what we think, too, Senor Chapman," Montano said, wringing his hands. "That is what we wish to avoid. That is why we come to you."

"Apparently, gentlemen, we all have peace with law and order in mind. We only differ in methods. I happen to believe an open meeting is the proper way to pursue those goals."

"The new governor is making progress," Judge Wilson said. "All of us think so, anyway. He says himself that he needs time. Let's give it to him. What difference will another month make?"

Chapman's response was, "I have a client to consider. To postpone the meeting would not be in her best interest."

"Sounds as though you're planning this meeting for selfish reasons, Mr. Chapman," Judge Wilson said.

The Las Vegas attorney pointed his index finger. "I'm sure it's within your province to issue a writ against such a meeting, Judge—say, in the interest of public safety. If you do so, however, I would suggest you prepare to defend yourself against a charge of being an accomplice of Colonel Dudley and the Catron store."

"That's a goddamned threat, Chapman," Ellis growled. "It might be a lucky thing you don't have two arms."

"I have nothing more to say to you gentlemen."

"*Muy bueno,*" Montano said. "When the blood, she flows, senor, it will be on your hands. Perhaps you should pray to the Virgin Mary that it will not be your own blood."

———— · · ————

The meeting overflowed. Even the Ruidoso men drifted back to Lincoln. Over a hundred men, women, and children listened in rapt attention as a born orator, Houston Chapman, opened with a ringing denunciation of a governor's pardon that allowed known murderers, rapists, and thieves to walk the very streets they'd desecrated by their villainy. Chapman then switched to a vitriolic denunciation of Governor Wallace because he'd failed to visit Lincoln to "acquaint himself first-hand with an anarchy brought about by determined outlawry, coupled with administrative acquiescence!"

James Dolan and John Riley rode into town at this point, accompanied by a dozen of their more prominent gunmen, including Jesse Evans, Billy Matthews, John Long, and the Mes brothers. Dolan's entourage pulled up just outside the crowd's perimeter and sat their horses, listening silently to the Las Vegas lawyer's harangue.

Chapman gave no sign of fear, continuing his fire-and-brimstone oratory, though some of the crowd edged away from the horsemen. Jethro Spring, standing beneath the spreading limbs of a nearby live oak, had to admit to the courage of the one-armed man. Finally Chapman wound up his hour-long appeal with an energetic accusation of military criminality. When at last Chapman stopped, he'd whipped the crowd into an ugly mood. Only the common sense reasoning of the respected community leaders dampened the crowd's passion—that and the discreet disappearance of Dolan and his cronies.

The very next day, John Copeland shot and killed Juan (Johnny Mace) Mes in a dramatic gun battle fought in the middle of Lincoln's single street. Once more, troops from Fort Stanton were rushed to Lincoln to install a tenuous peace and the Ruidoso farmers drifted back to the friendlier confines of their home valley.

Houston I. Chapman, by his venomous denunciation of the military, became a target for their animosity. He was arrested by a drunken detachment on trumped-up charges and no warrant, then released. Again, he was harassed by soldiers prior, during, and after his able defense of John Copeland in that man's acquittal for the Mes killing. Through it all, Lincoln seethed—a caldron ready to explode.

Mid-December brought the resignation of George

Peppin as Lincoln County Sheriff. In his letter to Governor Wallace, Peppin said he'd not received so much as five dollars of his salary, nor did he ever expect the county's empty treasury to be able to meet any sheriff's salary.

Though Peppin had for the past several months stuck closely to the shelter of Fort Stanton, there was at least the pretense of law in Lincoln County. Now, with his resignation, there was no law and little order in southeastern New Mexico.

———•—•———

Jethro Spring sat on the edge of the bed, elbows on knees, morosely smoking a cigar. He was clad only in his trousers, though the room was cold.

Susan lay on her side, snuggled near him, shoulders and head bare, index finger tracing the bullet scars on his neck and back. "Penny for your thoughts," she said.

"I'm leaving."

"What!" She sat up, bedcovers falling from her exposed breasts. "You're joking."

He pulled away, standing to face her. "I'm not joking, Susan. I'm going away for awhile."

Her lips pouted, but her eyes were calculating. "Why?"

"You don't want or need me around here."

"How absurd!"

"You've got Chapman. He's calling the shots. And I don't care much for the way he's calling 'em."

"But he's an *attorney*, dear. He's giving carefully considered legal advice."

Jethro grimaced. "He's leading this county back to war and you know it. I'll be no part of it. That was part of the deal when I came back the last time—I'd call the shots."

"Strategy. Not business decisions."

"That's right. Now it's Chapman who's making the strategy decisions." He sighed. "So it's time for me to leave."

"How can you?" she begged. "I've given you *every-thing*."

His eyes swept over her. Susan's hair hung over her shoulders and down to her naked breasts. "Yes," he said, "you have. Tomorrow, you can take me off the payroll. I won't be here."

"Jack, please."

He ignored her, donning his shirt.

"Well, where will you go?"

"I don't know. Maybe I'll see what these mountains look like in the winter."

"Will I see you again?"

"I don't know. Depends on you, I guess. If you need me—and you damn sure will—just send for me."

"Where? Where will I send?"

"Beats me. But I'll be in touch with somebody."

She fell back, then rolled onto her side and silently watched him slipping into his boots. When he turned to leave, she said, "There is still half a box of your cigars."

He paused, saying over his shoulder, "Do you want me to take them with me?"

"No. You may take them a cigar at a time. Like always."

He turned to face her. "I got a hunch they won't go stale before I'll be smokin' them again."

CHAPTER TWELVE

Jethro Spring helped his old regulator friends move their families from Fort Sumner back to their farms and ranches along the Rio Ruidoso. The move was completed December 21. All along the Ruidoso Valley, an air of optimism and jubilation reigned. Peppin's resignation, Colonel Dudley's discomfiture, the defeat of Selman's Scouts and their Seven Rivers outlaw friends, all combined to contribute to the holiday atmosphere.

Jack had just finished resetting the leather hinges on the Scurlock's front door when Billy the Kid rode in, followed by Henry Brown, Tom O'Folliard, and Charlie Bowdre.

"Hey, Jack!" Billy called from hailing distance away. "Bunch of us decided to go to town for Christmas. Why don't you come along?"

Scurlock and his wife came to the door to peer out.

"You, too, Doc. You and the missus."

Scurlock smiled and shook his head as the men wheeled and cavorted their horses before the house. They were freely passing a bottle between them. "Not us, Billy," Doc said. "It's plenty Christmas enough for us just to be home. We reckon we'll stay here."

Billy's buck-teeth flashed. "Suit yourself, Doc. How about you, Jack?"

Jethro shook his head. "No, I believe I'll pass, Billy. Maybe I'll kinda wander up in the mountains and see what a real Christmas looks like for a change."

"Aw, c'mon Jack. We'll have us a blowout like the town ain't never seen before."

Jethro smiled, but his eyes held a somber squint. "Just remember the terms of the governor's pardon, Billy."

"To hell with the governor!"

"Billy ..."

Bonney wheeled his horse in a full circle, "C'mon Jack. We're just out for a little fun. We got things to celebrate."

"Billy, dammit ..." But they were gone in a cloud of dust.

Scurlock watched them disappear, then said, "They'll be all right, Jack. They're young and just blowing off steam."

Jethro didn't head directly for the high Sacramentos as he'd planned. Instead, he pointed the sorrel mare over the Pajarito Spring trail he remembered so well. From there, he moved like a wraith between the Spring and the Rio Feliz and upper Penasco. He spent Christmas Day lying on a low knob between the two rivers, his horse concealed in a swale beyond, glassing the surrounding countryside for sign of his people's enemies. At night, he slept with an ear to the road. During the days, he lay still and invisible to a casual eye, even through frequent rain and snow showers. Finally, on the first day of the New Year, Jethro Spring returned to Scurlock's farm on the Ruidoso and collected his packhorse and camp outfit. Outside the farmhouse, he told Doc where he'd been and why:

"They'll come again, Doc. I know they will. The patrols have got to stay out watching for the bastards. I guess I expected 'em over the holidays, and I expected us to let our guard down a little."

"We'll be watchin' for 'em, Jack. Never you mind about that. Right now, though, you're headed up to the mountains?"

Jethro nodded. "Is Billy around?"

Scurlock's mood changed. "Naw, he cut and run for Fort Sumner." Jethro's eyebrows went up. Scurlock continued, "They got in a little trouble at Lincoln."

Jethro slammed his fist into the adobe wall of Scurlock's home. Dust and clay flew. Scurlock's jaw fell open when the gray-eyed man didn't even wince. "What happened?" Jethro growled.

"They was just havin' some fun, way I get it, Jack. I reckon they boozed up too much. And they shot things up a little."

"Was anybody hurt?"

"Not that I know of."

Jethro rubbed his fist. "Well, what the hell did they do?"

"I ain't real sure. I know they made enough waves that Dolan and his crowd run for the fort. And they pissed Ellis off enough so's he got his two sons and had Judge Wilson swear 'em in as constables."

"What happened then?"

"They th'owed Billy in jail is all I know."

"And he let them? He didn't fight?"

"He let 'em, I guess. You know how he is about the Ellis's. Maybe he was too drunk. I don't know."

"Property damage?" Jethro asked.

"Some, I guess. Shot up Catron's store and busted a few bottles in Wortley's saloon. Bad enough so Walz asked Dudley for troops to protect his store."

"And he sent them, of course."

"Yeah. George Coe said Dudley claimed he was protecting his military contractor."

Jethro's face tightened and the muscle along his jaw ticced, hinting at his burning anger. All the while, he rubbed his knuckles and stared a hole through Scurlock. For the first time, Doc actually felt a twinge of fear toward this man—his friend. "Goddammit!" Jethro blurted. "Now! Why now?"

"I didn't wanta be the one to have to tell you, Jack," Scurlock said. "We knew you'd be mad. Don't that hurt?"

"Don't what hurt?"

"Your hand," Scurlock said, pointing. "For God's sake, you most near knocked a hole in my 'dobe wall. Don't it hurt none?"

"Great shit! Yes it hurts. When did he get out?"

"Next day, I reckon. Promised Isaac he'd be good. They let him out for Christmas and him and the boys went on another tear."

Jethro rubbed a hand across his dark face. "Well, that cuts it," he said in disgust.

"Yeah, it ain't good. You got that right."

The two men walked back inside the house. "How's the coffee?" the darker man asked, moving to a chair.

"Should be hot. Mommy, fetch Jack a cup, would ye?"

After Mrs. Scurlock brought the coffee and shooed the kids from underfoot, Jethro sipped slowly and said, "That puts you back in command of the Ruidoso patrols, Doc. Can I count on you?"

"I already told you not to fret none about it. Go on up in the mountains and forget that lawyer feller."

Jethro's head snapped around. Red began creeping up the ruddy-faced farmer's neck. "Stuck my foot in my mouth, didn't I?"

"Can you carry a message for me to Patron?"

"Juan Patron? Don't see why not."

"With Billy gone, I'm putting him second in command of the mounted rifles. Any objection?"

Scurlock shook his head. "None that I can see. He'll make a good choice."

"In addition to being in command while I'm gone, he'll

be in charge of the Rio Bonito patrols."

"Makes sense."

Jethro set the empty cup on the table. "I'll write the note to Patron, then I'll pick up my other pony and gear and get the hell out of your hair."

"Ain't you gonna stay for supper?"

Jethro shook his head. "No. Thanks, though. I'm going to pull out while I can. Before something else falls apart."

———

Jethro Spring spent all of January and the first three weeks of February dwelling with the Mescalero Apaches, high in the fastness of their Sacramento Mountains reservation. He asked for nothing more than to be treated as an equal dwelling in the wickiup of the accepted reservation chief, Naiche Tana—also known by his enemies as Malvado.

Neither did Jethro come to the reservation village with empty hands and eating always-short Indian rations. Instead, his packhorse was loaded with corn and coffee and sugar. Twice during his stay the visitor saddled the packhorse and led him to Dowlin's Mill to purchase additional foodstuffs for the hungry band. Twice the gray-eyed-one, as the Indians now began calling him to replace their older choice of man-called-the-season-of-the-hunger-moon, disappeared deeper into the mountains, each time to return on foot, leading his horse with a fat deer slung across the saddle.

Within a remarkably short time, Jethro was speaking a few halting Apache words. Before the end of his stay, he'd acquired the ability for limited conversation with his Mescalero friends. Much of the visitor's rapid acquisition of the new language could be attributed to Naiche Tana, who'd long recognized the newcomer as a friend and ally to his people in their time of need. Primarily it was Naiche Tana's command that the gray-eyed man was seldom alone, seldom without some Mescalero carrying on a slow methodical conversation with their quiet guest.

Jethro found a hush to be the norm within the village. Conversation was carried on in a low murmur. Never, during his nearly two months with the Apaches, did Jethro hear a raised voice. Children almost never cried. Neither men nor women shouted. There, he experienced a quiet peace that had been rare for him since years before, when he'd visited in the home of Ling San Ho, his Chinese friend. As a guest in the wickiup of Naiche Tana, the chief, he was accorded respect from the beginning. But later, as he proved willing and able to provide more than his share of food for their village, he earned respect in his own right.

Besides learning the rudiments of their language, Jethro also learned much of their customs and a little of their religion and history. He learned the noted Apache fierceness was more an illusion shaped by the harshness of their environment and their constant struggle to sustain themselves against a succession of would-be conquerors: Commanche, Navajo, Spaniard, Mexican, and American. Because he was half-Indian himself, Jethro more readily understood their fatalistic mentality; how, clad in animal skins and rags and with little to eat, they could hold out for nearly three decades against Mexican and American armies ten times their numbers. And he could also understand their necessity for at last recognizing indisputable fact—that they could no longer resist their enemies' crushing numbers and devastating weapons.

Along the way to understanding, Jethro's respect for their steadfast leader grew immeasurably.

Fresh snow settled over the village. As it fell, the snow was little marred by hoofprint or moccasin track. The storm passed, however, and by mid-morning, a bright sun cast a blinding glare over the village. Inside the brush-thatched and mud plastered wickiup of Naiche Tana, only a half-light from a smokey, smoldering pine knot flickered uncertainly across the chieftain's face. Naiche Tana squatted stolidly near the fire, wearing only his loin cloth. His woman, Teonay Mizme, crouched by his side, occasionally stirring a simmering pot.

Teonay Mizme wore a simple dress of tanned deerskin designed as merely a sack with holes cut for arms and head. Many women belted the dress around their waist. The belts also served to support knife sheaths or drawstring bags of herbs or powders.

The men and boys universally wore deerskin breechclout and knee-length moccasins. The high-topped moccasins were developed, Jethro learned, for protection against spiny plants growing throughout Apache land. Many of the men also wore the white man's shirts of cotton or wool, often gaudily striped or calico in color.

Jethro Spring sprawled against the wickiup's wall. He wore his wool coat, turned up at the collar against a keening wind that blew through the hovel's cracks. He asked the somber chief, "How did you acquire the name *Malvado?*"

Speaking slowly in Apache so that his visitor could follow, Naiche Tana said, "From the Mejicanos to the south. The reason, I do not know."

"It means 'bad' or 'wicked' or 'evil' in their language, Naiche Tana. They must have feared you very much."

The Apache never moved, but Jethro could actually *feel* the man's piercing eyes seek him out in the wickiup's dim light. "Once, I wished them to fear me. Once, I wished all my people's enemies to fear all Apaches."

"But no more?"

"No."

"Why not, Naiche Tana? I know you wish to live in peace, but...." his voice trailed off.

"Naiche Tana does not wish to live in peace. Naiche Tana longs for war."

The measured statement surprised Jethro. "I don't understand. I thought you wanted peace for your people?"

"That is so. Naiche Tana wants peace for his people. For without peace there will be no Apache, no Mescalero. But for Naiche Tana, he longs for war."

Jethro moved a small pack of dried deerskins to make

himself more comfortable. The fire flickered out to mere coals. "Why?" he asked.

The Apache growled, "I am war chief! Naiche Tana was born to war, trained for war, led in war. It was as war chief the name Malvado was given to me by our enemies."

"I thought Victorio was Mescalero war chief?"

"Victorio is a great warrior. He is as a brother. We have been on many raids together. But it is I, Naiche Tana, who was chosen for war chief."

"Yet you lead your people in peace and he leads them in war."

The warrior chief shrugged.

"Why is that, my friend?"

Naiche Tana stared into the coals. "War is hopeless for the Apache, gray-eyed-one. Once there were many of us. Now we are but a few. If the Apache will live, we must fight no more. We must learn the ways of the white man."

"And you see that clearly, while Victorio does not?"

The fire sputtered back into tiny flames as the chieftain said, "Victorio also knows it to be true."

"I don't ... my eyes are clouded, Naiche Tana. I cannot see to understand."

"The Mescalero must survive, gray-eyed-one. We must go the white man's way in peace. But few wish to do so. All Mescalero Apache would fight until they have no life to fight more."

Jethro's brow wrinkled.

"It was our tribe who decided some should go to the reservation to live, while others stayed to fight."

"And so you ..."

Naiche Tana's expression had not changed. But suddenly his eyes blazed and he drew himself up, hesitated in that regal position for a moment, then said, "It was the only way our people would come to the reservation and live in peace."

Jethro nodded. "If you were the one to lead them to peace!"

Doc Scurlock rode into the village the next day. "Miz Susan sent me, Jack. She says to tell you she needs you."

"What's happened, Doc?"

"Aww, that damned lawyer fella went and got himself killed."

CHAPTER THIRTEEN

After Selman's Scouts suffered their series of crushing defeats, an uneasy peace settled over Lincoln County. Gradually those who'd fled the bloody disorders of the past returned to their homes. The earlier return of Juan Patron from Fort Sumner signaled a burgeoning confidence among the Mexican/Americans. Meanwhile, the Ruidoso Anglos dwelled in guarded optimism in their valley. Even John Chisum moved the center of his ranching dynasty back to Lincoln County.

Their opponents in the war also returned to Lincoln in force. James Dolan, the ring's field leader, maintained a low profile, but it was obvious by his frequent visits to Fort Stanton that the man still enjoyed the partisan good will of the commandant and his officers. Jesse Evans and others of his ilk also came and went at will.

The ingredients for open warfare still smoldered, however, awaiting only a brisk wind to again burst into flame. It was business as usual at Catron's big store. Now under the direct control of the territory's most well-connected political figure, Catron's wielded tremendous power. Under Edgar Walz's management and Dolan's tutelage, the store continued to squeeze small farmers and ranchers. Catron's also remained in control of southeastern New Mexico's military and Indian reservation supply contracts. And they still employed—so many folks thought—questionable practices in bidding their beef contracts, as well as still maintaining unsavory relations with men from shadowy bandit fringes who supplied livestock with smudged brands.

Amid it all, hatred for the big store festered among Lincoln County's ordinary citizenry. The truce, as it was, barely existed in the early days of 1879.

Amid it all, Houston I. Chapman, the Las Vegas attorney employed by Susan McSween, worked feverishly to bring peace to an end. He kept up a running stream of letters to Governor Wallace about circumstances in Lincoln County. Those letters were intemperate in content, abusive toward both the military and the newly appointed sheriff, George Kimbrell. The lawyer's role as an agitator can clearly be seen in an excerpt from one letter:

> Your own proclamation that peace had been restored in Lincoln County supersedes the necessity of further aid from the government and prevents the use of the military to aid the civil authorities in Lincoln County; and I have advised the citizens here to shoot any officer who shall in any manner attempt their arrest or interfere with their rights. I have counseled the people to observe it. While I counsel its observance, I question your authority to grant amnesty before conviction is had, for offenses against the law.

Then came the welcome news that Sydney M. Barnes had been appointed New Mexico Attorney General, replacing Thomas B. Catron. One of Barnes' first acts was to write a memorandum to Sheriff Kimbrell to the effect that as attorney general, he intended to pursue long-delayed pun-

ishment for the murderers of Englishman John Tunstall.
Kimbrell applied to Colonel Dudley for assistance in serving
warrants against Evans, Dolan, and Matthews.

Military aid was slow in coming.

It was during this period—middle of February, 1879—
that Billy the Kid and his friends chose to return to Lincoln
to raise a little hell. But this time, against opponents of
Catron's store, Dudley was quick to act. Bonney and his
gang to fled.

The diligence of the new sheriff and new attorney general in attempting to restore law and order to Lincoln
County caused the ringleaders of each faction's wilder elements to see wisdom in burying hatchets. Billy the Kid, tir-
ing of war and wanting to abide by the terms of the
governor's pardon, made the initiative. Jesse Evans, after
consulting with Jimmy Dolan, agreed and a parley was
arranged. Three men from each faction met in Lincoln during the evening of February 18 to discuss terms.

Billy the Kid, Tom O'Folliard, and Eugenio Salazar were
contractors for one faction; James Dolan, Jesse Evans and Bill
Campbell for the other. From the group's discussion came a
remarkable document, signed by each member present:

> I. That neither party would kill any member of the
> other party without first having given notice of hav-
> ing withdrawn from the agreement.
>
> II. That all persons who had acted as "friends" were
> included in the agreement and were not to be molest-
> ed.
>
> III. That no officers or soldiers were to be killed for
> any act previous to the date of this agreement.
>
> IV. That neither party should appear to give evidence
> against the other in any civil prosecution.
>
> V. That each party should give individual members of
> the other party every aid in their power to resist
> arrests upon civil warrants, and, if necessary, they
> would try to secure their release.

VI. That if any member of either party failed to carry out this compact, which was sworn to by the respective leaders, then he should be killed on sight.

Behind the agreement were several motives. The spring term of court was soon due. With an energetic new sheriff and territorial attorney general, it would be desirable for important witnesses to take the stand with closed mouths. It's possible, in view of what happened later the same evening, the document was merely an effort to compromise Billy Bonney....

With the treaty signed, the high-contracting parties set out for an evening of celebration. They were joined by Billy Matthews, Edgar Walz, George Van Sickle, and G.S. Redmond—all men of the Dolan faction. The group made the rounds of Lincoln, shouting, singing, and laughing one with another. On a Dolan whim, they stopped at the home of Juan Patron. Billy the Kid objected, but the group barged in. Soon they began badgering the indignant Patron. Campbell pulled his pistol and Patron ducked behind Bonney. A few ugly seconds passed before the celebrants were finally persuaded to leave Patron's. Bonney tried to slip away from the group at this point, but Evans and Campbell turned mean and the Kid went along rather than jeopardize their new peace. They'd not gone far when they met a man coming toward them in the darkness. "Who is it?" Campbell growled.

"My name is Chapman," came the reply.

Campbell drew his gun and punched it against Chapman's breast. "You're the bastard who's come here and stirred up all the trouble. But we settled all that now and we're all friends. Just to show us you're peaceable, too, you're gonna dance for us."

"Get out of my way," Chapman said. "I don't propose to dance for a drunken crowd."

Billy the Kid edged away but Jesse Evans seized him and held firm. The group milled around the one-armed attorney. Chapman, unable to clearly identify the men who surrounded him, asked of the man who held the gun, "Am I talking to James Dolan?"

"No," replied Jesse Evans, "but you're talking to damned good friends of his."

"Oh ho! You're the one who killed the Englishman."

Dolan broke into the exchange: "Why don't you go on back to Las Vegas, lawyer, and leave Lincoln County to Lincoln County people?"

"So you are here, Mr. Dolan!" Chapman exclaimed. "Yes indeed, you'd like to have things your own way again in Lincoln, wouldn't you? Well, I'm afraid that's over now. You see, I just came from Santa Fe and an audience with the good governor. He'll soon honor our little village with a fact-finding visit. Yes, Mr. Dolan, your days are numbered."

"Shut up!"

"Make him dance!"

"Rest assured, Mr. Dolan," the undaunted Chapman continued, "there will soon be a lawsuit and ..." A gun blazed in the darkness, then another. "My God!" Chapman moaned, then died.

James Dolan lifted his smoking Winchester back to his shoulder and turned to Bonney and O'Folliard, "He didn't sign our contract. he wasn't covered."

Billy looked at the circle of Dolan men now closing around him and swallowed. He wasn't a coward; neither was he a fool. "That's right," he said.

Dolan jerked a bottle of whiskey away from Billy Matthews and dumped the contents on Chapman's body. Then he scratched a match and threw it to Chapman's whiskey-drenched clothing. "Come on boys," he said, walking away from the blazing body, "let's go up to Wortley's. I'll buy a drink."

Bill Campbell watched the fire a moment. When he rejoined the group, he drunkenly said, "I promised my God and Colonel Dudley that I'd kill that goddamned lawyer. And by God, boys, I've done it."

———•◦•———

Chapman's body lay in the Lincoln street for over twenty-four hours. Sheriff Kimbrell, realizing how explosive the situation was and knowing the town crawled with armed and dangerous men, once again sent an urgent request to Fort Stanton for troops.

Colonel Dudley dispatched twenty men under the command of Lieutenant Dawson. The detachment included the post's Acting Assistant Surgeon, W.B. Lyons, who was charged with doing a post-mortem autopsy on the body. The troops were slow to depart for Lincoln, only doing so late in the afternoon following Chapman's murder—after its officer and surgeon first had a lengthy conference between Colonel Dudley, James Dolan, Jesse Evans, and Bill Campbell.

It was after eleven p.m. when Surgeon Lyons' examination of the badly burned body disclosed Chapman had died from two gunshot wounds in the chest, both fired at close range. The report also stated that Chapman's clothing was ignited by a muzzle blast from the killer's weapons—not from deliberate drenching of flammable liquid and its ignition.

An inquest was held the following day, but little was gleaned from local citizens fearful of their lives in a Lincoln crawling with heavily armed Dolan partisans. About sundown, however, hard-eyed men from the Ruidoso began to drift into town, followed by armed-to-the-teeth men from the Rio Hondo and Rio Bonito. The tide changed to favor the anti-Dolan forces and Colonel Dudley rushed a second detachment of soldiers to Lincoln.

Up in Santa Fe, a big, black-bearded man laid his pencil upon his writing table and took a late evening note from an aide. Governor Wallace read the note twice through, then slumped in his chair, rested his chin in one hand and deliberated for several minutes. Then he called his aide and issued instructions to arrange for the governor's immediate departure for Lincoln.

Meanwhile Houston I. Chapman's last remains were buried and Doc Scurlock rode hard for the Mescalero village of Malvado.

———•·•·•———

Susan McSween threw herself into Jethro's arms when she opened the door of her new store-building living quarters to his knock. He tugged her arms from his neck and pushed her gently away, then stepped into the room and nudged the door closed.

Her eyes were dull. "Well, Jack, once again it seems you were right and I owe you an apology. I was wrong."

He shrugged. "You wanted to see me?"

"Oh, yes! Jack, I'm frightened. The only time I feel safe is when you are near. Please, I want you here. I want you never to leave again."

He slipped off his heavy coat and hung it on a wall peg. She tried to come to him again, but he deftly held her at bay. Their eyes locked in a contest of wills. Hers' fell first.

"All right," he said, "what's the situation?"

They talked quietly for over an hour, standing by her door. She tried to lead him to a chair, but he shook his head firmly and asked additional questions. She answered them one by one; each becoming more searching and more pertinent to her goals. At last she exclaimed, "Jack, what is this—an inquisition?"

His smile was fleeting, but it was there. "Well, Susan, your answers seem right enough, as far as they go. At least they're in line with what I've already learned. There's still a lot I don't know, though—such as how much of this latest deal was Chapman's and how much yours."

"That is an insult, Mr. Winter!"

"And I still haven't figured where you're getting your money to buy ranches and stores."

"Why must I feel so ... so inferior around you?" she cried.

His mouth corners curled in irony. "Try giving answers some time."

Her voice chilled. "We've already been through this in the past. I simply do not feel compelled to answer your leading questions about my private business affairs."

"Your reply bent around several corners just then, Susan."

"So what if it did? I need not give credence to your insinuations about my business ethics."

"What is it I'm here for, Susan? Is it that you think you need a bodyguard? Didn't the new governor demand and receive a safeguard for you from Colonel Dudley? Why do you need me?"

"Don't you want to come back? Am I not good enough for you?"

"That's what I'm trying to make up my mind about."

"Oh, now I see!" she flared. "It's some Apache wench, isn't it?"

"I reckon you'd be surprised to find out how chaste—is that the right word?—their women are."

Susan McSween's was an internal struggle and her face mirrored it. She knew this man was unlike others she'd known. His quiet and intuitive intelligence continually surprised everyone with whom he came in contact. But wasn't it also that intelligence, competence, and masculinity that posed a danger? This man alone, of all the citizens of Lincoln County, suspected her of converting her dead husband's questionably acquired assets to her own use. Did he also suspect her of taking over the dead John Tunstall's Lincoln County assets by default?

Her face softened, "Please, Jack, let's not fight."

She was amazed that he could appear so cold and yet so calm. What was he thinking? Her only hold on him was through both his passion and compassion for her. No doubt she'd squandered some of the compassion by displaying her own forcefulness and business acumen. His passion? That was yet to be seen.

He leaned against the doorjamb. "I'm surprised the store isn't open."

"I'm afraid to do so. The shelves are stocked and ready. But without you, I'm afraid to open it. Catron is so powerful, and that awful Mr. Dolan is still around. So is Jesse Evans and that new hired killer, Campbell. I'm afraid by opening the store that we'd foment more trouble here in Lincoln."

Jethro pulled out his notebook and pencil. As he wrote F-O-M-E-N-T, he mumbled, "That's funny. Somehow I got it through my head your lawyer wanted to fan the flames. Does that mean to stir things up?"

"Does what mean—oh, foment. Yes. Fomenting trouble was Houston Chapman's idea, Jack. Not mine. I've already admitted you were right. Must I beg? What more can I do?"

"What more can you do?" he mused, staring down at the new word. "Well, you can start by bringing me a cigar."

It was all Susan McSween could do to keep from laughing aloud as she hurried to her bedroom for the cigar box she kept there. Why did she doubt that his passion for her would win out? With this man by her side she was safe. She could open the store, dismiss her enemies, flout convention or sanctuary, employ or deploy at will. She patted the cigar box maternally. And after her enemies were destroyed, it would not matter what Jack Winter thought.

Or knew, for that matter.

Susan handed Jethro the box. He took a cigar and pushed the rest back. She studied the man as he lit his cigar and blew out a satisfying cloud.

"I want to remind you," she said, "there are certain procedural stipulations that are attached to each of those cigars."

He smiled. "I'm not sure I'm up to it—having spent the last two months panting after a whole tribe full of Apache maidens."

"I was surprised to learn Eugenio was one of the signers

of Bonney's and Dolan's peace pact, my friend."

Antanasio Salazar shrugged. "The foolishness of youth, Senor Jock. This one time my own son, he did not ask his old father's advice. Perhaps he wanted peace too mucho, eh?" The ancient one glanced sideways at Jethro. "At the very least, *mi compadre*, my foolish son had enough of a head on his shoulders to slip away when he could. Poor senors Bonney and his other friend, they were not so fortunate."

"I'm not so sure, Antanasio. Billy's a witness. So is O'Folliard. They could make a difference as to whether Dolan is convicted of murder. They could be damned important, as a matter of fact."

"You are forgetting their peace contract, *mi compadre*. This contract, it says Senor Bonney cannot testify against the others who sign such a contract."

"That contract's not worth the paper it's written on, Antanasio. You know that. Dolan broke it within minutes after it was signed." Jethro fell silent, then added, "Yep, both Billy and Tom have got to testify."

"To do so, *mi compadre*, would be to sign one's death warrant."

"Don't you think it's already signed and sealed for them anyway, Antanasio? Awaiting only delivery?"

"Perhaps."

Changing the subject, Jethro asked, "What of the governor? What have you heard of him? What will he do, my friend?"

"We have heard he is to visit our village."

"Yes, that I know. Why has he not yet come?"

"If you wished for this governor to not find what evils have been done in this place, would you not work to prevent his coming?"

"How could that be done, if he really wished to come?"

"Ah, that thing a poor man such as I could not know. Are there not affairs of state; important matters that could not be set aside? Can not these things suddenly grow? Many such of these things and the governor, he grows late and forgets our poor county, no?"

Jethro shook his head morosely. Was this governor falling into the enemy camp, too? He stared bitterly at three soldiers strolling the dusty street.

"Senor Catron, he visits Fort Stanton only yesterday. It is known that he talked long with the Colonel Dudley and Senor Dolan."

"What was said?"

"Alas, *mi compadre*, but that is not known."

"What do you make of it, Antanasio?"

The old man gazed at the southern ridge. "Is *importante*, no?"

"It's important, yes.

"Si. For a great man such as Senor Catron, who has never before visit our poor county, to come just now is strange."

Jethro pounded a fist into a palm. "That damned governor *must* come!"

"Si. In this thing, the dead Senor Chapman was right." Jethro jerked around, a scowl on his face as Antanasio gently continued:

"The dead senor was not wrong in all things, *mi compadre*. Where he failed was because of greed. He wished only what was best for himself and Senora McSween. The senor wanted more evil to be done so that his *cliente* would appear more with the virtue to the new governor and to the world. It is sad the *hombre* forgot that many innocent people will suffer if this war, she begins again. But Senor Jock, the senor *jurisconsulto* was not wrong in all things. This you mus' remember."

They both stared at the mail coach as it rocked past their perch. A dusty black-bearded passenger stared back. They watched the coach pull up in front of Wortley's hotel and the traveler clambered down as mail sacks were swiftly exchanged. The passenger picked his valise from the coach and waved at the driver as the coach rolled away. The man glanced up at the Wortley Hotel sign, then turned to stare meditatively at the Thomas B. Catron & Co. sign over the big store across the street. The passenger glanced both east and west, up and down the street, then began trudging back the way the coach had come.

"Looks like a lost pilgrim," Jethro said.

"Si. Mos' visitors, they come on the stage, no?"

"Big man. High, flat-crowned hat. Expensive broadcloth suit. No tell-tale bulges to show he carries a gun. Looks like a carpetbagger to me."

"I do not *comprender* this thing—carpetbagger."

Jethro chuckled. "It's just a term southerners used for bloodsucking leeches who preyed upon them after the Civil War. What I meant by it is that this new bird looks like somebody Catron and Dolan might send out here to steal for them."

The dusty stranger paused to study the burned remains of Alexander McSween's home, finally walking over to peer through an open doorway at the adobe walls.

"I do not think so, Senor Jock," Antanasio said. "This hombre does not have the look of a bird of prey."

"Maybe not."

The stranger next took in the J.H. Tunstall & Co. sign over the boarded-up building nearby, and at the two men sitting on its porch. He came their way, saying, "Good morning."

"*Buenas dias,* senor. Welcome to our poor village."

"Why thank you, sir." The man set his valise down and began knocking dust from his clothing, gaze wandering. The chocolate eyes locked with Jethro's gray ones, flicked down to the tied-down Colt, then casually wandered back to stare diffidently at Jethro. "Perhaps one of you gentlemen could direct me to a man known as Antanasio Salazar?"

"I am that humble person, senor," Antanasio said, his chair jolting to the porch floor with a thump. "How may I serve you?"

"Well, well," the man said, "my luck is finally changing." He stepped upon the porch as Antanasio pushed from his chair. The old, stooped Mexican topped out only to the stranger's shoulder who, strangely, jerked off his top hat and extended a hand. "I've never met you, sir. But I feel I know you already."

Antanasio's brow wrinkled as the black-bearded stranger took and pumped his gnarled hand. "Yes indeed," the stranger went on, "through your letters, (pump, pump) I feel I know you. You are an articulate man, Mr. Salazar, and I've decided to (pump, pump) accept your invitation for quarters at Jose Montano's store. My name (pump, pump) is Lewis Wallace. I have the honor (pump, pump) of being governor of this great Territory of New Mexico."

Antanasio retrieved his hand at last. He bowed. "You do me a most high honor, Senor Governor Wallace. If I might be allowed, I will lead you to your quarters."

"Certainly. It is I who am honored."

Antanasio started away, then turned back to the dumbfounded Jethro Spring and said, "Please, may I first introduce Senor Winter? Senor Jock Winter, this is Senor Wallace, the honorable Governor-General of *Nueva Mejico*."

Governor Wallace smiled as Jethro scrambled to his feet. The black bearded man extended a hand, saying, "I believe I've heard (pump, pump) the name somewhere, Mr. Winter. It's a distinct pleasure (pump, pump) to make your acquaintance."

"Yeah, sure," Jethro mumbled. "Me, too."

Antanasio bustled away with the governor in tow, while Jethro stroked his chin and watched them all the way to Montano's store.

CHAPTER FOURTEEN

erritorial affairs had indeed interfered with Governor Wallace's visit to Lincoln until the evening of March 3. Then he brushed aside two impending crises and set out for Lincoln County in the darkness of night. His arrival March 5, 1879, via mail coach, caught everyone by surprise.

News of the governor's sudden appearance spread like wildfire. Within a half-hour of the governor's arrival, Edgar Walz, Catron's store manager, dispatched quick messages to Fort Stanton, then hurried to Montano's for an audience. James Dolan galloped in from Fort Stanton only two hours after the governor made himself known to Antanasio Salazar. Governor Wallace declined to see either of the two gentlemen that day.

Next was Colonel N.A.M. Dudley, properly escorted by a troop of his 9th Cavalry. The soldiers looked incongruous as they pulled up in formation in front of Jose Montano's tiny store. Dudley waited several decorous minutes hoping for an invitation from the governor. Instead, he received a courteous note, delivered by Antanasio Salazar, thanking him for his attentiveness and the military honor guard. Unfortunately, the note said, he was presently indisposed. The governor requested Colonel Dudley to retire to his military reservation taking all troops (the note was quite clear on the *all*) currently in and about Lincoln with him. The note also informed Colonel Dudley that Governor Wallace intended to call at Fort Stanton at his own convenience.

Colonel Dudley didn't take no for an answer. He sent his own note extending the full comforts of Fort Stanton to his excellency and deploring his present quarters in a "Mexican hovel."

Governor Wallace disdained a reply. Colonel Dudley waited for half an hour, then left Lincoln in a rage at the snub, followed by every bluecoat in town.

The governor's first interview was with Sheriff Kimbrell. His inclination was to like the big Rio Hondo farmer. That opinion changed noticeably when he discovered no arrests had been made for the killing of Houston Chapman. "Good God, man! Do you mean to stand there and tell me no arrests have even been attempted?"

George Kimbrell blushed and shuffled his feet. "We ain't had no warrants turned, Gov'nor."

"Why? Don't you know who the killers are by now?"

"More or less, I reckon. But getting anybody to swear to it is something else."

"Sheriff Kimbrell, need I remind you the killing was over two weeks ago. Rumors have even reached Santa Fe as to who was involved in this foul killing. Good Lord, man, their names have even been in the newspapers! It's common knowledge Mr. Dolan and a man named Campbell both fired their guns into Chapman! And by the gods, you're standing there saying nothing has been done about it?"

"That's about it Gov'nor, sir. There ain't a man in Lincoln whose got enough guts to go out to Fort Stanton and bring Dolan in. Fact is, I couldn't get up a posse if my life depended on it."

"Why didn't you apply to Colonel Dudley for men to help bring in the killers?" Wallace demanded.

"I did."

Wallace studied the solemn sheriff for a period, then asked, "Sheriff Kimbrell, is the weight of territorial law favoring one element in this feud more than another?"

"I ain't," the sturdy farmer replied.

"That's not what I asked, sheriff."

Kimbrell's silence was more eloquent than anything he could've said. Wallace then asked, "Tell me, Sheriff Kimbrell, what do you intend to do about arresting Chapman's murderers, now that you know the governor is interested?"

"Nothing without warrants, sir."

"And what's so difficult about obtaining warrants, sheriff? They're not tantamount to conviction, you know. They only allege suspicion. But they enable arrests to be made."

"Warrants take affidavits, Gov'nor. Somebody has to swear affidavits, and there ain't nobody in this town'll do that agin Dolan."

"A sheriff can swear an affidavit. It doesn't take a townsman."

"I'm a townsman, too, Guv'nor. Besides bein' sheriff, I gotta live in this county after you're gone. I ain't swearin' an affidavit to something I don't know for positive. I'll enforce and uphold the law when I got a chance to do it. But I ain't buckin' no stacked deck by myself. Give me a posse and a fair chance and I'll bring Dolan in. Campbell, too, for that matter. But try sending me out alone agin 'em and you'd best start looking for a new sheriff, 'cause you'll need one even if I was crazy enough to go."

"Thank you, Sheriff Kimbrell, for your time," Governor Wallace said, rising from his desk and holding out his hand. "I can assure you I'll carefully consider your comments."

George Kimbrell took the hand gingerly. "Lincoln County needs help, Guv'nor. You may be the only one with enough beans to supply it."

When Kimbrell had gone, Wallace asked for Antanasio

Salazar. The two markedly different men from different
social stations and different ethnic backgrounds discussed
Kimbrell's revelations for a long time. Antanasio quietly con-
firmed what the sheriff had said.

"Do you really mean to say in all of Lincoln County, no
one would assist the sheriff in arresting Dolan?" the governor asked in exasperation.

"Si, Senor Governor Wallace. In all this land, there is but
one who has such courage."

"My God, Antanasio, one man—two men—that's not
enough."

"Si, Senor Governor Wallace."

"Why won't honest people come forth to do their
duty?"

"There can be but one reason, Senor Governor Wallace.
They fear *manana*."

"Tomorrow? What could happen to them tomorrow if
the outlaws were all in jail?"

The governor's visitor shrugged and Wallace said,
"Thank you, Antanasio. We've probably discussed all I can
absorb for one evening. I hope I can call upon you if I have
further questions."

Antanasio Salazar bowed and shuffled for the door. He
was nearly out of the room when the governor called him
back. "The one with enough courage to brace Dolan—I
suppose you mean Billy the Kid?"

"No, Senor Governor. Senor Bonney, he is not in
Placito—Lincoln. He hides elsewhere for his life. The one
hombre I mean is the one you have already met, Senor
Winter. He is the one man Senor Dolan, Senor Evans, Senor
Selman, and Senor Matthews fear above all others."

"You don't say! He didn't look so imposing to me. Tell
me, why is it they fear him so?"

"Who can say? Like you, Senor Winter, he does not seem
malo to me. But I am but a simple old man. *Buenas noches*,
Senor Governor Wallace."

The following day, Governor Wallace interviewed Isaac

Ellis and Jose Montano about events leading to the battle of July 19th, and the part Colonel Dudley and the military played in Alexander McSween's death. Jose showed him the exact location of the mountain howitzer and told how it was aimed at his store. He also told how Dudley had threatened to use it. Both men told of the precipitous flight of the McSween forces from their buildings. Isaac Ellis added a sage comment:

"I'll tell you one thing, Governor Wallace, if it hadn't been for the warnin' from that fella Winter, we'd all be buzzard bait."

The governor snapped his fingers. "Now I remember! He's the man I'm told ran from the fight."

When both Montano and Ellis stopped laughing, Isaac growled, "Whichever told you that, Governor, you can mark him up for a liar. Winter was sent away. And then only when he tried to talk some sense into ever'body else. He stopped by my place on his way to tell us the army was comin' down the next day to help Dolan and Peppin."

"How could he know that?"

"I reckon I don't know, Governor. But it happened exactly the way he said it would." Ellis was silent for a moment, then added, "After a while, folks in this town gets to where they believe the man, no matter what."

"Si, Senor Wallace," Jose said. "The problem with our people is they have not always listened. And that is our mistake."

Governor Wallace studied the two men before him. Obviously these community leaders had a high regard for this man Winter. He dismissed his visitors and began poring over old Lincoln County records. He was surprised to find Jack Winter mentioned only twice, both on minor warrants covered by the governor's pardon. Wallace pondered his next move well into the afternoon.

Governor Wallace chose to interview Juan Patron. At one point in Patron's quiet monologue, the governor interrupted, "And Mr. Patron, these men had just left your home when you heard shots fired?"

"Si, Senor Wallace."

"And then you stepped from your house in the darkness and heard them talking?"

"That is correct."

"And then Dolan set fire to the body?"

"That is what I saw when the flames soared."

"That's wonderful. All we need is an affidavit from you and we'll arrest those men."

The tall, handsome Mexican/American shook his head. "No, Senor. To do so would end my life."

"No? How can you say that? You must! Juan, what you've just told me will hang some of those men, and rightly so!"

Patron shook his head.

Wallace studied the young man, muttering, "I'm beginning to understand Mr. Dolan's power. Look here, Juan, what if I guaranteed you military protection?"

Patron shrugged. "No, Senor Wallace. The colonel at Fort Stanton, he is hand-in-glove with the men who killed Senor Chapman. To place one's self in his protection would be worse than chancing a bullet from the darkness."

Wallace asked to see Lincoln's justice of the peace. After the two men had conversed for several minutes, Wallace asked, "Judge Wilson, you say you know positively who killed Chapman?"

"Yes. Who could help but see when the body was torched right in front of his house? Yep, Dolan did it, right enough."

"Well, at last we're getting somewhere. Although you cannot swear an affidavit on yourself, as justice of the peace, I believe I, as territorial governor, can take your testimony."

"No, sir."

"Oh yes, Judge Wilson. I'm sure of it. My legal training, you see …"

"That's not what I meant, Governor. What I meant was I won't swear it."

"Not swear it? But you just told me ..."

"Yep. But I won't put my name to an affidavit."

"Why not, man?"

"I ain't ready to die."

"But I can guarantee military protection."

"Dudley's? No thanks."

Governor Wallace interviewed three other men who heard the shots and witnessed Dolan's torching of Chapman's body. All three refused to sign affidavits. All three declined military protection citing lack of confidence in the Fort Stanton commandant's impartiality. One man told of Campbell's words as he walked from the blazing body: "I promised God and Colonel Dudley that I'd kill that goddamned lawyer, and by God boys, I've done it."

"You *must* sign an affidavit to that effect!"

The man mutely shook his head.

Wallace asked to talk to Antanasio Salazar. When the old man shuffled in, the governor said, "Mr. Salazar, we must have William Bonney. He's the man who could cut through all this confusion."

Antanasio held his sombrero, staring calmly at the governor with his sad black eyes. "Si, Senor Governor Wallace. That would be wise."

"Where can I find him?"

"*Quien saber?*"

"You don't know?"

The old man's eyes dropped to study the sombrero. "No, Senor Governor Wallace."

"Who does? Who can find him?"

"There is only one man who might find Senor Bonney, Senor Governor Wallace."

"Don't tell me. Let me guess. It's that man Winter, isn't it?"

"Si."

"Can you bring him to me?" the governor asked.

"No, Senor Governor Wallace."

"No? Why not?"

"Because Senor Winter is no longer in our village."

"Where did he go?"

"This I do not know. I only know why he goes."

"Well, why did he go?"

"Senor Jock left early in the evening you arrived. He only tells me he goes to seek Senor Bonney and bring him back to talk to your Excellency. Which way he went, only God knows. He is like a shadow, Senor Governor Wallace— this man who is a friend of all who wish to dwell in peace."

———•◦•———

Jethro Spring had indeed ridden from Lincoln on the trail of his young friend, Billy the Kid. He'd quickly reasoned that Billy was an essential material witness to the case against Chapman's murderers. He also reasoned that Billy was the one man who might have courage enough to testify against Dolan on a witness dock.

Antanasio Salazar had crossed his path as the sorrel mare plodded briskly from town. "*Hola, mi compadre.* You are about late."

Jethro reined in the mare to peer down at the old man. "You know, Antanasio, I think you are an old fraud."

"For you to think such a thing, Senor Jock, would distress me. Why is it you say *malo* words about a humble old man?"

"Here I been reading you newspaper articles and official notices and all the time you've been carrying on a letter writing exchange with the governor. Articulate, he called you."

Antanasio smiled toothlessly up at him. "Perhaps it would pain you less, *mi compadre*, if I told you the letters were written at my instructions, by my young *nino*, Jose. He read the governor's letters to me, also."

Jethro leaned down and patted Antanasio on the shoulder. "I still think you're a fraud. But a damned good one, at that."

"*Gracias.*"

Jethro straightened in the saddle and lifted the reins. "Way I got it figured, Antanasio, Governor Wallace will be needing Billy. I'm going to fetch him if I can. You got any idea where he might be?"

"Only that he is not at Fort Sumner where he is often to be found these days. We heard that report only yesterday."

Jethro nodded and clucked at his horse.

Billy the Kid was not along the Rio Hondo, nor the Rio Pecos. John Chisum's foreman, Jim Highsaw, said Billy had not lately visited any of Chisum's camps. The Kid appeared not to be hiding in the Capitans, nor was he at any of his friends along the Rio Ruidoso. It was finally in the camp of the Mescalero Apaches where Jethro at last struck the trail.

Naiche Tana nodded as he plopped a chunk of stew meat into his mouth. "Yes, the young-one-who-shoots-quick-as-a-striking-snake passed through our land during the darkness of the moon."

"Did anyone talk to him, my friend?"

The chieftain shook his head.

"Which way did he go?"

"Down the Rio Tulerosa. But he did not wish to be seen, and passed around the agency headquarters and the mill owned by Blazer in the dark of night."

Jethro came to his feet. "Thank you, Naiche Tana. You've been most helpful to me. May we always remain friends. The information you have given may also benefit your people."

The Apache grunted and shoved another handful of meat into his mouth. After chewing briefly, he swallowed and said, "Go with your Gods, my friend. Return to the camp of the Mescalero when you can. The gray-eyed-one is always welcome."

As Jethro Spring searched the Tulerosa Valley for Billy the Kid, Governor Wallace was holding a mass public meeting in Lincoln. The courthouse grounds were packed with men, women, and children who waited expectantly as the large black-bearded man mounted to an improvised speaker's rostrum. Governor Wallace raised his arms and the swell of noise subsided.

The governor began by introducing himself in a booming voice, then welcoming those present. He told them he called the meeting not to tell them what they must do, but to listen to their suggestions and complaints.

As a public speaker, however effective he might be on a one-on-one basis, the governor was slow and halting before an audience. But he received a tremendous ovation when he said, "My friends, before we really begin this hearing, before I open this meeting up to your statements and suggestions, I should first inform you that I've asked General Hatch, who commands all United States forces in New Mexico, for the removal of Colonel Nathan A. Dudley, commandant at Fort Stanton. I have, of course ..."

Lusty cheer after lusty cheer roared from the people's throats. Hats sailed into the air. Children clapped and screamed in glee, mimicking their parent's excitement. Women cried and laughed and hugged each other and clung to their husbands' arms. It was minutes before the governor could continue:

"I have, of course, concluded that Colonel Dudley's removal is absolutely essential to the restoration of peace in Lincoln County ..."

Again the governor's words were drowned amid bedlam. At last decorum was established and the governor opened the session to comments from his audience. For two hours Governor Wallace listened patiently to complaint after complaint. Each outlined past abuses by both military and civil authorities. Yet few had positive suggestions to make, other than that violent elements among Lincoln County's citizenry should be curbed.

After the meeting, Governor Wallace conferred privately with fifteen of the area's most prominent men in his room at

Montano's store. They all told the same story: dread of out-laws who seemingly were at James Dolan's beck and call, and fear of Dudley's displeasure and its manifestation through some misuse of his military authority.

"Gentlemen we have a problem," Wallace said to the group. "You're telling me you dwell in fear of the military because of its past misuse. You also tell me you have the same low regard for civil enforcement. I believe it essential for you to understand there is simply no other force available for the legal process to use in Lincoln County."

John Newcomb cleared his throat. "Wal, that ain't entirely so, Governor. There's the Lincoln County Mounted Rifles."

Governor Wallace looked around in surprise as each of the other men nodded in agreement. "What, pray tell, is the Lincoln County Mounted Rifles?"

"It would perhaps be best," Probate Judge Florencio Gonzalez said, "if the one who had the foresight to begin the Lincoln County Mounted Rifles was here to tell you, your Excellency. However, he is away just now, so ..."

"Let me guess," Governor Wallace drily said. "Jack Winter?"

"Si, Senor Winter, he ..."

"Well unfortunately, the illusive Mr. Winter isn't avail-able, nor has he been for the last few days. Perhaps one of you could enlighten me on the Lincoln County Mounted Rifles."

"Senor Governor Wallace?" Antanasio Salazar leaned forward.

"Yes, Mr. Salazar?"

"Juan Patron, he is the one to explain these Lincoln County Mounted Rifles to you. He is the second one to command, having been appointed by Senor Winter himself, more than two months ago. Also Juan is educated at your great University of Notre Dame, no?"

Wallace turned to Patron. "Very well, Juan, let's hear it."

After Patron finished explaining the development of the

volunteer force, their past function, and their present status, Wallace said, "I'm impressed. But you are suggesting circumvention of the existing legal system with such a force as these 'Mounted Riflemen'. I believe that could set a dangerous precedent."

Antanasio Salazar, still holding his sombrero, was helped to his feet. The room fell silent out of deference. "Senor Governor Wallace, does this territory have a—how you say it—militia?"

"No, no, that's one of the prob ..." Wallace stopped abruptly as the impact of the old man's question took root.

"I am but a humble old peasant who does not always understand. But is it not true that this militia exists in others of our *Estados Unidos?*"

"True."

"Could that not be our problem, Senor Governor Wallace? If our civil law fails for whatever the reason might be, is it not true that we mus' turn to *soldados* of the *Estados Unidos?*"

"Umm hmm."

"Would it not be better if *Neuva Mejico* had its own militia who could act in the absence of a sheriff and civil law?"

"You may have something, Antanasio."

"And can not you, Senor Governor Wallace, appoint such militia? Can not our own Judge Wilson charge them with serving warrants he issues? Can not these men perhaps be empowered to restore law and order to our county?"

Wallace nodded, his eyes narrowing as he gazed at the stooped old peasant wearing poor-grade cotton muslin clothing and clutching a huge straw sombrero to his waist.

"Thank you, Senor Governor Wallace," Antanasio said as he sat down. "You have been mos' helpful. This thing, it is not always clear to an old man such as myself."

CHAPTER FIFTEEN

The beardless youth appeared haggard and drawn, but his protruding teeth flashed in a happy smile as the trail-weary Jethro Spring rode into the Tulerosa Valley sheep camp. "You're somethin' else, Jack. I'll be damned if you ain't." The youth leaned his Winchester against a wagon wheel. "I didn't think nobody'd be able to run me to ground way out here. You are truly amazing."

Jethro leaned on his saddlehorn and squinted through red-rimmed, wind-burned eyes. "I come to talk you into giving yourself up, Billy."

Bonney's high-pitched cackle exploded. "Talk away, Jack. Talk all you want. But I ain't a-gonna do it."

Jethro swung from the saddle, leaning his head against it until his rubbery legs stiffened. "You really are a tough man to find, Billy. Seems like I've been riding forever. We've got to hurry." He turned and saw Billy had picked up the Winchester again; its muzzle pointed at the newcomer's feet. "Put the gun down, Billy. I don't give enough of a goddamn whether you go back that I'm willing to shoot it out with you."

"You couldn't win these days, friend." The smile was gone, but Billy leaned the carbine back against the wagon wheel.

"Maybe so, maybe not. I don't reckon ever to find out."

They stared at each other, then Billy called in a low voice, "C'mon out, Tom."

Tom O'Folliard brushed back the wagonsheet and stood there grinning, a double-barreled twelve gauge in his hands.

"You don't take many chances," Jethro said, eyeing O'Folliard.

"Pays not to when a man don't know who his friends are."

"You know I'm a friend."

"I know you ain't no enemy."

"Fair enough, Billy—if that's the best you can do. I'm looking for a cup of coffee."

"Too hot for coffee. Water will have to do."

Jethro ran a forefinger along his cracked lips. "Water'll do fine."

"C'mon around to the shady side of the wagon," Billy said, leading the way. He pulled the cover off a wooden cask and handed Jethro a dipper full of tepid water.

O'Folliard joined them. "Why you want Billy and not me?"

"I want you both, Tom," Jethro said. "You're both material witnesses to Chapman's murder. What you saw will hang Dolan. It's a chance to close out this war, once and for all."

"What makes you think it can be pulled off now, when Dolan's always had things his own way before?" Bonney said.

"The new governor, Billy. He's in Lincoln right now. He's staying at Montano's store, talking to people like Squire Wilson and Isaac Ellis and Jose Montano. When I left, he'd been there most of a day, refusing to see Dudley or Dolan or Walz. He really is trying to straighten this thing out. You boys may hold the key."

"We got an agreement with Dolan," O'Folliard said. "We can't testify against him or Evans or any of his friends."

"Tom, that agreement is a bunch of bullshit and you know it. Dolan broke it as soon as he made it. It was a stupid goddamned thing to do in the first place." Jethro knew he'd erred when he saw Billy's eyes blaze wildly.

"Damn you, Winter! All I wanted to do is live like other people. It's easy for you to say it was a mistake—you're a free man! You don't have no murder warrants over your head; that pardon never covered me!"

"Tom is free, too, Billy," Jethro said softly. "Maybe we can work it so you can go free if you testify."

"How?"

"Well, for starters, will you write the governor a letter?"

———•—•———

Never had Susan McSween taken such care in her appearance as when she prepared for her audience with Governor Wallace. Susan also took advantage of the room's arrangement to show to her best advantage, selecting a chair to catch the sunlight streaming in from the open window. She'd brushed her naturally wavy hair until it glowed. Along with a studiously augmented peaches-and-cream complexion, a ready smile, and eyes that seemed to reach out winsomely, she was well aware of her beauty and how to use it. When she saw the governor peeking quickly her way before returning to stare out the window, she knew her preparation and exhibition had its desired effect.

"I've so wanted a chance to tell you how much I personally appreciated your comments at the courthouse meeting, Governor. Your investigation here is such a marked contrast to Governor Axtell's, last year. He stayed only at Fort Stanton, never visiting Lincoln. And he was attended only by Mr. Dolan's and Colonel Dudley's inner circle. That is why I'm so impressed by your willingness to listen to everyone—a wonderful commentary on your effectiveness."

She shifted her chair so the sunlight struck her to even better effect.

"Yes, well, I appreciate your comments, of course," the governor said, turning back from the window. "Perhaps I should also say I admire your courage for persevering after your late husband's tragic death."

"Why thank you, your Excellency; you are kind. I'm just pleased to at last see Colonel Dudley getting his just desserts."

Wallace cleared his throat noncommittally and again glanced out the window.

"I feel I should tell you I still intend to continue my civil suit for damages, despite my attorney's untimely demise."

"My dear Mrs. McSween, that is, of course, your legal right. I should also say I was shocked by the nature of Mr. Chapman's death."

"It was terrible. So tragic. He'd just stopped by my store residence to tell me you'd agreed to visit Lincoln."

Governor Wallace started to chuckle, then shut it off and said, "The man wore me down. He was persistent, I'll say that for him. Even if he was—shall we say—grating in his manner."

"Yes. I must in fairness admit that. But he did have my interest at heart. I believe now, however, that he pursued the wrong course. Jack warned me about that."

Governor Wallace's head snapped around and his large brown eyes seemed to envelope her. "Jack? Do you perchance mean Jack Winter?"

"Why yes. He advises me often. Do you know him?"

The governor passed a big hand over his face. "I've met him," was his only reply.

Allowing a few seconds to pass for decorum's sake in changing subjects, Susan then asked, "Would it be proper for me to discuss Colonel Dudley's conduct the day my husband was killed, sir?"

"If you wish. I've read each of your affidavits, of course. But perhaps you'll shed some new light."

They talked for more than an hour, Wallace listening closely but maintaining a guarded neutrality; Susan waxing more and more impassioned in her efforts to present a conclusive and compelling case. At last, the governor said, "I'm sorry, Mrs. McSween, but I have other visitors I must see. Can we conclude our discussion soon?"

Susan leaped to her feet. "Of course. I believe I've finished, sir. Thank you for granting me this audience."

"Quite so, young lady." The governor also came to his feet. "I have but one further question."

"Yes?"

"You mentioned earlier, 'my store'. You mean, of course, John Tunstall's old store. I understand from other sources that it is now stocked and you plan to open it soon."

"That is my plan, sir."

"I wonder, in light of present circumstances, madam, if it might be better to postpone its opening for a period?"

"I believe not, sir. I shall be safe enough in any event, for I'll not attempt to open it until Jack returns."

"Jack? Jack Winter?" the governor asked.

"Yes," Susan answered smoothly. "No one would dare vandalize it when he's around—is something wrong, Governor?"

"No, no. Thank you for your company, madam. And for your confidence. I can assure you that I appreciate it."

Susan curtsied and left the room. Wallace sent for Sam Wortley.

"You are the proprietor of the local hotel?" Governor Wallace asked, studying the wiry, balding little man before his desk.

"That I am, Governor. For the past five years. Built her m'self."

"Mr. Wortley, as a noncombatant in this thing called the Lincoln County War, yet known as one generally considered to hold at least some degree of partisanship toward the, ah, Dolan faction, I'm interested in your opinion of past incidences in the 'war'. Would you be kind enough to share them with me?"

"Well," Wortley guardedly began, "I reckon wrong was did by both sides—some anyway. It's right hard to pick them as was at fault. Easier to pick the good ones—them as caused no trouble, or wa'nt at fault for the trouble they got in." Wortley paused, then asked, "You ain't gonna make me sign no affidavit, are you?"

"No, Mr. Wortley. No affidavit. Tell me about the 'good' people. That would be fine."

"Well, in McSween's and Tunstall's outfit, my idea of the best one is that feller, Winter. If they'd all listened to him ... is somethin' wrong, Governor?"

Wallace peeked at Wortley through the fingers of both hands. "No, Mr. Wortley. Nothing is wrong. Please continue."

By Thursday, March 13, 1879, Governor Lewis Wallace was prepared to act. General Hatch's suspension of Colonel Dudley went into effect and Captain Carroll was placed in temporary command at Fort Stanton. Wallace forwarded a list of thirty-six names of men with major warrants outstanding. All were to be arrested and impounded at the fort by military forces in Carroll's command. The list was nearly a muster roll of prominent participants in the Lincoln County War. Along with the list was a personal note from the Governor to Captain Carroll. The note informed the officer that Wallace was privy to information that Jesse Evans, Billy Matthews, and Bill Campbell could be found at Murphy's old Fairview Ranch, only a few miles from Fort Stanton.

Captain Carroll acted immediately and the three desperadoes were brought in by a squad of cavalry within the day. Recognizing that two of these three men were wanted for the death of John Tunstall as well as Houston Chapman, Wallace ordered the three held incommunicado at the fort.

James Dolan now came to the governor's attention. Placing himself under Colonel Dudley's wing directly after Chapman's killing, Dolan was already at Fort Stanton when the governor instituted his dragnet. But he was still allowed to come and go as he pleased. When Wallace discovered Dolan was visiting Lincoln at will, he sent Carroll a peremptory note:

> J.J. Dolan was down here (Lincoln) tonight. Please arrest him on his return to the Fort, and put him in close confinement for the murder of H.I. Chapman.

It was during this period that Jethro Spring's sorrel mare plodded tiredly into Lincoln. He turned the mare into Wortley's stable and was unsaddling her when a shadow appeared at the door. Jethro spun, gun in hand, hammer clicking back. Then he saw who it was.

"Sorry, Mr. Wallace. I'm tired, I guess." He let the hammer down on the Colt and thrust it back into its holster. "Just don't reckon to see many governors hanging out around Lincoln stables." He turned back to the mare, muttering, "Probably wouldn't be in the county's best interest to go through a change of governors right now, either."

"I'm certainly not in favor of it, young man," the governor said, color beginning to creep back into his face. He stepped into the stable from the doorway. "I've been wanting to talk to you for days. So many people in Lincoln know of my wishes that I've had three separate reports of your return. I'd like to talk to you privately, sir, if I may. That's why I chose to come myself."

The governor could finally smile. He brushed a dust-covered cobweb aside and said, "Obviously I called in a manner unacceptable to people in Lincoln County. Forgive me."

Jethro was too tired to see humor. "I doubt your coming to Wortley's stable is any secret, sir. But of course I'll talk with you. I'll do anything I can to help."

"No doubt you are tired, Mr. Winter. And hungry, too. Would you be available, say, at eight this evening? That would give you time for supper and two or three hours of sleep."

Jethro nodded. "Certainly. Where?"

"My room at Montano's."

"I'll be there."

—·—·—

Jethro Spring knocked on Governor Wallace's door promptly at eight p.m. "Come in," a muffled voice said. Jethro pushed the door open. The governor sat at a desk, his jacket off and his shirtsleeves rolled up. Sweat rings stained the shirt's armpits. Jethro hesitated until the big man said, "Please close the door, Mr. Winter, and have a chair."

Wallace's large brown eyes seemed almost to swallow him. "If I had not already met you, young man, I would have thought you nine feet tall."

"Sir?"

"The only thing really exceptional about you are the eyes."

Jethro's brow wrinkled. "I don't ..."

"You are merely average height and weight, though well set-up, no doubt."

"Is this an interview, Governor? If so, it's a strange one."

"Not unusually handsome or striking. One gun, only, where really dangerous men wear two. Working man's clothing...."

Jethro pushed to his feet, his mouth pinched.

"Oh don't be so touchy," the governor said good-naturedly. "Sit down."

His guest settled back into his chair.

"You are held in extremely high regard by your fellow citizens of Lincoln County, you know."

"I doubt that, Governor," Jethro said testily. "I've got reason to believe some hate my guts."

"No doubt. But your enemies still hold you in high esteem. They respect you."

"That's nice to know, sir. May I ask where this conversation is leading?"

"I understand you took it upon yourself to contact young William Bonney on my behalf."

"No, sir. On his behalf."

The governor smiled. "... even before I knew how important he was to the settlement of affairs in this county."

Jethro said nothing.

"And will Mr. Bonney surrender and testify against Chapman's killers?"

"Aren't you pushing things a little fast, Governor?"

"Perhaps. It depends upon what you mean."

"I mean William Bonney has a murder charge hanging over his head. It might be a little simple to believe the man would just walk in and give himself up because Lewis Wallace asked him to do so. You're not the first governor to ask Billy to surrender, sir."

Wallace's expression never changed, nor did his gaze waver. "Do you know where Bonney is?"

"Yes."

"Will you tell me?"

"No."

"Did you see him—talk to him?"

"Yes."

Wallace picked up a pencil from his desk and began tapping it on his chair arm thoughtfully. "I need Bonney, Mr. Winter. We all do. His testimony would convict Dolan and break the back of the ring that has been controlling and exploiting this area for years."

The dark eyes swallowed Jethro again. "You're considered to be thoughtful and intelligent in action by your contemporaries. Obviously your seeking out Bonney without first being asked to do so is an example of just such talents. Therefore, you must have a plan. Do you have one? A proposal?"

"No, sir. I have a letter."

"A letter? From Bonney?"

"Yes, sir."

"For some reason, I didn't expect the man to be educated."

"He's smarter that most people think, Governor. He's sometimes given to raising a little hell, but basically good stock."

"Lots of today's youth fit that same definition," the governor said. "When may I see the letter?"

Jethro handed it to him. Wallace unfolded the carefully penciled letter. It was on rough brown paper, such as might be used to wrap perishable goods in a mercantile store. Bonney's letter read:

> To his Excellency the Governor
> Gen. Lew Wallace
>
> Dear Sir:
>   I have heard that you will give one thousand ($) for my body, which as I can understand it, means alive as a witness. I know it is as a witness against those that murdered Mr. Chapman. It was so I could appear at court, I could give the desired information, but I have indictments against me for things that happened in the late Lincoln County War and am afraid to give myself up because my enemies would kill me. The day Mr. Chapman was murdered I was in Lincoln at the request of good citizens to meet Mr. J.J. Dolan, to meet as a friend so as to be able to lay aside our arms and go to work. I was present when Mr. Chapman was murdered and know who did it, and if it were not for those indictments I would have made it clear before now. If it is in your power to annul those indictments, I hope you will do so as to give me a chance to explain. Please send me an answer by bearer. I have no wish to fight any more, indeed I have not raised an arm since your proclamation. As to my

character, I refer to any of the citizens, for the majority of them are my friends and have been helping me all they could. I am called Kid Antrim, But Antrim was my stepfather's name.

> Waiting an answer I remain,
> Your obedient servant,
> W.H. BONNEY

Governor Wallace read through the letter a second time, then asked Jethro, "I trust this letter is genuine?"

"It is."

"Are you aware of its contents?"

"Yes, sir."

"How much of a hand did you have in drafting it?"

"Are you asking if I wrote it, Governor?"

"That's not what ... never mind. He's proposing a pardon in exchange for his testimony."

"Yes, sir."

"What do you think, Mr. Winter? Is he reliable? Would he break faith?"

Jethro's gray eyes shifted thoughtfully to his scuffed boots. "He has the courage to testify and I suspect, the knowledge to convict. As to staying peaceably within the terms of a pardon, I honestly don't know. I know it's his intent to do so. But he sometimes gets a little wild."

"If you were me?"

"I'd chance it, Governor," Jethro said quickly. "I would think the chance to break the ring's power too important to lose."

Governor Wallace shifted in his chair to study a far wall. His pencil began tap, tap, tapping the chair arm again. He shifted back to stare at Jethro. "I suspect, Mr. Winter, that you are the engineer behind this plan. But it may well be a workable one. I shall need some time to think. How soon would you be ready to undertake delivery of a return message?"

"Just the time it takes to saddle another horse."

"No need for such urgency. Can you be ready by mid-morning tomorrow?"

"Yes, sir."

———•◦•———

Jethro was at the governor's room at nine a.m. Wallace let him in and handed him a letter. "Read it please, Mr. Winter."

"That's not necessary, sir."

"I wish it, please."

Jethro read:

(Saturday)
Lincoln, March 15, 1879

W.H. Bonney

Come to the house of old Squire Wilson (not the lawyer) at nine (9) o'clock next Monday night alone. I don't mean his office, but his residence. Follow along the foot of the mountains south of the town, come in on that side, and knock at the east door. I have authority to exempt you from prosecution if you will testify to what you say you know.

The object of the meeting at Squire Wilson's is to arrange the matter in a way to make your life safe. To do that the utmost secrecy is to be used. So come alone. Don't tell anybody—not a living soul—where you are coming or the object. If you could trust Jesse Evans, you can trust me.

Lew Wallace

When Jethro had finished reading, Governor Wallace asked, "Will that give Bonney enough time? Can he be here by Monday evening?"

Jethro nodded. He handed the letter back. Governor Wallace took it, folded it carefully, scratched a match alight and melted a puddle of candle wax at the overlap. At last, he took his Territorial Governor's seal and imprinted the hot wax, then handed the letter to Jethro. "Go with God," he said.

—•—

Billy the Kid knocked on the east door of Judge Wilson's Lincoln home promptly at nine p.m., March 17, 1879. A muffled voice called, "Come in."

Billy pushed the door open a crack, then a bit more. He saw a large bearded man that fit the description his friend Jack had given of Governor Wallace. Beyond the bearded man was Judge Wilson. Billy pushed the door open farther. He carried his Winchester in his right hand, a revolver in his left. "I was sent for to meet Governor Wallace here at nine o'clock," Billy said. "Is he here?"

"I'm Governor Wallace," the bearded man said, rising to his feet and holding out a big hand. Billy thrust the rifle in the crook of his left arm and accepted the governor's hand. After they'd exchanged formalities, Wallace invited Bonney to take a chair at the kitchen table.

"Your note gave promise of absolute protection?" Billy asked.

"Yes. And I've been true to my promise." Wallace pointed at Judge Wilson. "This man, whom of course you know, and I are the only persons in the house."

Billy looked at the judge who nodded. Satisfied, Bonney lowered the rifle and returned the Colt to its holster. When he'd taken his seat, the governor sat once more and said, "I'd like for you to voluntarily surrender, Mr. Bonney, and testify as to what you saw in the Chapman killing in the upcoming spring term of court."

"I'd like to do it, Governor. But there's several reasons why I can't."

"Tell me what they are, please."

"First off, I wouldn't live long enough to testify. They'd be after me like flies to a dog turd. Cut off in a jail cell and without any way to defend myself, hell, they'd poison me or gun me down during the night."

"I can order you held under close confinement at Fort Stanton. I can guarantee your safety. We already have Dolan, Evans, Campbell, and Matthews there—did you know that?"

Billy nodded and flashed his buckteeth. "That's what makes me double nervous."

"Colonel Dudley is no longer in command. I can assure you of your safety."

"Then there's the matter of the warrants against me."

Wallace took a deep breath. "In return for your testimony against Chapman's killers, I will let you go scot free with a pardon in your pocket for all your misdeeds."

Billy said, "Is that the truth?"

"Yes, so help me God."

"How should I give myself up?"

Wallace's heart leaped, but he merely said, "I'd prefer it looked authentic. I hope you realize and appreciate that I'll be criticized extensively for this agreement and the less it looks like a staged affair, the better it will be for both of us."

"You could have a posse take me."

The two men talked for another half-hour about the Kid's proposed fake arrest. Then Bonney rose and held out his hand to the governor. "Thank you, Governor Wallace. I ain't quite ready to make a decision now, but I'll let you know one way or another in a few days."

Then Billy the Kid was gone.

Two nights later, Jesse Evans and Bill Campbell escaped from the Fort Stanton guardhouse, accompanied by a deserting soldier known as "Texas Jack."

The governor's fist slammed the top of his desk. "Gentlemen, I must know if Evans' and Campbell's escape will jeopardize my negotiations with Billy Bonney!" It was the first time Jethro had seen the man angry.

Antanasio Salazar turned to Jethro and spread his palms.

Jethro said, "I'm sure Billy will have second thoughts about security at Fort Stanton, Governor. And he'll sure as hell be lookin' over his shoulder to see if Evans and Campbell are coming after him. Remember, he's the only remaining witness available who can identify Evans with Tunstall's murder. And Campbell sure as hell has reason to want him dead because of Chapman's killing."

"What can we do to speed him into custody?" Wallace asked. "We must have the man!"

"The best advice I can give is don't try to force him, sir."

"Will you talk to him once more?"

"Certainly, if that's your wish. I'll do my best to persuade him, Governor. But don't expect too much."

"How soon can you leave?" Wallace asked.

"Right away. Saddle a horse is all."

"How soon might I have an answer?"

The tiniest smile flitted across Jethro Spring's drawn face. "Perhaps sooner that you think, Governor. Could be Billy is closer to Lincoln than anybody realizes."

After Jethro had gone, Governor Wallace said absently, "Remarkable man, that Winter. I'm beginning to believe as the rest of you—that he can move mountains. With luck, we'll find the key that will bring peace to southeastern New Mexico."

"That *hombre* is the key, Senor Governor Wallace," Antanasio Salazar said, still staring at the door Jethro Spring had softly closed.

Five hours later, Jethro ambled back into Jose Montano's Store and was hurriedly ushered into the governor's presence. In silence, he handed Wallace a letter. The black-bearded man slit the seal and read swiftly. A smile softened his features and he breathed an audible sigh of relief. "You've read it?" he asked, glancing up at Jethro.

"No, sir. But I know its contents."

Wallace passed the letter to him. Jethro read:

San Patricio
Lincoln County
Thursday, (March) 20th, 1879
General Wallace,
Sir,
   I will keep the appointment I made, but be sure
and have men come that you can depend on. I am
not afraid to die like a man fighting but I would not
like to die like a dog unarmed.... All I am afraid of is
that in the Fort I might be poisoned or killed
through a window at night....

Bonney's letter continued by lining out arrest details.
Jethro finished reading and paused to consider.

"It sounds as though he's willing to submit to military
confinement." the governor said.

"He's resigned to it, sir. But he has no confidence in it."

"Neither do I after last night's escape. What do you
think?"

"I think it would work to deputize a bunch of people
known to be friendly to Billy and hold him here in Lincoln
in loose confinement."

"I have another idea, Mr. Winter—may I call you Jack?"

"Certainly, sir."

"Good. You call me Lew or Lewis."

"I wouldn't do that, out of respect for your office, sir."

Wallace waved dismissively. "I understand you are familiar with the Lincoln County Mounted Rifles?"

Jethro nodded.

"I'm thinking of activating it into a territorial militia.
Have you any comment on that idea?"

"Only that it's an excellent one, sir."

"The 'Mounted Rifles', as I understand it, are made up
largely of men favorable to Billy Bonney."

"Well, I don't know if that's exactly right. But most of
'em was on the same side Billy fought for."

"Suppose I activate them and use them for Bonney's
arrest?"

Jethro nodded again. "It would ease Billy's mind, I'm sure. And I think it would sure as hell send a message to the outlaws in this county if the Lincoln County Mounted Rifles had the governor's blessing."

"All right, I'll do it at once. You shall be appointed Captain of Militia and ..."

"No, sir."

"No?"

"I'm sorry, sir. But I think I have a better suggestion. Appoint Juan Patron. He's young, courageous and respected by both Anglos and Mexicans. He's well educated. He lives here and was born here. He's part of the landscape. I'm a newcomer and I might be gone tomorrow. For the long-term welfare of the county and of the Mounted Rifles as a militia, the appointment should go to Patron."

"But," Wallace protested, "it was your idea. You created them."

"That's damned unimportant in the long run, isn't it, Governor?"

Wallace found more to like about this strange gray-eyed man all the time. "Very well, it shall be done. The Lincoln County Mounted Rifles, commanded by Captain Juan Patron, will bring in Billy the Kid."

CHAPTER SIXTEEN

Governor Wallace's official endorsement of the Lincoln County Mounted Rifles, their elevation to the level of territorial militia, and the group's apprehension and escort of popular Billy the Kid and Tom O'Folliard into Lincoln was "cause celebre" in southeastern New Mexico. It was common knowledge that Billy had voluntarily surrendered and was to testify against James Dolan, Jesse Evans, and Bill Campbell. As a result, there were few in all New Mexico who failed to understand that their territorial governor was actively maneuvering against the architects of the Santa Fe ring. In Lincoln County, street celebrations resulted.

Bonney and O'Folliard were ensconced at the home of Juan Patron. There, they received a steady stream of friends and well-wishers. Even Governor Wallace stopped in to see his star witness.

The governor asked Billy if his accommodations were suitable and was told they were. Though handcuffed to give authenticity to the charade, Billy was in great spirits, basking in the glow of his notoriety. Their conversation drifted to the reputed shooting skills of Billy the Kid, and the governor, basking in the aftermath of successful events, asked for a demonstration.

Billy's guns were brought and the young gunman slipped his small hands from his handcuffs to lead the way out to the base of the hills back of Patron's home. There he proceeded to demonstrate his considerable skills with both rifle and six-gun to an admiring crowd. Walking back to Patron's, Wallace said, "Billy, isn't there some trick to your shooting? How do you do it?"

"Well, Governor," Billy replied, "there is a trick to it. When I was young, I watched a man shoot who was really good. That man taught me a lot. He said to point a gun just like an extension of your forefinger. Think of it that way. Treat it like that. Practice with that in mind. A man can point a finger at something and with enough practice, he learns to point with exact aim. I decided to follow suit with my shooting. When I lift my revolver I say 'Point with your finger' and it makes the aim certain. There is no failure. I pull the trigger and the bullet goes true to its mark. That's the trick, I suppose, to my shooting."

"Remarkable," Wallace said.

"Yep," Billy continued. "The man who taught me that is a friend of yours and mine and he's here in Lincoln right now. He's a dinger with any kind of gun, I'll tell you. I think I could beat him now, but I hope to God I never have to try, 'cause even if I got him first, that gray-eyed sonofabitch would kill me before he ... s'matter Governor? Don't believe me? You would if you saw him shoot. He really is good. I'm talking about ..."

"I know who you're talking about, young man," Wallace interrupted.

On Monday, April 14, 1879, the District Court convened in Lincoln after a year's lapse. Compared to his biased last year's charge to the jury, where he vilified Alexander McSween and attempted to prejudice the jury's decision against the man, Judge Warren Bristol's current charge was carefully neutral, attempting only to moralize against lawlessness and violence.

During the three weeks the Lincoln County Grand Jury was in session, they considered dozens of cases, among which, to Billy the Kid's surprise, was his old indictments against the murder of Sheriff Brady and George Hindman. Bonney appeared and pled not guilty.

True to his promise, Billy the Kid also appeared to give testimony in both John Tunstall's and Houston Chapman's murder cases. His testimony was largely responsible for Jesse Evans being indicted in absentia of being an accessory to Chapman's murder, while Bill Campbell and James Dolan were indicted on the direct charge of murder in that case.

Dolan, for the first time, sensed the hounds snapping at his heels. In a series of legal moves supported by District Attorney William Rynerson and allowed by Judge Bristol, Dolan's case was continued and a change of venue ordered to Socorro County, where he could hope for the ring's influence to better manifest itself.

The burning of McSween's home and its attendant killings brought forth a raft of indictments against former Sheriff George Peppin's forces, including an indictment against Colonel N.A.M. Dudley for arson in connection with the torching of the McSween house. George Peppin and John Kinney were also indicted on the same charge. Kinney was immediately arrested and placed under bond, pending trial at the next term of court. Peppin and Dudley were held on their own recognizance for $2,000 each. Both men asked for and received a change of venue to Socorro County.

Others of the Dolan Faction, indicted in the July five-day fight pled what Thomas B. Catron—their attorney—called the "Wallace amnesty" and were released.

At the close of the grand jury sessions, Jethro Spring asked for an audience with Governor Wallace just as the governor prepared to return to his Santa Fe residence.

"Billy expected to walk away from this session a free man, Governor."

Wallace tapped a pencil on his chair arm. "That's the way I planned it, too, Jack. For your information, I asked the prosecuting attorney for Billy to be allowed to turn state's evidence, but Rynerson rather indignantly refused. Do you suppose that man is tied in some way with the ring?"

"I know damned well he is, sir. But what Billy's concerned about is how and when you intend to fulfill your part of your agreement? He feels he's kept his."

"No doubt he has, Jack—up to a point. However, his testimony is still vital, you know. Dudley has asked for an Army Court of Inquiry into his conduct. The inquiry is slated to begin May 2nd. Then there will obviously be a need for the young man to appear at the actual trials during the July court terms."

"Can't he do that as a free man?"

"Will he? I must wonder that. Look, Jack, let's reason this out. You admit yourself the young man is somewhat wild—given to impulses. As governor, responsible to an enormous degree for a successful conclusion to events I've begun, I cannot risk losing Bonney. As you must know, the ring's newspapers are fiercely vilifying me. I cannot risk Billy's disappearance, whether he decides to leave the territory under his own power, or whether he's shot down by his and my enemies. It's my studied opinion that young Mr. Bonney is much safer being held in protective custody by the Lincoln County Mounted Rifles than by being free to become a target for our enemies. Do you not agree?"

Jethro pondered the governor's argument.

"His captivity certainly isn't too confining, is it?" the governor continued. "After all, he's being held at the home of his friend, protected by an impenetrable cordon of other friends."

"Couldn't that be done just as well if he was free, sir?"

"Do you really think so? I don't. His guards quite likely

would not feel the urgency of sheltering a free man that they do in protecting a criminal with whom they are in sympathy. Be reasonable, Jack. We still have the governor's pardon as a tool. It's a tool I fully intend to utilize at the proper moment. He must trust me. So must you."

"I'll talk to him," Jethro said.

Colonel Nathan A.M. Dudley's Court of Inquiry finally began session at Fort Stanton, May 25, 1879. The charges against Dudley were classified under the articles of war as (A) conduct unbecoming an officer and a gentleman, and (B) disobedience to orders. Article A revealed the extent to which Colonel Dudley was suspected of having shown partisanship:

I. Conspiracy with the Dolan-Riley party to aid and assist them in measures of violence against McSween.

II. An agreement with one of the parties of the feud to afford them protection and aid against the other party.

III. Allowing the McSween house to be fired, and thus endangering the lives of women and children therein.

IV. Failure to protect these women and children after they had left the burning house.

V. Not preventing the pillaging of the Tunstall store after the burning of the McSween house.

VI. Failure to protect Chapman after the aid of the military had been sought to this end, but referring to him as 'one of the murderers, horse thieves and escaped convicts infesting the country,' thereby excluding Chapman from the protection of the forces at his command.

VII. Aspersions on the character of a woman.

VIII. The publications of newspaper articles reflecting on the policy of Governor Wallace.

IX. The publication with improper motives of certain official documents furnished him to aid his defense before the board of inquiry.

The second charge, Article B—disobedience to orders—merely set forth three instances in which specific orders from superiors regarding the interference of troops in civil affairs had been disregarded.

The inquiry ground on for six long weeks. Governor Wallace occupied the witness dock for a full week, and was questioned at length in cross-examination by both Dudley's defense attorney and the board of inquiry recorder, whose role corresponded with that of a prosecuting attorney. Billy the Kid, Jose Chavez, Martin Chavez, Sam Corbett, and Dr. Ealy were among those testifying from the McSween side, while Fort Stanton officers such as Captain Carroll, Lieutenant Goodwin, and Dr. Appel, as well as civilians Buck Powell (from Seven Rivers), George Peppin, and Marion Turner were among those testifying for Colonel Dudley.

All in all, Dudley supporters were more numerous in testimony than his detractors, but Wallace, Bonney, Susan McSween, and Judge Wilson provided more weighty evidence.

The board of inquiry concluded taking testimony during the first days of July and, following military procedure, forwarded its decision to General John N. Pope, commanding the Department of the Missouri, of which New Mexico Territory was a division. The board of inquiry's decision exonerated Dudley of all charges. However, Dudley's record was so questionable that General Pope, upon review, disapproved the board's findings and transmitted the record on to the War Department in Washington with a recommendation that court martial proceedings be instituted against Dudley.

It was during this period, directly after the board of inquiry's whitewash of Colonel Dudley and before General

Pope disapproved their findings, that William Bonney began to tire of his restraint.

"Juan, dammit, I feel 'em closing down on me," Billy said around noon of that particular July day.

Juan Patron nodded gloomily. "Yet they are squirming, my friend. Perhaps they will go free, but it is obvious they will never rise from the ashes."

"That's no consolation to me when my toes are swinging three inches from the ground."

"The governor has promised. He is a man of honor."

"That's what I thought, too. So why ain't I free?"

Patron chewed the end of his moustache. Billy the Kid was growing restive and irritable, and the leader of the Lincoln County Mounted Rifles could hardly blame him. Others in Lincoln County felt similar frustration—without their necks at stake.

More and more, Juan Patron had come to depend upon the leadership and counsel of the man he knew as Jack Winter. "I think I will discuss this thing with Senor Jack, Billy. Let's get his thinking while it is uppermost in our minds, eh?"

Bonney shrugged. "Suit yourself. Ask him to drop down to see me when he gets a chance, will you?"

Juan nodded at Antanasio Salazar as he entered Susan McSween's store. He looked around at the busy place. Certainly the re-opened J.H. Tunstall & Co. enterprise was doing a land-office business, neatly undercutting the big store owned and operated by Thomas B. Catron. The captain of the Lincoln County Mounted Rifles found the man he sought working in an aisle. Patron studied Jethro before approaching. *Something is wrong with this eagle,* he thought. *Perhaps it is that he looks out of place stocking shelves in a store.* He cleared his throat

"Oh, hello, Juan. Be with you in a minute."

Patron looked about at the busy store. Sam Corbett and Susan McSween both worked with customers. *That woman! Aiee, she is beautiful. But she will be the death of the eagle. Why cannot he see it?*

"What is it, Juan? What can I do for you?"

"It is about Billy, our friend. Can we not find a place to talk?"

Jethro looked around with a harassed air. "We can certainly talk, Juan. But can we do it here? Between customers?"

"Of a certainty—Billy feels the governor has abandoned him."

"I've been over that with him before, Juan. You know that. Wallace promised him and me that he'll go free. He must hold to that belief."

"Word here is that Colonel Dudley has been exonerated."

"I've heard that, but I'm hoping the gossip is wrong."

"But what if it is right?" Patron persisted. "Billy wonders what Dudley will do to those who testified against him."

"Billy's a man, dammit, Juan. He's got to take a man's approach to nightmares and idle speculation."

"The court will convene in Don Ana County soon. It is not idle speculation that Sheriff Kimbrell intends to appoint Senor Redmond to escort Billy to Mesilla—I have that very fact from Kimbrell myself. You know as well as I that Redmond was with the Dolan party the night Chapman was killed. Billy does not yet know this thing. He is like a caged lion already. He is frightened. I shudder to think what will happen when he learns Senor Redmond is to take him to Mesilla. I beg you not to turn your back on your friend."

Jethro sighed. "What the hell can I do?" Juan's gaze was so imploring that Jethro finally said, "All right, Juan. I'll talk to Kimbrell. See if I can get him to change escorts. Okay?"

Patron shrugged. "Perhaps you could also come talk to Billy?"

Just then, a Ruidoso farmer walked in with a list and Jethro turned to help him. He said to Patron over his shoulder, "Not right now, Juan. Tell Billy I'll come see him later."

Patron strode from the store. "*Hola, mi compadre,*" Juan said to the old man sitting in the sun.

"*Buenas Dias,* Senor Juan."

Quietly, Juan recounted his reservations about Billy the Kid's situation to Antanasio Salazar. He also told of Jack Winter's distracted manner, of the rumors of Dudley's whitewash, and Redmond's pending appointment to be Billy Bonney's Mesilla escort. "I fear we will not long hold Senor Bonney, Antanasio. What shall we do?"

The old man bowed his white head. At last he mumbled, "It grieves me to add to your troubles, my son."

"What do you mean?"

"Word just comes to us here in Lincoln that Senor Dolan has been released by Senor Judge Bristol, at Senor District Attorney Rynerson's request. The bond, it is rumored, is only $3,000. And that is for two counts of murder." The old man lifted his head to stare at a distant ridgeline. "What are we who are poor but honest, to do, eh?

It was an hour before Juan Patron returned to his home. When he did he told Billy the Kid, "There is a horse across the street. The horse carries your saddle. In its rifle scabbard is your rifle. Your *pistoles* and cartridge belts swings from the horn. Though I will not advise you, I will not stand by to see one I call a friend linger to a slow and certain death without trying to help. In a moment, I will leave this room. All other guards have momentarily gone to the cantina. Whatever you wish to do, I will support you."

Billy the Kid slipped from his handcuffs and left Juan Patron's home in broad daylight. No guards were in sight. He swung into his own saddle, which was strapped to the best horse in Lincoln. And he pointed the horse toward Fort Sumner and freedom.

At that very moment, in Washington, the Secretary of Interior finished reading a letter written to him some time before by a harassed Governor Wallace. The Secretary read its key paragraph again:

> ... The people of the county go to Fort Stanton,
> witnesses on one side or the other of the Dudley

court of inquiry, and witness strange sights; they see
Dolan, admittedly the leader of the fiercest refracto-
ries, at large and busy in Col. Dudley's behalf,
although he is under two indictments for murder,
one a murder in the first degree. They know that he
is not at large by the consent or the connivance of the
sheriff. They know that the commandant of the fort
has my official request in writing to keep him in close
confinement. Knowing this, and seeing what they
see—Dolan free to come and go, a boarder at the
trader's store, attended by a gang well understood as
ready to do his bidding to any extreme—they are further met by threats of bloody things intended when
Col. Dudley is acquitted by his court and restored to
command of the post, and are afraid, and so con-
stantly as to find it impossible to settle down....

"What do you mean Billy's not here?" Jethro Spring
angrily demanded.

Juan Patron said, "He is no longer here. That is all."

"He was here this morning when you talked to me."

"That was this morning."

"Goddammit, Juan, I'm telling you, Billy better not
have flown the coop."

"And if he has? What will you do, Senor Jack?"

Jethro's face tightened. "Did you help him?"

"Our enemies have friends to help them. Should not our
friends also have friends?"

"Do you realize, Juan, that Billy may just have shit in his
own nest? That he may have thrown away his last chance to
be a free man?"

"I realize he is free, Senor Jack. Just as Colonel Dudley
and James Dolan is free."

"Dolan? What's he got to do with this?"

———•—•———

The following week's edition of the *Mesilla Independent* editorialized about Dolan's release on bail. An excerpt read:

> The examination of J.J. Dolan before Judge Bristol on a writ of habeas corpus strikingly illustrates the condition of affairs in Lincoln County. That such fiendish and dastardly murders should be committed in a civilized community, and no arrests or efforts made to bring the guilty parties to justice for weeks after the murders—notwithstanding the guilty parties remained in the town and at Fort Stanton—is strange to say the least of it....

Jethro finished reading the *Independent* and lay the paper on a nightstand. He reached over and raised the lamp's globe to snuff out the flames. Then he eased back upon the bed and tucked his hands behind his head. "I've got to find Billy, Susan."

She stirred. "Did you say something?"

"I've got to bring Billy back. It's the only way he'll have a chance to amount to something."

"Ummm."

"I'll leave in the morning."

She bolted up in bed. "What did you say?"

"I'm going to find Billy."

"That's absurd. You can't leave now. We're too busy. I can't spare you."

"You'll find a way. Did you read the *Independent?*"

"Yes. They're right, of course. But that has nothing to do with you and my store."

"It has a lot to do with Billy and why he left. So does General Pope's disapproval of Dudley's whitewash. Billy's future life is at stake."

Her voice actually snapped. "Well, I can't spare you, and

that's that!"

"You'll have to, I reckon. I'm not cut out to be a store clerk. I told you that a long time ago. Fact is, as I recollect, you told me you didn't expect me to be one."

She snuggled down beside him, trailing fingertips over his chest. "You won't be a clerk much longer, Jack. But right now we're so busy. Catron's store is reeling from our taking so much business from them. I simply can't spare you now."

"There must be somebody in town who can take my place as clerk."

"But no one can protect Tunstall and Company from Catron and Dolan, except you." She wriggled even closer, her naked body soft and cool to his bareness.

"I'm going, Susan."

"Ummm. Let's talk about it in the morning."

The following morning came and went. So did many others. Then one day Doc Scurlock showed Jack a short item in an issue of the *Las Cruces Thirty Four*:

> Kid and Scurlock and others are still in the county. They are reported as getting a crowd together again. No effort is being made to arrest them.

"What does this mean, Doc?" Jethro asked when he'd finished reading.

"It means I'm being accused of going on the owlhoot," Scurlock said, his face flushed in anger.

"Everybody knows better than that, Doc," Jethro said soothingly. Then the import of the newspaper article sank in. "Wait a minute! That means Billy is also accused!"

"Yeah, that's where it's comin' from. But I ain't."

"Is Billy?"

"Could be," the Ruidoso farmer conceded. "But I ain't."

Jethro Spring left Lincoln that very day, riding for Fort Sumner, fearful in his heart that he was too late.

Chapter Seventeen

"**H**ey, Jack!" Billy the Kid roared over the cantina noise, his happy face shining, standing out among a room filled with men of dark countenances. Jethro Spring glided through the throng, crowding and pushing his way when required. Billy met him with a hug, shouting to be heard over the din. "God, it's great to see you, boy! You're looking peaked, though. Store clerkin' ain't too good for you?"

Jethro nodded, smiling at the slender youth. Billy led him to their table. Tom O'Folliard and Charlie Bowdre were there, as well as two men Jethro had never seen. He shook hands with Sesturce Garcia and Dave Rudabaugh while worrying about Billy's choice of companions. Billy ordered beer for all, then he turned to Jethro and shouted, "So what brings you to Fort Sumner, friend? As if I don't already know."

Jethro said he'd came to visit his friend. Billy leaned forward, cupped an ear, and shouted, "Huh?"

"Later," Jethro shouted in return. "We'll talk later, not here."

Billy waved in agreement, then settled down for some serious drinking. Jethro bit his lower lip as he watched the youth. All evening, Billy spent money carelessly. The party broke up well after midnight and Jethro was at last able to talk to his friend.

"I want you to go back to Lincoln, Billy."

Bonney propped his chin in both hands, elbows resting on the table. "Wha' for?" he mumbled.

"I want you to go back and stand trial. I'll talk to the governor somehow, and get you free."

The blue eyes momentarily cleared, then glazed again. "Hell, I'm free now." Billy's chin slipped from his hands and he would've tumbled to the floor had not his companion caught him.

Jethro finally stood, smiling down at Billy as the young man tried in vain to focus on his friend. "Come on, pardner," Jethro said. "Let's go home to wherever you're sleeping. We'll talk tomorrow."

"Maxwell's," Billy mumbled, staggering to his feet. "I'm sleepin' at Maxwell's. Jus' ask fo' Pete Maxwell. You ... can sleep there, too."

Billy was up when Jethro first stirred the following morning. Though he looked the worse for wear, the youth flashed his buck-toothed grin and said, "I wasted part of that drunk, Jack, for there's some of it I don't remember."

Jethro nodded and sat up on the rawhide cot, swinging his bare feet to the floor. "Looked like you was swilling in competition with everybody else in the cantina, Billy."

"Fact? Damned if I know."

Jethro studied the youth. Billy met his gray-eyed gaze without flinching. "Time to talk, Billy?"

"Naw. Sure as hell we do, we'll get into an argument. Let's leave it for a day or two. Meantime, we can play like it's back in the good ol' days."

"Our good old days never was very good, Billy. Way I remember it, there was always something going on, somebody dying. A Tunstall, or a McSween, or a Buckshot

Roberts. I'd like to live for the future, where a man don't have to always look over his shoulder to see if somebody's chasing him."

Billy knocked over the chair as he leapt to his feet. "I said I don't want to talk about it now!"

Jethro never moved a muscle, sitting naked on his cot, seemingly relaxed. The tenseness went out of the youth and he gruffly said, "I'll see if Elvina has something to eat."

Jethro was dressed when Bonney returned. He followed the Kid down a porch that ran the full length of the rambling low adobe building. Many rooms opened upon the porch. "Got a friend in Elvina's kitchen I want you to meet," Billy said. "He's got a ranch hereabouts. He's a good man. Tough, too."

"Who's Elvina?" Jack asked as they turned the corner along the building's north wall. The porch continued on.

"Pete's wife. I'm in love with her."

Billy turned into an open doorway. Elvina Maxwell was of an indeterminate age, a huge woman of Mexican and Indian descent. Jethro guessed her weight at well over three hundred pounds. She had unusually long gray-flecked hair which was pulled back in a severe bun. By the way she smiled and bustled about them, Jethro soon discovered why Billy loved her.

A tall, broad-shouldered, slim-hipped man brought his plate of half-eaten food from a corner table and joined them. "Jack," Billy said, "this here is another friend of mine, Pat Garrett. Pat, meet Jack Winter. You're both hell-on-wheels."

Jethro took the extended hand and pumped it. Garrett's hair was as dark as his own. The cheekbones were prominent, as was the nose, giving the face an aquiline appearance. The man wore a heavy, full moustache. Jethro liked the way he looked.

"Heard a lot about you, Winter," Garrett said, smiling down from his greater height. "All of it damned good, and not all from Billy, either."

"My pleasure," Jethro said. "A pleasure to meet you,

too, Mrs. Maxwell."

"Ha! Is little pleasure I give men these days, Senor Jock, except through their bellies. Sit down now. Hurry and I will bring you steak and potatoes and coffee."

After they were seated, Jethro said, "Billy says you're a rancher around here, Mr. Garrett?"

The tall man chuckled. "Only of sorts. Upriver a piece. My spread ain't worth much—not enough for the attention of Billy and his boys."

Garrett, Billy the Kid, and Elvina Maxwell all laughed at Garrett's joke. Jethro concentrated on his steak.

"Billy tells me you taught him what he knows about guns and how to use 'em, Winter," Garrett said.

"I doubt that. I taught him some of what I know. He went on from there."

"Some?" Bonney broke in, only half-mockingly.

Jack grinned. "I'd like to keep you guessing, Billy. Otherwise you might get too cocky."

"I can beat you," Billy the Kid said flatly, his eyes guileless.

"I never have said I doubted you."

Billy's eyes wavered to his plate, then flickered back to Jethro and Garrett. "Tell you the truth," he said, "the only two men in the whole world I'd hesitate to match guns against are sittin' at this table right now."

Jethro and Garrett's eyes met. The rancher asked, "Why are you afraid of us, for Christ's sake?"

"I'm not afraid of you," Billy flared, "nor nobody else, dammit!" There was an awkward silence, then Billy said, "Hell, I'm better'n either one of you. I know I'd get you. Trouble is, I know you'd get me, too. I don't know anybody else like either one of you. When you set your mind to something, it gets done. I suspect you'd kill me, even with your dying breath."

Jethro's eyes flickered again to Garrett, then returned to Billy. "I can't speak for Pat, Billy. But it's all right with me if you feel that way, for I never figure to match guns with anybody again, not if I can help it. Let alone you."

"Amen," Garrett murmured.

"Billy," Jethro said the following day as the two men sprawled in the shade of a Pecos River cottonwood, "since I've been here, I've figured out for myself that there's some truth to the rumor you're using a long rope and a straight iron."

Bonney's gaze was across the river. "You ain't askin', so I ain't sayin'."

"Billy, if you ever want to live free, you've got to give yourself up."

"Like Dolan, huh?"

"Dolan's trial is coming up in Socorro soon. So is Dudley's civil trial. It's likely they'll get theirs."

"If you believe that, you'll believe anything."

Jethro broke off a dried grass stem and began methodically breaking it into tiny bits. "Let me talk to the governor about you, will you?"

"Sure. Talk all you want. But don't expect me to abide by anything cooked up without me."

"Will you keep an open mind about it, though? Until you hear it?"

"Yeah, I'll do that." Curious, Billy asked, "What'll you talk to old blackbeard about?"

"I'm going to ask him to honor his agreement made about freeing you on your old indictments—up to the time you rode away. I'm going to tell him I'll try to talk you into standing trial for whatever crimes—if any—you've committed since your escape."

"Fat chance I'll do that," the youth said.

"He'll never pardon you for crimes after your agreement, Billy."

Bonney took out the makings and began rolling a cigarette. "I got the impression he was going to welsh on our deal anyway."

"Billy, you know better than that. You left because it looked like Dudley and Dolan were going free. Wallace never had a damned thing to do with that. He didn't make an agreement with the courts to release them bastards. Fact is, he tried every way he could for conviction. What he did do, however, was make an agreement with you to pardon you for any crimes committed to that point. That's all."

"I'm free now," the Kid said. "What do you make of that?"

"And you're happy with the kind of freedom you've got?"

Bonney said nothing, staring moodily at nothing.

"Look, Billy," Jack pressed, "you and I both know the law's not looking very hard for you. But continue the way you're going and you must know that'll not last forever."

"A cow here and there. Chisum can stand it."

"Is Chisum the only one you've hit so far?"

"Yeah. Me and the boys figure he owes 'em to us for standing off the Seven Rivers bunch from his herds for a year or two. Them bastards would've picked him clean if it hadn't been for us."

"Then I'll tell Chisum that before I talk to Wallace; see if he won't agree not to press charges. If he says he'll go along, and with the governor's pardon, you're a free man."

Billy puffed silently, staring across the river.

"Do you have any other bones in your closet?" Jethro softly asked.

The youth shook his head.

"Will you mind your manners and give me a chance?"

Billy pitched the butt into the slowly flowing water and turned to his friend. "Here's my hand on it."

Jethro grinned, took Billy's offer, and grasped the slender youth's shoulder with his free hand.

Jethro was in luck—John Chisum was at his Bosque Grande Ranch. "Lemme get this straight, Winter," the old cattleman growled, "you're asking me to drop charges agin Billy Bonney for stealin' my cows?"

Jethro nodded.

"In exchange for what?"

"Billy says it's in exchange for services rendered against the Seven Rivers gang. He says you agreed to carry the expenses of the fight against Dolan after McSween and Tunstall died."

"That's what the young whelp said to me, too. But that's all a bunch of bullshit." When Jethro said nothing, Chisum demanded, "Well, ain't it?"

"Billy might have thought it was true," Jethro replied.

"You never struck me as being an idiot," Chisum said. The old cattleman turned to glare down a lane shaded by half-grown cottonwoods. Two cowboys herded a small band of mares and colts toward them.

Jethro was dusty and tired. He resented it that Chisum hadn't asked him into the coolness of the ranchhouse; nor even volunteered trough water for his horse. But without showing his rancor, he asked, "How many head has Bonney got away with?"

"How the hell would I know? I don't count 'em."

"Have your losses been substantial?"

"If they was, Highsaw would've swung that buck-toothed whippersnapper from a cottonwood limb."

Jethro swung his gaze from the oncoming horses to the old cattleman. "How about thinking of withdrawing charges against Billy as insurance that it won't happen again?"

Chisum spat into the dust. "Water yore hoss at the trough yonder. Then come on into the house. We'll talk."

Billy the Kid wasn't in Fort Sumner when Jethro Spring passed through on the way to Santa Fe. He left a note for Billy with Pete Maxwell telling of his favorable agreement with Chisum and begged Billy to continue the peace until Jethro could talk to Governor Wallace. The gray-eyed man then spent the night at Pat Garrett's ranch, on the way to the Las Vegas stage line.

"Billy ain't a bad sort, Jack," Garrett said that evening as the two sat in front of Garrett's ramshackle ranch house to watch a vivid sunset. "He just don't think the same as we do about other folks' property."

"People have used him, Pat. McSween used him. So did Chisum, I think. Billy thought an awful lot of Tunstall. He figured to get even with the ones who killed the Englishman and I suspect he got a lot of encouragement from some who lacked the guts to do it on their own."

"Always the way of it," Garrett murmured.

"How did you get to know Billy?" Jethro asked the taller man.

"Through Maxwell. Billy stayed at Sumner a lot. Let's see, that was a few months ago. Pete's place is one where folks just naturally come and go. We hit it off, Billy and me."

Jethro yawned and stretched. "And how was it you never got drug into the Lincoln County War? One side or the other?"

"I guess I mind my own business. Unless I got a personal stake, that is. I don't think it was 'cause I was scared."

Jethro laughed and yawned again. "You'll make sure Billy gets the note I left at Maxwell's?" he asked. "It's damned important for Billy to know Chisum won't press charges if he stays clean."

"I will. If you can make honest men out of Billy and his bunch, you'll be doing a service to the whole damned country."

The smaller man nodded. "I guess I'll hit the hay, Pat. I want to get an early start for Las Vegas."

The "Palace of the Governors" was a disappointing place to Jethro Spring. After his travels through many of America's cities as a rising middleweight prizefighter known as "Kid Barry," Jethro was familiar with many major edifices. The name Palace of the Governors conjured up an image of castle turrets and cathedral architecture. Instead, Jethro found a long two-story adobe building that fronted the north side of Santa Fe's main square. The Palace of the Governors sported a block-long porch along the square; the porch was every bit as squat and cheaply constructed as Pete Maxwell's in Fort Sumner and only a bit longer.

Jethro stepped inside the lobby and moved to a counter where a bored, wizened, unusually pale man sat perched on a high stool. A pair of Franklin wire-framed bifocals hung on the end of a long nose. "Yes?" the man said distastefully.

"I'd like to see Governor Wallace."

"A lot of people would like to see Governor Wallace."

Jethro stood uncertainly in this outer hall of the seat of New Mexico power. The clerk sighed and eyed the unwanted visitor up and down. "Do you have an appointment?"

"No, but I'm sure he'll see me if you will be kind enough to announce that I'm here."

"Then I'm afraid it's impossible for you to see Governor Wallace. And I shall make no such announcement."

"How does one go about making an appointment?"

"In your case, write a letter. If the governor deigns to acknowledge your need, he'll notify you as to the time of your appointment."

"I'm not from Santa Fe."

"The clerk sniffed at the travel-stained man. "That, sir, could be to the everlasting credit of Santa Fe."

Jethro grinned despite his irritation. "I'm from Lincoln."

"I should have guessed when I saw the tied-down gun."

He tried again: "I'm sure Governor Wallace would see me if only he knew I'm in town."

"Perhaps it's fortuitous the governor doesn't know, then. He has quite a busy schedule."

"Tell him it concerns Billy the Kid."

"I shall tell him nothing, my good man. Especially not anything concerning that notorious outlaw."

"Then," Jethro said with no change of expression, "tell me where I can find him and I'll tell him myself."

"You'll do no such thing! As a matter of fact, you smelly man, you will leave the Palace of the Governors immediately or I shall have you arrested."

Jethro leaned on the desk and began indifferently scratching at his sweat-stained shirt, his gray eyes settling on the clerk.

"Guard!"

Jethro heard a chair scrape in an adjoining room and a squat, broad-shouldered man appeared at the door. "What's going on?" he growled.

"Escort this gentleman out, please," the clerk said. "He refuses to take my suggestion."

The guard tugged at his revolver. "Okay, you heard the man. Let's go."

Jethro continued to scratch and stare blankly. The guard, whose powerful chest bulged beneath his shirt, stomped forward, holding his gun steadily on Jethro. He reached out and grasped the travel-stained newcomer and jerked him roughly away from the reception desk.

The guard should not have came within reach.

As Jethro spun away, a foot and a hand lashed out. The hand's edge snapped into the guard's right wrist a split second before the foot kicked his knee and leg from beneath him. The second mistake the guard made was in trying to catch the spinning revolver. As he did, the edge of Jethro's second hand chopped at the base of an ear and the guard collapsed on the floor with a thud.

The travel-stained newcomer scooped up the revolver, then straightened, stopping at eye level with the frightened clerk. He leaned forward until his nose was only inches from the other man's nose and said, "Now, my good fellow. What room is the governor in?"

Involuntarily the clerk's eyes flicked to the unconscious guard, then returned to Jethro's level gray ones. His mouth opened a time or two, but no sound came out. At last, the man pointed down a hall.

"Lead the way, please," Jethro said, motioning.

Somewhere the clerk found courage to shake his head. But when Jethro nudged his chin with the muzzle of the guard's revolver, he slipped and nearly fell from the stool in haste to rush down the hallway with Jethro at his heels. Finally the clerk stopped before frosted-glass double doors.

"This is it?"

The clerk was near collapse. His head bobbed. Jethro turned the knob and pushed both doors open. Governor Wallace looked up startled from a head-to-head conversation with a man in a U.S. Army general's uniform. Wallace took in the frightened clerk and the unkempt man holding a gun who stood in his office doorway.

"Sorry to use this method, Governor," Jethro said as he handed the gun to the clerk, who promptly dropped it. "I tried to explain to this fellow that I needed to talk with you, but he's a little dense."

Governor Wallace's amused glance swept to the general, then back to the men at the door. "Well, your—ah—entry is a bit unorthodox. But it is always a pleasure to see you, Jack. Have you met General Hatch?"

"No, sir."

"Come on in then and do so." Wallace turned to the officer. "This, General, believe it or not, is Jack Winter—the man we were about to send for."

As General Hatch stood to hold out a hand to Jethro,

the clerk, still at the door, whined, "We tried to stop him, sir. He assaulted the guard. Knocked him unconscious, he did. I'll call a squad ..."

"Assaulted a guard, eh? Knocked him unconscious? Apparently took his gun?" The governor's brown eyes enveloped Jethro once again. "Someday, I'd like to see you in action, Jack, rather than merely hearing of your exploits."

"Sorry, sir. But I had to see you."

"Governor Wallace, do you want me to ..." the clerk began.

"I want you to close the door, Giles. Pour water on the guard and give him back his gun. Then," Wallace said in perfectly good humor, "I want you to cancel the rest of my appointments this afternoon. General Hatch and I—if the good General is willing—will be tied up with Mr. Winter for the rest of the day."

General Hatch grinned at Jethro. He was small and wiry, with thinning white hair, a ramrod-straight back, and sun-tanned skin that looked as though it had recently been shed by a bull snake. "I'm available, Lew. Even if I wasn't, I would be after the entry your young friend just made."

Wallace gestured at a chair and Jethro sat down, placing his battered hat on the floor near his chair. "Now," Wallace said, "to what do we owe this honor?"

"Billy," Jethro said. "Billy the Kid."

The corners of Wallace's mouth turned down. "Well, he's low on my list right now, Jack. It's other things we wish to talk to you about just now."

Jethro decided to take a chance. "I can't imagine what it could be, Governor. But will I be able to discuss Billy briefly with you sometime while I'm in Santa Fe?"

"We'll see."

"That's what brought me here, Governor. A later appointment will be fine."

"I said we'll see. I must tell you I have a very low regard for William Bonney, after he broke our agreement."

"There're two sides to ..."

"Mr. Winter! I do not wish to discuss Billy the Kid just now. There are more important things to consider."

Jethro pushed slowly to his feet. "Then I'm sorry to have interrupted you and General Hatch. I'll make formal application for an audience concerning William Bonney with your clerk, then go on back to Lincoln and await your summons."

"Confound it, Winter, I told you your being here is especially propitious! General Hatch and I have other vital matters to discuss with you."

"But my being here is because I'm seeking an audience about the William Bonney matter. While I'm certainly willing to yield to your greater urgency, your Excellency, I'm not eager for you to dismiss consideration of my own concerns."

General Hatch smiled as Governor Wallace's face turned red. "That's blackmail, Winter!"

"Oh, I hope not, Governor," Jethro said, putting his hand on the doorknob.

Wallace sighed, "Sit down, Jack. You're a better poker player than I. You'll have your audience."

Jethro returned to his chair. After he was seated, Governor Wallace said, "You know about Victorio?"

Jethro nodded. "I know he's a Mescalero Apache."

"Do you know he's been raiding in southwestern New Mexico?"

"Yes, sir. But I'm not sure to what extent."

"He's been giving us a devil of a time. He's slippery, vicious, and always doing the unexpected."

"That's typical Mescalero—Apache—traits, isn't it?"

"Yes. That's true, Mr. Winter," General Hatch broke in. But it's not really Victorio that worries us so much as the Mescaleros on the reservation, near Lincoln. They are, according to every report, growing restless. While we know individual warriors have slipped away to join Victorio, we've managed to placate a sub-chief called Malvado, who seems to wield some obscure power over them."

Jethro waited. The governor picked up the thread. "This Malvado rascal, so we're told, grows more bellicose daily, apparently out of jealousy for Victorio's success. We understand from our sources that Malvado has aspirations to become war chief to replace Victorio and we're afraid he will lead a significant portion of his people from the reservation. Malvado could be instrumental in bringing our entire southern frontier into flames."

"Our soldiers out of Fort Stanton appear largely ineffective," General Hatch interjected. "We've tried sending out patrols to guard the reservation perimeter, but the agent requested we stop because it seems agitation was the result, rather than pacification."

Jethro asked, "Have there been raids, General?"

"There hasn't yet been overt hostile activity—only unrest. But it's fair to say we're worried."

Wallace said, "It seems this Malvado fellow is the key. We did a check on him and can find very little reason for his influence. I suppose it's because he's some sort of an undercover rascal."

When the governor paused for breath, Jethro asked, "Then you think there's a genuine danger the Mescalero will break from their reservation?"

"Absolutely."

"All signs point to it," General Hatch added. "The Army, of course, can handle it, but if this Malvado leads the reservation Mescaleros away, it could compound problems on every Apache reservation throughout the frontier."

"Since it appears army patrols only exacerbate an already sensitive situation," Governor Wallace said, "we began a search for a civilian with influence among the reservation Mescaleros. You'll never guess whose name came up."

"What do you want me to do?" Jethro Spring asked.

CHAPTER EIGHTEEN

Governor Wallace flashed a smug smile at General Hatch, then turned to the man he knew as Jack Winter. "Perhaps we should ask if you can help us in pacifying the reservation Mescaleros?"

Jethro Spring shrugged. "I can try."

"How?"

"I don't know. And I won't know until I go there and learn what's going on."

"Do you know this Malvado rascal?"

"Apparently better than you do."

"What do you mean?"

"First off," Jethro began ticking off a count on his fingers, "his name is not Malvado. It's Naiche Tana. He's not a rascal; neither is he a sub-chief or a minor chief. He has no desire to climb the ladder to greatness because the man is already at the top. He's not an undercover rascal. His power is not mysterious. He is not in the least jealous of Victorio. Nor does he aspire to become war chief of the Mescalero Apache for the very best of reasons: Naiche Tana—Malvado to you—is already war chief of the Mescalero Apaches."

"Impossible," General Hatch said. "Victorio is war chief."

"General Hatch, Victorio is only a sub-chief. The real Mescalero war chief dwells on your reservation, and has for several years. He only did so—and only does so now—because he is so revered by his people that the only way they would agree to go to the reservation is if he led them there. *That,* sirs, is the reason for your Malvado's mysterious power. He is a great man, as well as a great chief."

One could've heard a feather thump the floor before the governor said, "Jack, in the short time I've known you I have come to understand, both from my own observations and from others, that your comments are not to be taken lightly. Yet surely you see why we must ask how you can be privy to information not even available to the War Department?"

Jethro leaned back in his chair. "Do either of you speak the Apache language?"

Hatch and the governor exchanged glances. "Is that another of your accomplishments?" Wallace asked.

"We have men available to us who do, though," Hatch said belatedly.

"And have you lived with the Mescaleros?"

"Have you?" the Governor asked.

Jethro nodded. "I have. I have lived in the wickiup of Naiche Tana—Malvado's wickiup—for two months and have talked for many hours with the chief in his own language. I have seen the love and respect his people have for him. From their lowliest to their mightiest, I have talked to them of the past exploits of their great war chief, Naiche Tana. Gentlemen, I assure you Naiche Tana—Malvado—is what I say he is."

"All the more reason then for him to be jealous of Victorio," General Hatch said, "and to want to lead his own people to war and victory."

"No, General, you're wrong. Victorio is no more or less

than a Mescalero sub-chief, subject in some degree to their war chief. Naiche Tana led his people to the reservation for a reason. He does *not*—please understand this—he *does not* desire peace for himself; but for his people, he knows there is no other way."

Jethro spent the next hour explaining the Apache society and Apache hierarchy to the two men who held the very future of those Indians in their hands.

When he'd finished, General Hatch said, "Mr. Winter, if this is all true—the things you've told us—I've learned more about these Apaches in the hour with you than with a lifetime of Indian agents."

"It's all true, General. You must believe that."

"And if Malvado is that important, perhaps we'd better put him under detention."

"Arrest him? Jethro exclaimed. "Do you mean arrest Naiche Tana?"

"Protective custody," Hatch growled.

"Do that, General, and by the time the morning sun touched Sierra Blanca, there wouldn't be an Indian on the reservation."

"You seem pretty positive, Jack," Governor Wallace said.

"I am. In the first place, I doubt you could take Naiche Tana. If you did, I doubt you'd take him alive. And even if you were able to pull it off, it wouldn't make a damned bit of difference, his people would feel betrayed and would flee the reservation."

"So what do you suggest?" Hatch asked.

"Let me go down there and see what I can learn. You gentlemen are right about one thing—the man you know as Malvado is the key. If we can persuade him it's best for his people to stay, they'll stay. It's as simple as that."

The governor's eyebrows arched as he turned to the general. Hatch nodded. "All right, Jack. You have our blessing. You also can have access to whatever you need to accomplish your mission. General Hatch and I will issue blanket authority for you to requisition anything at all at any territorial or federal installation. I'm sure you'll need time to plan your program—say tonight? Can you return in the morning with some kind of schedule in mind?"

"I'll try, Governor. But I need more information. You mentioned a word a while ago I've never heard before; I believe you said Malvado grows more 'bellicose.' What, exactly, does that mean?"

"Hmm." Wallace looked at Hatch. "Angry? Ready to fight?"

"You're the literary man, Lew, not me," Hatch said. "But I'd guess that's right."

Jethro nodded, almost to himself. "Naiche Tana brought his people to the reservation because he saw it as the only way the tribe could survive. If he's changed his mind and has grown angry and ready to fight, I'm curious as to why."

"So are we, Mr. Winter," Hatch said. "If it's not jealousy of Victorio's success, then we have no idea why."

"Do you, Jack?" Governor Wallace shrewdly asked.

"Not really, sir. But I'd be willing to place bets it's why I'm here in the first place."

"Billy the Kid? I don't understand."

"No, not Billy, Governor. Billy's problems and the Mescaleros' problems more'n likely stem from the same source—greed. Indian reservation and military supply contracts have been shaved and cheated on for years. Murphy, Dolan, Riley, Catron. It's all the same. The big store extorting and milking the land and people. Red, white, or Army blue—what difference does the color make—gold is yellow from any of them. Maybe they went too far this time; beyond the Mescaleros' ability to tolerate. It'd be my guess if Naiche Tana is really considering war, the Mescaleros have been cheated one hell of a lot more than in the past. And that's already plenty!"

Governor Wallace harrumphed from behind his desk. General Hatch said, "That's some speech, young man. If you can bring proof that such things exist, both we and the

Mescalero will be eternally grateful."

"Yes, Jack," Wallace added. "If that's true and we can get proof, we'll act immediately to correct it."

"Even against Catron?"

"Especially against Catron!"

Jethro stood. "I'll think on it tonight and come back with something in writing before I leave. Will eight o'clock be too early in the morning to call?"

"Not at all, Jack. I'll be here," Wallace said.

"We'll talk about Billy, then?"

The governor smiled. "Yes, we'll talk about William Bonney then."

After Jethro had gone, General Hatch said, "A remarkable man, Lew. Do you think he knows what he's talking about?"

"I'd be afraid not to believe it, Edward. The man has an unusual record for saying little and doing much."

"Do you think he's right about the supply contracts?"

"Yes. There's entirely too much smoke for there to be no fire. If he can only bring us proof, we'll pin Catron's ears to the wall once and for all."

"If it's true and anyone gets to sniffing too close, that man's life may well be in danger."

Governor Wallace smiled. "In that case, Edward, we may have the best man available for the assignment."

———————

The following morning, after reading Jethro Spring's Mescalero pacification plan, Governor Wallace said, "Your requested authority to requisition appears pretty broad, Jack."

"You said yesterday that you and General Hatch would issue blanket authorization, Governor."

"For *personal* acquisition. And at territorial and federal installations. This proposal gives you authority to make bulk purchases from the private sector."

"You should look at the proposal more carefully, sir. It clearly states *only* if in fact my suspicions are true and the Mescaleros have been cheated of their rations. Only then does my proposal give me authority to take emergency steps to help them."

"God bless me, though, Jack—you're asking me to approve a pig in a poke!

"I'll not use it unless there's no other way, sir."

Wallace's brown eyes enveloped Jack. "Very well," he said laying Jethro's proposal down on his desk.

"About Billy?" Jethro asked.

"My, you are determined. Go ahead."

Jethro asked the governor to honor his agreement to pardon Billy Bonney for crimes up to mid-July.

"What about crimes since?" Wallace demanded.

"He is willing to stand trial for them if charges are pressed."

"He is?" the governor said in surprise. Then his eyes narrowed. "There's something I'm missing here, isn't there?"

"Nothing underhanded, sir."

"You've struck a deal with Chisum, haven't you?"

Jethro sighed. "He's agreed not to press charges."

Wallace picked up a pencil from his desk and began tap, tap, tapping. At last he said, "Why do you do this for that young outlaw, Jack? Why do you extend yourself for him?"

Jethro's chin sank to his chest. His reply came while he studied his boots: "Same reason I would for you, sir. Or for Naiche Tana and the rest of the Mescaleros. Or for Susan McSween and the rest of the good people of Lincoln County. Because basically they are fine people trying to survive in a part of the world that's somehow gone clear out of kilter. Billy's a good boy who was stuck into a man's shoes by circumstances beyond his ability to handle. He faced forces even a territorial governor, for God's sake, is having trouble getting a grip on. And he fouled up a little. Well, I think there's something in Billy worth saving. And I'm betting you will, too."

The pencil continued tap, tap, tapping as Governor Wallace studied Jethro. "Extraordinary," he finally said. "You combine rare talent with real compassion and an ability to act quickly and concisely when necessary."

"About Billy?" Jethro prompted.

"I don't share your faith in the man."

"Understandable," Jethro said. "But will you pardon him?"

Wallace threw the pencil to his desk and stood to walk to a window. There, with his back to the room, he peered out at the plaza. He clasped his hands behind his back and returned to pace back and forth before Jethro. At last, the governor said, "I'll make a counter-proposal, young man. Four months. Let's give Billy the Kid four months. If John Chisum does not press charges against Bonney for cattle rustling, *and* if there are no other crimes against the Kid or his gang by New Year's Day, I'll pardon him at that time."

Jethro ran a rough hand over his face in relief. "Thank you, Governor Wallace. I'll tell Billy right away."

"By mail, I hope."

"Yes, sir."

Wallace went back to his desk and sat down. "When will you leave to see Malvado?"

"The Mesilla stage is at noon. I'll be on it if you'll have my requisition authority ready by then."

"I'll send a clerk to the station with your authority."

Jethro nodded and stood. "I'll try to keep you informed, sir, as I can."

Wallace rose and extended a hand. "You are on official assignment, Jack, as of now. As such, you'll receive a salary. The requisition order should cover most of your expenses. Those not covered will be reimbursed upon presentation of a proper expense account."

"Thank you, sir."

"If your suspicions are correct and it is at all possible, General Hatch and I earnestly need proof, Winter. Proof! If it takes you more time to uncover and obtain the proof, take the time. Pacify Malvado first, then send us proof."

"Yes, sir."

The governor said, "You may be in some danger."

"Yes, sir."

"And upon conclusion of your assignment, I'll want a personal report."

"Personally written, you mean, Governor?"

"Yes, that too. But I mean I want a report in person."

"Need I make a formal request for an audience, through proper channels, sir?"

Wallace roared. "Mr. Winter," he said when he subsided, "I doubt seriously if you'll ever have to do that again."

CHAPTER NINETEEN

"**W**ho is it?" Susan McSween said to the persistent knocking.

"It's me, Susan," came a muffled voice.

"Well, I never! Go away. You're fired!"

"Susan, I must talk to you."

"Jack Winter, if you don't go away, I'll call the sheriff."

"Are you on better terms with this one, Susan? You wouldn't have called any sheriff before."

"I tell you—go away! It's after midnight and I won't open this door."

He began pounding again. "If you don't, I'll cause a ruckus that'll wake the whole town."

"Quit it now, Jack. Please! Are you drunk?"

"Open up I say." He began kicking the door.

She threw the bolt and swung the door wide. "I'll swear I don't know what has come over you. Gone for three weeks and you're acting like a lunatic."

He leaned against the doorjamb. "Eighteen days. Did you really fire me?"

"Yes. Now go away."

He pushed past the woman into her living quarters. He smelled of sweat and dust and saddle blankets. "I need some supplies, Susan."

"What's the matter, Jack?" she said in alarm. "You're not in trouble are you?"

"None that I know of. Except with you. Light a lamp."

"I will not! Do you want the whole town to know about us?"

"Light a lamp, Susan. I don't give a good goddamn what the town knows." His voice was low and cold and flat. And there was something about it that made her hurry to obey.

When the lamp flared, she turned to face him. Her hair flickered straw-colored in the uncertain light, long and wavy and framing her face. She wore a floor-length flannel night-gown. Bare toes peeked from beneath. Sleep was still upon her. "What is this now? I insist on knowing." She moved closer to sniff his breath and was even more puzzled when he appeared not to have been drinking.

"What's the price of cracked corn from Bartlett's Mill?" he demanded.

"You are absolutely crazy! You've been out in the sun too long."

"Come on, Susan. What's your price, wholesale?"

"Go on. Leave my house. Get out."

"I'm serious."

She studied him. "I believe you are," she finally muttered.

"The price?" he said again.

"This isn't a game?"

"No game."

She told him.

"And how much do you have in storage?"

"Here or there?"

"At the store and at Bartlett's," he said after a pause.

"Offhand, Jack, I don't know. What is this all about?"

"What about flour?"

"White or dark?"

"Both."

"I would imagine a ton of each."

He stared at her, but she could tell he was looking through her, beyond her. "How about Dowlin's or Casey's Mills? Do you have anything there in storage?"

She shook her head. "Jack, what ..."

"Do they have any excess on hand? Do you know?"

"No! I don't know-w-w!" she screamed. "Now, will you tell me what this is all about?"

She'd seen him smile this way before—when only his mouth twisted. He sometimes used it just before he went into action and she shuddered. "Jack, I insist on knowing what we're talking about."

His altogether grim smile softened and stretched to reach his eyes. "I've been fired, huh?"

She sniffed. "You were removed from the payroll the very day you left."

"Hell of a life, ain't it?"

"Are you going to tell me what you are doing in my room late at night, gabbling like an idiot."

"Yeah. I came for a cigar."

"Oh no you don't," she said, drawing her gown more tightly about her.

"Well, what the hell? If I'm not on the payroll and not eligible for cigars no more, I won't feel bad for doing what I have to do."

"What are you talking about, Jack Winter?"

"I want all your cracked corn, all your wheat of any kind, all your stock of potatoes, all your coffee, sugar, every basic staple you have in your store, or in storage. On top of that, I want you to try to procure every basic food grain available in any of the local mills at a reasonable price."

"That's all?" she said, grasping him by an arm and shoving him toward the open door.

He threw off her arm and said, "I'm serious, Susan."

"You're also either drunk, insane, or sleepwalking. Get

out."

He kicked the door shut. "Now, Mrs. McSween, will you get it through your thick head that I'm not joking. I want every goddamned item I listed, and in the quantities described. I will pay what it costs you, plus ten percent. Now, you can damn well get to work figuring out what you have, where it is, and when I can get my hands on it."

"And how will you pay for these things, Jack Winter?"

He handed her his requisition authority, signed by Governor Wallace and General Hatch, then watched in amusement as it finally dawned on the woman that he was serious.

"What is this all about, Jack?" she asked quietly.

"Indian reservation. They're starving. Catron apparently hasn't delivered for six months or more. Time is important."

She sank to a chair, still holding his papers and said vacantly, "The cigars are in the right-hand top dresser drawer."

When he returned with his cigar, she looked up and smiled sweetly. "I never really fired you, Jack. And I'll see that you get all your back pay."

"No."

"Jack," she said, appearing as if the thought had just struck her, "we can make a very handsome profit off this—you and I."

"I said no, Susan."

"But Jack, this is a blanket authority. They needn't know how much my costs are. I'll bet they don't even care."

"No, Susan. Cost plus ten."

"You could become wealthy."

"Cost plus ten."

"I won't sell at that," she said.

"Yeah you will, Susan."

"These papers do not give you the right to commandeer except at government installations. It gives you the authority only to *purchase* from private sources."

"You'll sell," he said matter-of-factly. "Because if you give me any more shit, I'll go up the street and rattle the door at Catron's store and you'll lose your chance to nose into some fat government contracts."

"You wouldn't dare. Not if they've been cheating the Indians already."

"The Indians, Susan. Think of the Indians. They're starving. Do you think I'm going to quibble about the merits of one store versus another when people are starving? Besides, as Catron's have already stolen from the Indians, they're certain to have a ready supply of everything I need."

"Jack, we can't let this chance for a really big profit slip by!" She was almost in tears.

He laughed. "I thought you already knew tears don't help with me. Cost plus ten, woman. Take it or leave it."

She stopped sobbing and sighed. "When will you need it?"

"As soon as possible."

"How will you transport?"

"I'll work on that while you work on the volume, location of supply, and price."

"You won't reconsider, Jack?"

"Positive," he said.

"I might take you off the payroll again."

He laughed.

The morning after pounding on Susan McSween's door, Jethro sent a telegram from Fort Stanton advising Governor Lewis Wallace that Mescaleros were starving, that they'd received no supplies for six months, that because the approach of winter made their situation even more desperate, he was therefore invoking his authority to buy emergency supplies from the private sector.

After sending the telegram, Jethro jogged back to Lincoln on a fresh cavalry mount commandeered using his requisition authority. He thought over events of the past week and his jaw muscle ticced when he remembered Fairfax Wheeler, the temporary agent in charge of the Mescalero reservation....

"Yeah, Winter," the agent had said to the gray-eyed man seated before him, "we've received all supply deliveries as scheduled."

"No, I'm not sure of the amount of beef or flour or corn." "Yes, I suppose it was listed on the waybill." "No, I don't have the waybills handy. Reckon I sent 'em in when I sent the request for proper payment to the suppliers." "Yeah, I suppose you're right, I should've kept the waybills." "No, Winter, I guess I've got no way to prove deliveries was made now. I guess you'll have to take my word for it." "No, come to think of it, I can't recall exactly when the last delivery was made, but I imagine it's on the waybill."

The man blatantly lied, Jethro knew. He found out how much when he entered the wickiup village of Naiche Tana and saw the emaciated people. He'd dismounted before the chief's shelter where the stern old warrior squatted, waiting for his visitor. Jethro actually "felt" the pair of deep-set coals the warrior chief used for eyes burn into him. This was the *real* Malvado!

"It is good to see you, Naiche Tana," Jethro said in the Apache tongue."

"Why?" Malvado said in English.

"Why?" Jethro repeated. "Do you mean why is it good to see you?"

"*Esta hombre Indio Mirar muy malo,*" Malvado said in guttural Spanish.

"*Ni loco; que esperanza!*" Jethro replied angrily.

Malvado stared fixedly back. Then he changed back to Naiche Tana, speaking in slow Apache so Jethro could follow: "Why does the gray-eyed-one come to the wickiup of Naiche Tana?"

Jethro told him, speaking in halting Apache. He told the chief of Governor Wallace and General Hatch and how he'd been commissioned by them to investigate the wrongs being done to the Mescalero, not neglecting that he had authority to temporarily help them in their need.

The Indian listened impassively throughout Jethro's fumbling Apache speech, then said, "Naiche Tana led his people to peace, forsaking the ways of war forever. We do not go to war even as we should when the white man starves us to extinction. Naiche Tana said no! We will try to walk in peace as long as two breaths remain. We will rise in war when there is but one breath left."

"How many breaths does the Mescalero have left, Naiche Tana?"

"Yesterday we had but one. Today, the gray-eyed-one brings us another."

———•+•———

Antanasio Salazar had several wagons and teams ready in Lincoln, as he'd promised during the night of Jethro's arrival. He also had twenty men of the Lincoln County Mounted Rifles drawn up to act as escort.

"I didn't ask for an armed guard," Jethro said to the old man. "Do you really think we'll need them?"

"No, Senor Jock. I do not think so—if you have them. If you do not have them, that is when you will need them, eh?"

Jethro chuckled at the logic and patted the old man affectionately. He entered the J.H. Tunstall & Co. store, where Susan McSween and Sam Corbett were hard at work.

"Just about ready, Jack," Susan called. "I've tied up all the grain Bartlett's have, but my messenger isn't back from Casey's Mill yet. Dowlin's, of course, is too far away to find out before tonight."

"I'll check there on our way up the Ruidoso." He moved to her desk. "Do you have your billing list?"

She handed over several sheets of foolscap. He glanced at the list. "Too much, Susan. Re-do them. You quoted me your cost on cracked corn last night. I said cost plus ten. You got what amounts to cost plus twenty."

"Prices have gone up, Jack. You must understand that. Anytime there's a sudden demand, prices go up."

He moved to Sam Corbett's desk. "Make out new billings, Sam," he said, thrusting the sheets to the man. "Cost plus ten on everything."

Sam looked at Susan who nodded, her face tight with anger.

It was not until the next day, as their wagons lumbered up the Rio Ruidoso toward the starving Mescaleros, that Jethro worked out the method Susan used to feather her profits on the sudden demand for food grain.

"Yes," Juan Patron said, "she is a shrewd one, that woman. She wakes Edgar Walz in the middle of the night and purchased most of Catron's grain stocks at bulk prices. I find it humorous, do you not? The woman now controls the remaining grain supply in Lincoln County."

————•·•————

The famished Mescaleros fell greedily on their supplies. The farm wagons, on their way back down the Ruidoso, met the hundred head of beef cattle Jethro had earlier contracted from John Chisum. The cattle, delivered by Jim Highsaw and six Chisum cowboys, arrived at the happy Mescalero village early the following morning.

"How is Billy getting along, Jim?" Jethro asked the rangy Jinglebob foreman.

"You shore castrated him, Jack. I don't know how you done it, but John and Pitzer are about as happy as if they had good sense. They ain't heard nothin' from Billy. He's been so good, I reckon he's prob'ly a tophand church deacon these days."

When Highsaw and the Jinglebob men left, Jethro turned his attention to a long-term solution to the Mescalero problem.

"We must have proof, Naiche Tana, that your people were cheated by their contractor and their agent." The two men again squatted before the chief's wickiup, watching the Mescaleros moving about their village.

"Naiche Tana say it is so. Is that not proof?"

"Not in a white man's court, my friend. It is your word against that of the agent, who says otherwise."

"He lies."

"I know, but we need to be able to prove he lies."

Malvado called a young child over. Upon questioning, the child said he could not remember the Mescalero people receiving any supplies throughout the entire summer. "You see," Malvado said, "now it is this child and Naiche Tana who says it is so. There are two of us who say the truth against our agent's lies. That is proof."

Jethro smiled as he shook his head. "No, Naiche Tana, that is not how the white man's courts work. You see, both the contractor and agent swear delivery has been made."

"Then all Mescalero will say truth!"

Again Jethro shook his head. "We need proof without anyone saying anything."

Malvado pondered the question. At last, he said, "Does not my people starving speak the truth?"

"Yes it would, if a court could see it." Jethro snapped his fingers. "Daguerreotypes! Of course! If we can get someone to take pictures!"

To think was to act with Jethro Spring. The next day he was at Fort Stanton to send a second telegram:

TO LEWIS WALLACE
GOVERNOR
SANTA FE NEW MEXICO TERRITORY
FROM JACK WINTER
FORT STANTON

REQUEST PHOTOGRAPHER TO DOCUMENT STARVING CONDITION OF MESCALERO STOP WILL WAIT FOR REPLY STOP END OF MESSAGE

TO JACK WINTER
FORT STANTON
FROM LEWIS WALLACE
GOVERNOR
SANTA FE NEW MEXICO TERRITORY

JOSIAH COOK COMMISSIONED AS PHOTO-
GRAPHER STOP ARRIVE LINCOLN OCTOBER
TWELVE STOP GOOD LUCK STOP END OF
MESSAGE

However, Josiah Cook did not arrive on the Lincoln stage. "No," the driver said, "I ain't seen him, nor heard of him." Jethro waited three days. Josiah Cook was never heard from again.

Jethro's three day wait for the stage wasn't a total loss, however. The stage brought news from Socorro, where a fall term jury found James Dolan innocent of two counts of murder in the first degree. The jury also freed former Lincoln County Sheriff George Peppin and Colonel Nathan A. Dudley of complicity.

Jethro Spring was in Santa Fe two weeks later. He hand-ed several papers to Governor Wallace, who pored over them.

"Interesting," the governor said. "Very interesting. Is Dowlin's, Bartlett's, and Casey's the only mills where Catron could've obtained their grains?"

"No sir." There are mills at Roswell and Tulerosa. But I checked and they made no shipments to Catron."

"How about purchases under another name?"

"No sir. All their sales are accounted for."

"So the alleged deliveries to the Mescaleros and report-ed deliveries to Fort Stanton, along with the bulk purchases by Susan McSween, amounts to more grain than was pro-duced in all the available mills?"

"That's the way it appears to me, sir," Jack said.

"So someone says they delivered more grain than was

possible to have accomplished?"

"Yes."

"And they didn't stint on deliveries to Fort Stanton, for there are no reports of the troops starving. How about Mrs. McSween's store? Has she obtained delivery of her purchase?"

"Yes sir."

"Then there can be but one answer," Wallace said, slapping his desk. "They didn't make their Mescalero deliveries."

Jethro nodded. "If you'll look closely, sir, the shortfall in reported production compared to reported delivery almost exactly matches their fake Mescalero deliveries."

"Yes indeed," the governor mused. "Ver-r-ry interesting."

Jethro watched the governor closely for several minutes as the man pondered. "Is that adequate proof, sir?" he asked at last. "Is my job done?"

Wallace sighed and shook his head. "I'm afraid not, Jack. Speaking as a lawyer familiar with our court system, this is good material—certainly an indicator of *probable* chicanery. But hardly enough for certain conviction. You know these people better than I. They will develop outside sources to explain the discrepancy, or buy off some of the producers to suddenly come forward on a witness stand to swear something that's not true."

Jethro twisted in his chair to gaze out the window. "We could nail down bulk deliveries to the mills by grain payments to farmers, affidavits, that sort of thing. As for outside sources to explain their over-supply? I'm sure the cost of shipment from the Mesilla Valley or the upper Rio Grande would show that to be damned tough."

The governor swiveled to gaze out the window with Jethro. "You're right, of course. And I think you should go on back to pick up whatever proof of supply you can from farmers and millers. Meanwhile, I'll take your suggestion and see if I can get an account clerk on cost comparisons for any imported grain they might have brought in from outside the area. But as time permits, I'd like you to do more checking on the theft of Mescalero cattle. I'd like to know just where the Indian herd went."

Both men turned from the window at the same time. "Some of those cattle went into their bellies, sir. When people are starving, they're not really too interested in keeping a few critters for breeding next year."

"But your report demonstrates clearly that they lost the bulk of their herd through theft, doesn't it?"

"Yes, sir, it does. I'll do what I can, but cattle are hard to trace unless you get on it right away."

Wallace nodded. "Do the best you can."

The governor changed the subject. "You've still uncovered nothing about the photographer?"

"No, sir. Not on my end. Have you?"

"No. The man got on the stage here. Apparently he was the lone passenger. He was still on at Bernalillo, so the driver says, but gone at Albuquerque. All his photographic equipment stayed on the stage."

"Any ideas?"

"No," the governor replied. "Foul play was suspected. But we later found the man had completely closed his studio here in Santa Fe. We also have witnesses who say he came into considerable money just before he left town. He may have sold his soul to the ring."

Jethro yawned and crossed his legs.

"Another photographer?" Wallace asked.

"No. Too late. The Mescaleros have been stuffing themselves with everything they could eat for nearly a month. By the time we could get another photographer there, they'll look fat and happy."

"Well, that's it for now. Do you have anything more to add, Jack?"

"No. But maybe somebody should ask what we're going to do about these Indians when their emergency rations are gone?"

"I'm not sure what you mean. Bids for their new supply contracts will be let soon. We're moving supply dates forward. What is perhaps most important—we've taken steps to remove Thomas B. Catron and Company from the list of approved contractors. There may not be enough evidence to convict, but there certainly is enough to warrant removal of his firm from bidding on future federal contracts."

"What about Wheeler? That agent is as crooked as a dog's hind leg. As long as he's ..."

"Wheeler's appointment is only temporary, Jack. I'm preparing a package that I intend to forward to the Secretary of Interior about the Mescaleros. I'm asking the Secretary to hurry through permanent appointment of Wheeler's replacement."

Jethro nodded and yawned again. "Good. It can't come too soon."

"I will need one thing from you before you leave town, though," Governor Wallace added. "I'll need an affidavit from you as to the Mescaleros' general condition when you first saw them. I'll need it to include in the Secretary's package. I mentioned that need to my clerk."

"Yes sir. I'll swear one out for you."

Switching subjects, Wallace asked, "You've heard about the Socorro trials of Dolan and Dudley?"

Jethro nodded, turning glum.

"Well, it's distressing news, though somewhat expected, given the two men's importance to the ring." When Jack made no comment, Wallace continued, "What is of importance is the ring is on the run. They've recently incurred several costly adventures into litigation; the switch in officers and personnel at Fort Stanton is virtually complete; their power is broken, Jack. At least in Lincoln County."

"I'm sure that's some consolation to the ghosts of John Tunstall and Alexander McSween."

"No sarcasm now, my boy. My objective has always been to stop outlawry and bring peace to the region." The governor gazed at his frowning visitor and sighed. "I might as well add to your burden now, rather than wait until later."

Jethro's heart leaped. He waited.

"Word came in from Las Vegas just last night."

Jethro's heart sank. "What kind of word?"

"John Chisum lost an entire herd of Panhandle cattle. They've traced the cattle to Colorado buyers. Billy the Kid and his gang are implicated."

Jethro sighed. "I'll go back to Lincoln County through Fort Sumner."

"It won't do any good, Jack," Wallace said as kindly as he could. "Our agreement was that Billy had to stay out of trouble until January. It was also contingent upon John Chisum not pressing charges."

"Governor, dammit, we don't know if any of this is true. I want to find out. Even if it is, you know it happened because he got pissed off at that Socorro business."

"That may well be, Jack. Even so, as Governor of New Mexico Territory, I'm not about to pardon a known incorrigible criminal."

"By your leave, Governor, I'll be about my business."

"Certainly, Jack. But I'd urge you not to go back by Sumner. You've done all you can for young Bonney. You'll be wasting your time in attempting more."

"I reckon I have to go back that way, Governor. My old sorrel mare has been in a stable in Las Vegas for near onto two months now. It's time I took her out for a ride."

As Jethro Spring left Governor Wallace's Santa Fe office that first day of November, the wizened reception clerk he'd had words with some months before called out to him.

"Yes?"

"Governor Wallace asked me to make an appointment with ... with a local justice of peace, so you could swear an affidavit."

"Yes, that's right."

"Well, you have a three o'clock appointment with Justice Loveall, down on the Paseo de Peralta. Do you know where that is?"

"No. But it makes no difference. Three o'clock is too late anyway. I'm going to catch the one o'clock stage to Las Vegas."

"Oh no! You can't do that."

"Why not? I'll find another judge to swear the affidavit."

"No! It must be Justice Loveall," the little man said. "I'll make you another appointment."

"Why must it be this Judge Loveall?"

"Because I've already made the ... your appointment."

"Well, cancel it." Jethro left the Palace of the Governors, angered at the clerk and his persistence. Gradually anger turned to curiosity. Why was the man so obstinate about Jethro going to see this Judge Loveall? An alarm bell went off in Jethro's mind and he turned into a plaza saddle shop.

A moment later, the guard Jethro had knocked unconscious in an earlier altercation paused at the door, then continued around the plaza. Jethro brushed past the startled saddlemaker and out the shop's back entry. A few minutes later, he sauntered into the Palace of the Governors and handed the wizened clerk the sworn affidavit. "Wasn't too much trouble to find a judge willing to accommodate a governor's need," he said good-naturedly. "Now I'll be able to make my one o'clock stage to Las Vegas."

The clerk's head bobbed as he took the affidavit. "Very good, sir. I'll see that Governor Wallace gets this immediately. Have a good trip, sir."

Despite a lady waiting to board, Jethro was first on the stage. He took a seat against the far door, his back to the driver. The day was cool and he wore a light wool jacket. For additional warmth, he carried a heavy wool military greatcoat over his arm.

The lady clambered into the stage, sniffing at Jethro's lack of chivalry, taking a seat opposite him.

Next was a drummer who took the window seat diagonally away from Jethro. He was followed by what appeared to be a rancher, then an old stove-up cowboy. A beefy-faced army sergeant in uniform boarded last. The rancher and his cowboy sat next to Jethro, the rancher by the window. The sergeant took what was left, between the drummer and the girl. Jethro pulled his hat down over his eyes and pretended to fall asleep.

Which one would it be? Jethro wondered. He dismissed the stove-up cowboy as too old to be a hired killer. The rancher? No, he's friends with the cowboy and he fits the cowboy's description as too stove-up. Okay, the drummer or the soldier. Both of 'em took opposite seats, and that's where an assassin should make his play from. Let's see now, the soldier took what was left, while the drummer made sure he was into the coach early enough for a choice.

The stage rolled out of Santa Fe, heading for the Glorieta Summit. Jethro's head lolled on the seat cushion in mock-fatigue while he continued his evaluation of his fellow passengers. The drummer is too fat—a man'd think a hired killer would stay in better trim. The soldier, now, he's in uniform and dressed to kill. Campaign hat, white gloves. Shuck that uniform under a cutbank somewhere and switch to ranch clothes and nobody'd ever in the world identify him. But why would an assassin wait to take the last seat? It didn't make sense.

The stage slowed as it neared the summit. Then at the top, its driver pulled in the team for a rest. This would be where the attempt was most likely to be made. Jethro steeled himself for action.

The girl dipped her hand into her handbag and pulled out a derringer. "I'm sorry to awaken you, Mr. Winter, but you and I will be leaving the stage here. There's a man outside who would like to talk to you."

Jethro couldn't believe it! The woman! The roar of the Walker revolver he'd concealed under his greatcoat since Santa Fe was deafening inside the coach! In an instant, the gray-eyed man kicked open the opposite door and dived between the drummer and the rancher, hitting the ground rolling. He'd guessed right, because the crack of a rifle came from the coach's far side. Jethro continued to roll while snapping quick shots in the rifle's general direction.

Belatedly, the driver whipped the team into action and Jethro jumped for a sheltering rock as the stage rolled away. It hadn't gone far before the driver pulled up his horses in response to cries from his passengers.

Silence descended. Then Jethro heard hoofbeats pounding away. The gray-eyed man limped down the road to the stage. The soldier and the rancher held guns but Jethro thrust his into his waistband and climbed into the stage where the old cowboy and the drummer worked over the girl. "How is she?" he asked.

"Shoulder's nothin' but jelly," the cowboy said. "Losin' blood bad."

"Let's get her out on the ground," Jethro said. "Then we'll take a better look."

The sergeant stuck the muzzle of his service revolver against Jethro's backbone and said, "Don't you think you've done enough for the girl? You're under arrest." He pulled Jack's Colt neatly from his holster, apparently overlooking the Walker in his waistband.

"For what?" Jethro said, turning to face the sergeant and the angry rancher. "She pulled a gun on me. I shot in self-defense. I tried not to kill her."

"People in these parts don't shoot women, mister," the rancher said. "For whatever reason."

"Then people in these parts are damned fools if the woman pulls a gun with the intent of shooting them." To the soldier, he said, "Give me back my Colt."

"I'll hold on to it if you don't mind," the sergeant said. "At least until I find out what's going on."

Jethro carefully pulled out his papers from the territorial governor and handed them to the soldier. "I'm about as curious as you are, sergeant. Now will you give me back my gun and help us get the girl out of the coach before she bleeds to death?"

The seat of New Mexico government was closing for the day as Jethro Spring strode into the lobby of the Palace of the Governors. The clerk paled and the guard's hand dipped toward his gun.

"I wouldn't," Jack said, thumbing back the hammer on his Colt.

"I ... I thought you'd left S-Santa F-Fe, Mr. W-Winter," the clerk stammered.

"I did. I came back. Let's go see the governor."

"Wha-what for?"

"Because I want us to."

"He's busy," the guard interrupted.

Jethro smashed the barrel of his Colt against the man's ear and the guard went down like he was axed. Jethro stooped to slide the man's revolver from his holster and thrust it into his own belt. Then he grasped the unconscious guard's collar and started dragging him down the hallway. "Come on, Giles," he said, waving his Colt at the clerk.

The governor looked up from his desk, exclaiming, "Goodness!" Then he lapsed into silence, leaning back in his chair, a bewildered expression on his face as Jethro prodded the clerk forward, dragging the inert guard into the room.

"The clerk babbled hysterically: "He ... this man attacked us!"

"Shut up, you bastard!" Jethro said as he kicked the doors shut behind him.

Wallace said blankly, "I trust there's a good explanation for this?"

"He's savage, Governor Wallace! A killer!"

Jethro kicked the clerk into a heap in the room's far corner.

"Stop it!" the governor shouted, leaping to his feet.

Jethro took a deep breath while struggling with his own

fiery anger. "Did he give you an affidavit from me today, Governor?"

"No. Why? I asked about it. I thought you'd forgotten."

Jethro whirled back to the cringing clerk. "Where is it?"

"I burned it," the man whimpered.

Jethro spun back to the governor. "We thought our leaks were coming from the telegrapher at Fort Stanton."

Governor Wallace spread his palms. "Can somebody tell me what is going on?"

"And all the time, you had spies for the ring right in your own office!"

CHAPTER TWENTY

Jethro Spring spent several unsuccessful days searching for Billy the Kid in the vicinity of Fort Sumner. He did learn from Billy's friends, however, that Bonney had reverted to his old ways, forsaking a future pardon in the wake of Dolan's Socorro trial travesty. Finally, knowing that Billy avoided him and concerned about his Mescalero friends, Jethro pointed the sorrel mare down the Pecos. He stopped at Chisum's South Springs Ranch and found the old cattleman committed to Billy the Kid's destruction and nothing Jethro said or did made the slightest difference.

Jethro spent the next several weeks gathering statistical information on grain deliveries to and from various Lincoln County mills, continuing to sew up one end of the theft case against the Catron store. His search took him throughout the county on many lonely rides, calling at first one farm, then another. He examined receipts and check stubs and took depositions that he asked the farmers to sign before a judge the next time they were in Lincoln.

His efforts to track down the stolen Indian cattle was less rewarding. He did find one cowhide carrying the Indian brand slung over a corral rail in a remote Seven Rivers cow camp. It was during the cowhide discovery that Jethro Spring's investigation almost came to an abrupt end.

The man had been meticulously careful not to develop an identifiable routine during his movements, turning up in the Rio Bonito one day, the Ruidoso the next. Tomorrow, he might be in the vicinity of Agua Negro Spring, yesterday he was along the Rio Penasco. He was a wisp by design, here today, gone tomorrow, never a target for unseen bullets. Only when he felt the keen edge of his mind and body fading did he seek refuge; always in the wickiup village of Naiche Tana, war chief of the Mescalero Apache. But during one particular search through the Seven Rivers country, he'd been spotted by an unseen observer. Then the cowhide had been placed where he couldn't miss it....

Jethro rode into the trap and nearly out of it before it was sprung. The waiting men in the sod hut had expected him to come to the little cabin to ask questions. But instead, he'd merely examined the hide, then rolled it up for evidence and tied it behind his saddle. He glanced at the line-hut and something ticked within. *Is it too quiet? Would anyone leave such a damning piece of evidence lying in plain sight?* He mounted his mare and pointed her toward the hut as if he intended to ride to it. Then he wheeled the horse and buried his spurs, bending low over the saddle as he did.

There were a few scattered shots from behind. His mind raced: *Where are their horses? Must be a horse-holder back in the hills—where? Are there other bushwhackers?* His answer came as three riders dashed from an arroyo, cutting him off from the left. He slipped out his Winchester and pointed the mare at them, firing as he went!

The sheer audacity of his swerving to meet the oncoming riders saved him as the three ambushers reined aside. By the time their friends from the cabin joined the three mounted pursuers, Jethro Spring had an insurmountable lead.

He made it to South Spring where he borrowed a Chisum horse. Daylight found him back at the sod line cabin where he'd found the hide. The cabin was deserted. And in several more days of cautious scouting, he failed to find another trace of the missing cattle.

----·•·----

The travesty of New Mexico Territory's justice continued on: In early December, Susan McSween's civil suit against Colonel N.A.M. Dudley was tried in Mesilla and the jury found in favor of Dudley. After Dudley's triumph, other suits against Peppin and Dolan died a quick death.

Immediately following the Mesilla trial came news from the War Department in Washington. The Judge Advocate General's report to the Secretary of War concerning Colonel Dudley read:

> ... While the evidence does not substantiate the principal charges against Colonel Dudley, yet it is to be granted that the presence of soldiers did give a certain degree of moral support to the sheriff's posse and stimulated them to more drastic measures than otherwise would have been undertaken. As for the minor matters, there appears to be little proof to support them except for the one concerning Dudley's extorting from Judge Wilson a warrant against McSween personally for shooting at the courier. Dudley did appear to have been too violent and arbitrary in that matter, as well as unnecessarily rough in means and intemperate in language on other occasions. Further, though Dudley's acts might have been irregular and without sanction from orders, it should be taken into consideration that he was in command of a frontier post in a country overrun with contending bands of outlaws toward whom he could hardly hold a consistently neutral and passive attitude, especially when invoked to protect women and children and other defenseless persons.

It is the recommendation of the Judge Advocate General that charges against Colonel N.A.M. Dudley, Commandant, Fort Stanton, New Mexico Territory, be dropped.

And so, with that strange combination of tar and white-wash, Colonel Nathan Dudley returned on January 1, 1880, to command at Fort Stanton. It was a command far different to the one previous. Most of his officers had been exchanged with officers from other posts throughout the Territory. Similarly, the enlisted men were largely new.

The citizens of Lincoln County, at first apprehensive about Dudley's return to command, soon found a changed man; an officer largely content to spend his time reviewing training drills.

The civil situation had also drastically changed in Lincoln County. Catron's store was under direct fire for cheating on Indian contracts, their mercantile leadership taken over by the enterprise of J.H. Tunstall & Co., operated by Susan McSween. Gone, too, was John Selman's outlaw band. James Dolan's influence was at its lowest ebb and the Seven Rivers toughs were lying low. Lincoln County courts were functioning and a reasonably aggressive and impartial sheriff was in office.

Susan McSween, rebuffed at bringing Colonel Dudley to account, was more successful in other endeavors. In the wake of Thomas B. Catron & Co.'s decline, her J.H. Tunstall & Co. store wound up winning most of the lucrative military and Indian reservation supply contracts formerly held by Catron's. Though unsuccessful in manipulating transfer of the deceased John Tunstall's two cattle ranches to her name, she did, as administratrix of his estate, arrange a favorable long-term lease. With the lease in hand, Susan soon joined with John Chisum in developing a large-scale southeastern New Mexico cattle venture.

From Fort Sumner came the news that Billy the Kid killed a man named Joe Grant in a saloon argument. Billy, so the same report said, was greatly expanding his cattle rustling operations.

Amid it all, Jethro Spring labored for his Mescalero friends. Though without official capacity, he was at agency headquarters in early February when the first contract deliveries were made by J.H. Tunstall & Co. He examined waybills, weighed sample sacks, and methodically counted the bags as they were unloaded. When the agent Wheeler signed for delivery, Jethro insisted the man also sign the list he'd made on his own.

"Why should I do that?" Fairfax Wheeler asked.

"For my records, Wheeler. I want to pass it on to the governor."

"I work for the Indian Bureau, not for the territorial governor."

"True. But I work for the governor," Jethro replied, "and I promised him I'd send a receipt on delivery."

"So send it."

"I will—just as soon as you sign it." When the man still hesitated, Jethro's voice dropped. "You will sign it, won't you, Mr. Wheeler? After all, it's just you and me. Or do you want it to be just me?"

The man signed. When he handed the paper back, Jethro said, "Fine. Thank you. Now, I want you to know I have persuaded Malvado to keep a record of all food distributed to the Indians from agency stores. We're going to account for every sack of grain, every side of bacon, every pound of coffee."

"What's that mean to me?"

"Nothing, I hope. I just want you to know it, is all."

Jethro was still at the agency the day a telegram was delivered to him by a cavalry patrol on their way to the Tulerosa Desert, searching for marauding Apaches under Victorio. The telegram read:

TO JACK WINTER
INDIAN AGENT
MESCALERO AGENCY
NEW MEXICO TERRITORY

FROM LEWIS WALLACE
GOVERNOR
SANTA FE NEW MEXICO TERRITORY

TEMPORARY APPOINTMENT MESCALERO
AGENT FAIRFAX WHEELER WITHDRAWN BY
INTERIOR SECRETARY STOP PERMANENT
REPLACEMENT NOT DETERMINED STOP
NEW TEMPORARY AGENT ASSIGNMENT
MADE STOP YOU ARE IT STOP APPOINT-
MENT EFFECTIVE WHEELER NOTIFICATION
FROM INTERIOR STOP CONGRATULATIONS
STOP END OF MESSAGE

"You sonofabitch!" Fairfax Wheeler exclaimed when he opened his official letter a week later and learned of his dismissal. "You undercut me, didn't you?"

"Well," Jethro agreed, "I sure as hell tried."

"I try to do right by you and you stab me in the back."

"Yep. I told them you weren't worth the powder to blow you to hell, right enough. I was beginning to wonder if my advice took, though."

"What did I ever do to you?" the ex-agent whined. "I did everything you asked."

"Yep. You sure as hell did. And I hope you keep it up, because I'm asking you to get the hell out of this agency and off the reservation by noon tomorrow. I don't want a crooked, lying, thieving bastard like you around to stink up the place any longer than it takes for you to trot out of sight. Understand?"

Fairfax Wheeler left at daylight.

"It is good," Naiche Tana said, squatting by the agency door, "to have the gray-eyed-one as Mescalero agent. The white chief in Santa Fe is wise."

Jethro glanced up from a desk where he pored over old

agency records. "I'm not sure the governor had anything to do with my appointment, Naiche Tana," he said in English.

"If he did not, then he who did is wise."

Jethro slipped from his chair and joined the chief in watching the sunset. In his improving Apache, Jethro said, "Victorio still raids, Naiche Tana."

"Yes."

"He strikes deep into New Mexico—the last time was into the great desert near the shifting snow-sands."

"Yes."

"It is said Victorio grows more cruel—that he even tortures women and children when he kills."

"Yes, that is the way of one who becomes desperate," Naiche Tana said.

"It is said some of his warriors leave him because he is too cruel even for them. Does Victorio grow desperate, Naiche Tana?"

"Why else would he torture women and children? To torture is not a warrior's way. My heart saddens for him."

"My heart saddens for all who suffer in this war between Apache and white."

"Were it not for the will of our people, Naiche Tana would be Victorio and Victorio would be Naiche Tana."

"Would Naiche Tana be so cruel?"

The Apache simply said, "No."

Jethro shifted from the fading sunset to stare across the flat at Blazer's sawmill. "Would it not be better, Naiche Tana, if Victorio comes to live on the reservation, too?"

"Why do you not ask him?"

Jethro was so unprepared for the chief's answer that his jaw dropped. He blurted in English, "How? Where? I mean, is it possible?"

"It is possible."

"Where could the one-called-the-season-of-the-hunger-moon meet Victorio and talk with him, my friend?" he asked in Apache. "And when could such council be?"

The war chief grunted something unintelligible. He

came to his feet and said, "Naiche Tana will come for the gray-eyed-one when it is time."

———•••———

Jethro Spring trotted up the sandy bed of the dry arroyo, sheer rock cliffs towered on either side. Once, he glanced behind, suddenly fearful Naiche Tana had abandoned him to his fate. It was a senseless fear—the war chief trotted easily behind, knee-length moccasins only whispering on the arroyo sand.

Much earlier, while the land was still steeped in darkness, they'd left their horses somewhere near the headwaters of the Rio Tulerosa. From there, Naiche Tana led off west, Jethro following, climbing a rocky defile where no horse could travel, into the mid-April snows clinging to these eastern slopes of the highest Sacramentos.

Jethro was sure they'd left the reservation boundary shortly after they'd trotted across the high summit, Naiche Tana leading. They then began a laborious descent along a treacherous game trail that followed a narrow cliff slash. At the bottom, the two men again set out at a steady ground-eating trot down canyon to a fork, then up canyon to another fork, then another. Mile after steady mile, climbing now to the east, the two churned on. Sweat ran freely through Jethro's pores and he envied the bare torso and loin cloth of his companion. He marveled that the chief, at his age, could run so steadily and easily.

In his early twenties, as a well-conditioned middleweight prizefighter known as Kid Barry, Jethro had put in thousands of miles of roadwork. Now, as his lungs screamed and eyes dimmed with fatigue, he was everlastingly grateful for those miles. As it was, all he could do was concentrate on the dark form ahead. Then Naiche Tana stopped. "We rest," the chief said. "Then the gray-eyed-one will go first."

Jethro stared around. They were in a narrow canyon of sheer rock walls, only ten to twelve feet wide from bottom to top. He glanced at Naiche Tana and concentrated solely on breathing as easily and shallowly as the old chief.

A few minutes later, with Jethro leading, an Apache warrior fell in beside him! The move was sudden, but so deep and trusting was his faith in Naiche Tana that he gave no hint of surprise. When the next warrior fell in on his other flank, he was prepared. Then another fell in to lead.

They trotted on in that way, Jethro surrounded by Naiche Tana and the three Apache warriors. Gradually the warrior in front increased his speed; faster and faster, until the four Indians and one half-Indian pounded headlong up the arroyo. Jethro's lungs were near bursting and his eyes began to dim. Then they rounded yet another bend and the lead warrior stopped. Jethro, rushing pell-mell caromed off the first warrior and bumped into another before he could stop. He staggered, wobbling in a circle as his eyes slowly focused. He was in the middle of ring of Apaches—warriors all. Dimly he saw Naiche Tana. The war chief stood haughtily outside the circle, his legs spread and arms folded. Just the hint of a smile was on the stocky chief's lips and the black eyes flashed with a mischievous glint.

Slowly, Jethro turned, peering at each warrior in turn. A tall, broad-shouldered Indian with wide, cruel-bent eyes and unruly black hair hanging to his shoulders said, "I am Victorio." He spoke in English.

Jethro still panted, fighting for breath. He studied the man as he did. Victorio, Jethro decided, had an uncontrolled fierceness about him that seemed foreboding—actually a wildness. "Greetings," he said in halting Apache. "I am Jack Winter. I am called the gray-eyed-one by your people, the Mescalero. I am agent for the Mescalero Apache people on the reservation to the north. I am their friend. I would be your friend."

Victorio rattled something in rapid Apache. Jethro caught only a few words: "Enemy," "white eyes," "kill," among them.

"I do not understand," he said. "I speak Apache poorly.

Please speak more slow."

Again, Victorio rattled more garbled Apache. Jethro looked casually around. He was getting his breath now and thought more clearly. Only hostility met his eye. He turned back to Victorio. And this time his voice was flat when he said, "If we are to talk, we must both understand. If we are not both to understand, then Victorio and the gray-eyed-one came for nothing."

"What is it the white man would say?" Victorio said coldly, but slowly.

"I came to ask you to come to the reservation and dwell in peace amongst your people."

"How can we live at peace with the white man who kills us and drives us from our homes?"

"How can the white man live at peace with Apaches who do the same? I tell you, there has been enough war. You are tired. The white soldiers are tired. Would it not be better for both to say we are tired? Can we not live in peace without one defeating the other in war? Those who truly want peace can seek peace with no loss of honor."

"Any who seek peace are women with neither honor nor friend."

Jethro still wore his Colt on his hip. And he, like Naiche Tana, carried his Winchester. There was a knife in his left boot, too. The Mescaleros had deliberately left him armed. But they all carried weapons, too, and at least twenty of them surrounded him. "How," he asked Victorio slowly, putting as much disdain in his words as he could muster, "can I prove to you I am not a woman?"

A look of greater wildness came over Victorio. "All white eyes are women, and women can never prove themselves to be men."

Jethro's breathing had returned to normal. Still, he was tired from his all-night ride and long morning run. He measured his chances and shrugged. Then he bent, laid his Winchester at his feet and unbuckled the Colt from around his waist to lay alongside the carbine. He straightened and stared hard into Victorio's malevolent orbs. Then he bent again, this time to his boot, and removed the small knife. Straightening, he glanced at Victorio then spun the knife to its hilt in the ground between them.

"Many whites," he growled in guttural Apache, "have the courage of Naiche Tana or Victorio. I am one of those. To prove to you this is so, I will fight any warrior Victorio chooses to send against me. But he will be armed with only a knife and I will have only empty hands."

A low murmur swept the circle of Apaches before Jethro continued: "Or alone and with no weapons, I will fight three"—he held up three fingers—"of your warriors, who are also unarmed."

Victorio stared coldly at the newcomer, then barked three names. The three warriors who'd escorted Jethro and Naiche Tana up the winding little arroyo laid their rifles at their feet and divested themselves of pistols and knives.

Jethro backed cautiously until the rock wall was at his rear. As he did, he subconsciously mumbled a prayer to his one-time mentor, Ling San Ho, who'd taught him many lessons in the art of unarmed fighting.

The first Apache to disarm himself—the lithe warrior who'd led their pounding run through the arroyo—leaped to the attack before the other two were ready. He came with arms wide-spread, intending to grapple. It was too easy. Two hard straight lefts, a vicious right to the body and a full left uppercut to the jaw stretched the man full length between his two partners as they advanced. They paused momentarily in shock, then separated and went to a crouch, each advancing more cautiously than had the first warrior.

The man on Jethro's right was first within range. The gray-eyed man's arm snaked out and iron-like fingers clamped on a brown wrist, jerking at once. As the warrior tumbled off balance, a hand edge slammed against the bridge of his hawk-like nose and the warrior tumbled to his knees. It was so skillfully and quickly done that Jethro was set for the warrior on his left when that man made his move.

As that third warrior lunged, a soft boot came from nowhere and smashed him full in the face. Then, as the Indian staggered back, Jethro grasped his long hair and jerked him forward and down, while slamming a knee into his jaw, sending the Apache into oblivion.

Jethro wheeled back to the second warrior, who wobbled to his feet. "I am truly sorry, my friend," Jethro growled in Apache just before a measured blow to the man's jaw laid him in a crumpled heap between his two partners.

The quick and violent action had Jethro panting again. He wiped sweat from his eyes with a grimy shirtsleeve. As he did, Victorio chattered a name and instructions and a squat, powerful warrior pitched his rifle to a comrade, whipped out his knife and sprang to the attack. Jethro dodged the first thrust and stumbled over one of the unconscious warriors lying at his feet. The knife wielder was on him in an instant. Still off balance, Jethro knocked the darting knife arm aside once, twice. The second time a dark red stain spread over his lower sleeve.

The warrior paused, then began stalking his prey as Jethro regained his balance and backed against the rock wall. When the warrior thrust again, Jethro was prepared. He neatly kicked the man's pivot knee from beneath him, caught his knife wrist in a vice grip, and kicked his attacker in the crotch. Ignoring the other hand clawing at his face, Jethro threw the man off balance, using both men's full weight to fall upon the knife wrist.

All within the circle heard the snap, but there was only a grunt from the squat warrior. Jethro clambered to his feet, pulling at his shirttail. His eyes widened as the squat warrior picked up the knife with his left hand and crawled to his knees, eyes savagely intent. A measured kick sent the man to temporary oblivion and Jethro tore a strip of shirttail with his teeth. He was wrapping the torn cloth around his bleeding forearm when he heard Victorio snarl three more names.

Three Apache warriors pulled knives and began their advance. He glanced at the squat warrior's knife laying in the sand four feet away and realized he'd never reach it in time. With only one alternative left, he began to back along the rock wall, sidling toward the nearest advancing knife wielder.

"Halt!"

The sharp command broke the eerie scrape of moccasins on sand and the three advancing warriors stopped.

"It is enough," Naiche Tana said.

Victorio spoke swiftly in Apache; so swiftly Jethro could not follow. But Naiche Tana snapped imperiously back, "And I say it is enough!"

The warriors turned sheepishly from Jethro, but Victorio roared, dropped his rifle, snatched his knife, and leaped forward! Naiche Tana fired from his hip and a spurt of sand whipped at Victorio's feet. The maddened sub-chief whipped around to face the Apache war chief and the wildness ebbed from him. At last Victorio said in slow measured words, "I would fight this white man. I will do so hand to hand, knife to knife, gun to gun—however he would wish. It is Victorio's wish to pit his strength and cunning against this white eye, to see who is the better man."

Naiche Tana said, "Gray-eyed-one, do you understand what Victorio asks?"

Jethro gathered his wits about him. He looked at the wild-eyed Apache. No doubt the big Indian was a redoubtable warrior amongst his handful of terrible men. But because of his own professional training as a fighting man, Jethro knew it would be a poor contest, probably resulting in his having to kill the Indian. "I hear, yes, Naiche Tana. But I do not wish to further prove myself. There is always a time to fight and a time for peace. Sometimes it takes more courage not to make war than it does to make war. No, I will fight no more Mescaleros today."

Naiche Tana turned to Victorio. "He has spoken," the chief said. "It is the words of a man with great courage."

Victorio wheeled and stalked away, his long unkempt black hair jerking with every stride. Naiche Tana spoke crisply. Two warriors gathered Jethro's weapons and handed them to him. As he buckled on his Colt, the old chief said, "We will go now." Without another word, Naiche Tana turned and jogged off down-canyon. Jethro followed.

They trotted steadily for an hour. Then Naiche Tana halted in the shade of an overhang and said, "We will rest. Now we are far enough so that Victorio will not see that his chief is tired."

Jethro grinned wearily at the man squatting against the canyon wall. The old warrior was sweating but little and breathing easily, while he himself sprawled upon the sand, gasping for breath.

"The arm?" Naiche Tana said.

"Nothing. Just a scratch."

A glint of humor lay in the war chief's eyes. "It is as the young-one-who-shoots-quick-as-a-striking-snake says, the gray-eyed-one is a great warrior. To see it was an honor for an old chief who has forgotten how to fight."

"But I failed. Victorio will not listen."

"No, the gray-eyed-one did not fail. For Victorio, it is too late. But for others in his band, they saw honor and courage among a people not of their own. It is they who will come to the reservation before it is too late."

CHAPTER TWENTY ONE

Naiche Tana's prophecy proved true. All through the summer and fall of 1880, Mescalero Apaches from Victorio's dwindling band straggled to the reservation. As followers ebbed and his power eroded, the warrior leader turned to even more violence toward the hated whites. Even so, the pulsing power of his savagery withered until the dreaded Mescalero's raids were little more than annoying pinpricks to frontier life.

Finally in October, Mexican and United States troops, working together, trapped Victorio and the remnants of his band in the Tres Castillos Hills, between Chihuahua and El Paso and slaughtered them. About thirty warriors escaped. Victorio and seventy-seven others died.

Billy the Kid's outlaws gradually turned into the scourge of southeastern New Mexico. From Fort Sumner to the Tulerosa, and Carrizozo Springs to Seven Rivers, his gang pilfered cattle with impunity, not even neglecting cattle belonging to Jethro Spring's reservation Mescaleros. So notorious did the young outlaw become that murders occurring hundreds of miles away were attributed to his feared guns. Throughout all southeastern New Mexico, however, friends were ready to give young Bonney timely warning and enemies dared not deny him supplies and concealment. Only in the vicinity of White Oaks, a new and bustling mining town some forty miles northwest of Lincoln, did citizens show any inclination to resist the Kid's activities. At the slightest hint of the presence of Billy's gang, White Oaks' popular Deputy Sheriff, Will Hudgens, easily organized a posse to drive the outlaws from their section.

One such time, early in September, a small band of White Oaks possemen surrounded Billy and his men at the Greathouse Ranch, northwest of White Oaks. The ranch was a suspected way station for cattle stolen along the Las Vegas road.

Bonney at first laughed at the posse, as his gang was merely on the move and had no stolen goods in their possession. But finally it dawned on the Kid that this posse was serious about arresting them. He thought, given enough time, his gang could talk their way out of danger and he struck a plan to exchange hostages while the two sides negotiated. The rancher Greathouse acted as a hostage for Billy's gang, while a popular White Oaks blacksmith, Jimmie Carlyle, became a White Oaks representative inside the ranch house.

Negotiations crept tediously on while, within the house, nerves tightened. Bowdre in particular grew belligerent toward the young blacksmith. "Kill him, dammit. Leastways that'll be one less we gotta fight our way through."

"Charlie, if you was half as kill-crazy as you let on, you'd be dangerous," a harassed Billy the Kid said. "Now shut up and let me think."

"At least tie him up while we make our break."

Carlyle was the excitable type. "You said the hostage

exchange was to work out surrender terms!"

"Both of you shut up," Billy said as he paced the room.

"I'm leaving. This exchange is off." And Carlyle jumped from his chair. Tom O'Folliard and Dave Rudabaugh shoved him back.

"You'd best sit," Bonney ordered. Then, more to himself than anyone else, the young outlaw said, "They ain't got enough people out there to take us in a fight. I think we ought to unlimber and take right at 'em. They'll cut and run, I'm betting."

"What about Greathouse?" O'Folliard asked.

"Luck of the draw," Billy replied.

Suddenly, Carlyle leaped to his feet and dove through a window. Bowdre, standing nearest, shot the blacksmith down as he scrambled to his feet. Billy the Kid, acting decisively as always in times of danger, shouted, "Let's go at 'em, boys!" and led the way out the door, shouting like a wild man.

It was as he predicted. The outnumbered posse of White Oaks shopkeepers fled before the determined outlaw assault. But the next day, White Oaks returned en masse for the recovery of Jimmie Carlyle's body and the burning of the Greathouse Ranch.

As a result, the mining town's hostility became even more implacable. A public subscription raised two thousand dollars as a reward for the "dead or alive" capture of William H. Bonney, wanted for the wanton murder of Jimmie Carlyle.

"We deserve a better relationship, Jack."

"What relationship? I don't think we've seen each other more than four or five times since I left to talk to Billy and the governor a year ago."

"That's what I mean. A woman can starve for a little affection, you know."

Jethro Spring and Susan McSween sat quietly talking in the lobby of agency headquarters. Only minutes before, he'd watched her drive in unescorted and admonished her about traveling alone through dangerous county. She'd "pshawed" at what she called his "groundless fears," and they embraced.

Inside, he served coffee and exchanged pleasantries. She laughed and said, "Always the gallant, aren't you?" Then Susan bluntly admitted her loneliness....

His piercing gray eyes calculated while she stared unwaveringly back. "I know you too well, Susan, not to believe you have something else in mind."

"Several things," she admitted. "But first things first—I'd like you to kiss me again."

"I can afford that."

"That's merely the first payment."

They came together hungrily, overwhelmed by unspent passion. Afterward he said, "I'll see if I can rustle up a bite to eat. You must be starved after your long drive up the Ruidoso."

She giggled. "Actually I left Scurlock's only this morning. I've had a leisurely drive. The Mescalero reservation is a beautiful place, isn't it?"

He nodded, buttoning his shirt. "Beautiful, yes. Productive, no. It will always be difficult for these Indians to produce what they need to live in this high mountain country."

"Isn't it better than most reservations, though?"

"I don't know, Susan. I haven't seen many. But from what I have seen, this is better. What's most important is they're happy here."

She marched ahead of him to the kitchen. "Who would have thought you, of all people, would make an effective Indian agent?"

"I don't know that I am. I only know that I try to do my best."

"You always have been too modest. Dr. Blazer says your Indians are the most passive and happy of all the Apaches.

Now, with Victorio's death, word is that there soon will be no Mescalero hostiles. That is remarkable, you know."

"What's remarkable is U.S. troops and the Mexican Rurales cooperating in actually catching the wily devil."

"You deserve more than your share of the credit for their pacification," she said with finality.

"One thing I try to keep in mind is that I'm not an Indian agent. I'm merely on temporary assignment until a permanent agent is appointed."

"And why shouldn't that be you?"

No doubt several reasons," he said. "A couple I can think of right off are: One, with a new administration certain to come into office next year in Washington, I might not be wanted. Two, I might not want the job."

"Not want the job? That's ridiculous. It's one of the more prestigious ones in the county. And certainly well paid."

He paused in the kitchen door. She smiled her most winning smile and, from a fold of her skirt, pulled out a cigar and handed it to him. Coyly, she said, "There may be another for you if you mind your manners and perform well."

He took it gingerly and she said, "Now sit, sir. What is it you'd like to eat?"

"You're my guest," he protested. "I should cook."

"Oh no. I've had but little chance to apply my culinary skills of late. However, recognizing that it's your kitchen, it appears we probably should collaborate."

Later, as they ate, she asked, "Have you heard of Billy's latest? At White Oaks?"

He nodded. "He digs himself deeper and deeper."

"And you will soon be galloping to the rescue."

He searched her face to see if there was deliberate sarcasm, but saw none. So he shook his head and said, "I don't know if anyone can help Billy now."

"What do you think of Roswell's Mr. Garrett as sheriff?"

"I've met him and like him. He lived up at Sumner then. Strangely enough, Billy introduced us. Apparently they're friends—Sumner is where Billy met him, too. I don't really know if Garrett would work very hard against Billy or his bunch."

"John Chisum just threw his weight behind Garrett—did you know that? John isn't often wrong, either."

"Have you met Garrett?"

"Yes," she said. "Incidentally, he's terribly impressed with you."

"What do you make of him?"

"Perhaps something different than you. I think he's potentially capable and very ambitious. Frankly, I think past friendships will mean very little to the man in the performance of his duty."

"It shouldn't."

She studied him. "Would it to you?"

His eyes dropped to his plate. "I don't guess we'll find out, will we?"

She laughed. "Perhaps sooner than you know, Jack."

Jethro Spring discovered what Susan meant the very next day as he drove her slowly through stately yellow pines, on her way back to the Ruidoso Valley.

"Jack, as you know, new bid specifications are being released soon for next year's reservation supply contracts."

"Yes. I've already forwarded my paperwork for them."

"Perhaps this is a forward question, Jack, but has J.H. Tunstall and Company's supply performance been adequate this past year?"

"Why, yes. I guess so. There were those two incidents of undergrade flour, but you straightened that out as soon as I called it to your attention."

"Then—and my goodness, I know this is forward—would it be proper to ask you to make note of the excellent record of J.H. Tunstall and Company on your bid review sheet?"

Jethro pondered the question. As he did, he turned to check his saddlehorse plodding behind the slow-moving carriage. At last he said, "I suppose that's a request any legitimate supplier might ask. All I'll tell you right now, though, is that I'll consider it."

"That's fine, Jack. Wonderful, in fact. Believe me, that's all I could hope for you to do. Now, could we discuss something more?"

"Certainly, Susan. What is it?"

She flounced her skirt and turned to better face him. "The Mescalero population is quite fluid, isn't it, Jack? I mean with your success with the reservation and Indians and all, and Victorio's defeat and death, aren't there more and more Indians?"

"The reservation population is growing. Yes."

"And no one really knows what it is on a daily basis, right?"

"I keep a fair handle on it."

"Of course you do. But you couldn't give anyone an absolutely exact figure today. Right?"

"Maybe," he said cautiously.

She paused, obviously thinking. "Jack, you mentioned last night that, with a change in Washington, you quite possibly will no longer be the Mescalero agent."

"That's possible, yes."

"Are you concerned about the Mescaleros if you leave?"

"Of course."

"Then I have an idea how you may help them even if you are no longer their agent."

He thought he could see where she was leading, but he played her game. "How?"

She stared steadily at him. "The reservation numbers are so fluid, Jack. How many do you have?"

He glanced at her. "Around fourteen hundred."

"Then report two thousand—eighteen hundred—and J.H. Tunstall and Company will supply to those numbers. You can stockpile at the agency—you have storage and can build more. That way you can add stores—more than you need—for your Mescaleros as a hedge against your possibly not being reappointed agent. It'll be a wonderful tool against their facing future shortages. You'd be prepared in case of legitimate increases and hailed as a genius who prepared for anything the future might bring."

He waited for her to run down. "You want me to pad the agency rolls?"

"No, no, Jack. Not for the reasons you think."

"Godfroy claimed two thousand when he had only, at best, nine hundred."

"I know, Jack. And I know J.J. Dolan only delivered supplies for seven hundred and charged for two thousand. I know Dolan and Godfroy split fortunes between them. But I'm not asking for that. My company will deliver hard supplies based on the head count you present. But, Jack, what I'm suggesting is just prudent business. Stockpile for your wards while you can do it. No one needs know. Goodness, there's no way anyone could find out."

Jethro studied her thoughtfully while her matched team broke into a trot. "Overstocked, huh Susan?"

"What did you say?" she asked, face reddening.

"I said you must be overstocked."

"For the life of me, Jack Winter, I don't know what you're talking about."

He laughed. "I'm talking about the overstuffed mills down there; how everybody's talking about nickel-a-bushel wheat because of the overproduction. I'll bet you went out and bought a bunch speculating on the price going up, didn't you? Now, you want to unload a few tons of it to the Mescaleros for last year's prices. Tell you what I'll do, Susan. I'll bet a double eagle against a hatpin I'm right. What do you say?"

Later, after he'd left Susan McSween near civilization and was jogging back to the agency on the sorrel mare, he wondered whether she'd visited him for business or pleasure.

———◦·•·◦———

The flickering firelight barely reached the man, reflecting from his glasses. He leaned back against a tree, picking his teeth with a sharpened twig, his mind miles away. Then something caught his attention and he peered into the darkness. Suddenly Dave Rudabaugh dropped his tin plate and leaped to his feet.

Jethro Spring chuckled and stepped into the firelight.

Billy Bonney swore a string of oaths and put his gun away. "That was the stupidest goddamn trick I ever seen you pull, you dumb bastard. You trying to get yourself killed?"

"Billy, Billy," Jethro said, "when you going to learn? How many times does that make when I've come into your camp unannounced? Suppose I'm wearing a star?"

"Then it'd have a nice, neat hole in it."

Jethro picked up one of the cups the men had dropped and poured coffee. He set the blackened pot back on the coals, glancing at Tom O'Folliard and Charlie Bowdre as he did. Turning back to Bonney, he said, "Kind of high up the Ruidoso, aren't you boys?"

"What's wrong with that?"

"Close to the reservation boundary."

"So what?"

"There's cattle grazing just across that boundary."

"That so?"

Jethro's and Billy's eyes locked over the gray eyed man's cup rim. "When Malvado brought word you and your boys were up this way, I asked myself, 'What could possibly bring Billy and Tom and Charlie this far from Fort Sumner?'"

"Get to the point, Jack," Billy said.

"Okay. So I said maybe I'd better call on Billy and tell him I've organized a band of Apache police to patrol the reservation."

Bonney's pale blue eyes glinted.

"I've armed them, too. All two dozen are packing brand new Winchesters."

"Why you telling us this?"

Jethro took a sip from his cup. "Some of those Apache police are real hardcases—just back from Victorio's bunch before he got his."

"That's goddamned mean—givin' bastards like that guns!" Dave Rudabaugh exclaimed.

"If you think I can slip around, Billy, you should see Malvado and his outfit. Did I tell you he's captaining the outfit?"

"I'll ask you one more time, Jack. Why are you telling us this?"

"Just personal pride, I guess. I'm proud of 'em. To get 'em started, I got 'em watching the cattle. I guess I just thought ..."

Bonney shifted and waited. Tom O'Folliard blurted, "You thought what?"

"Well, I thought maybe, Tom, you and the boys ever get up around those cattle ... well, I thought maybe you could tell me what you think of my Apache police."

Billy the Kid said, "Could be we'll do that someday. Right now, though, me'n the boys are headed for Sumner."

Jethro pitched the dregs of his coffee on the ground. "Too bad, Billy. I kind of hoped I'd get a chance to talk to you again. You ever see your way free to get away on a pure-ly social call, I'd be obliged if you stopped by the agency."

"I'll do that, Jack. Someday I surely will. And thanks for dropping in, huh?"

CHAPTER TWENTY TWO

Pat Garrett was over-whelmingly elected sheriff of Lincoln County in November to take office the following January. George Kimbrell took his defeat in good grace, appointing Garrett as his deputy for the remaining two months of his term. Garrett took the field immediately. One of his early forays was to the Ruidoso Valley and on to the Mescalero agency headquarters. Jethro Spring awaited him when he rode in.

Garrett leaned from his horse to shake hands with the gray-eyed agent. Jethro took the hand warmly, saying, "Light and sit a spell, Pat. You're welcome to spend the night if you've a mind to."

"It's sure a pleasure to see you again, Jack. I reckon I'd look favorable on a bed and a grubline meal."

"Then turn your pony into the corral and pitch him some hay. Meanwhile, I'll peel a couple more potatoes."

When Garrett came in a few minutes later, Jethro thrust a bottle and glass his way. "Congratulations on your election. Lincoln County got a good man."

"That's rare praise, comin' from you. All I told 'em was I'll try." The sheriff-elect raised his glass and said, "To a friend."

Jethro raised his glass. After returning to the stove, he said over his shoulder, "I assume this is a social call?"

"Yes and no. I'm not much more than a deputy just now. But I'm going around trying to get acquainted."

"I see."

"Yeah, I stopped along the Ruidoso to make a few calls; Scurlock, the Coe boys, Sanders, a few others."

"How is George?" Jethro asked. "I haven't seen him or Frank since they came back from Colorado."

"Looked okay, I guess. I hardly knew 'em before, but they seem law abiding enough."

The statement caught Jethro by surprise and he turned from the stove. "That's a strange thing to say—they always were."

Garrett poured two fingers into his glass and set the bottle on the table. Then he raised his brown eyes to study Jethro. "I'm surprised to catch you in. Word in town is you spend a lot of time in the field."

"You aren't the only one getting 'word', Pat—I heard you were on the way." Jethro returned to the stove and slapped two thick steaks into a big cast iron skillet. "There's little going on anywhere on this reservation that I don't know. I made a point to get here when you did."

"Well, that's good luck for me." Garrett tossed off his whiskey and set the glass on the table with a thud. "I plan to get Billy, Jack."

"That's your duty."

"I won't let friendships stand in my way."

"You shouldn't."

"Any friendships."

Jethro turned slowly from the stove, his gray eyes veiled. "What's that supposed to mean?"

Garrett's gaze fell to Jethro's Colt. He hitched himself around in his chair and said, "Nothing. If the boot pinches, don't wear it."

Jethro jerked out a chair, reversed it and sat down facing Garrett, his arms across the back. "Maybe it is that I don't know you well enough, Pat. But what the hell is the purpose of this visit?"

Garrett met his eyes straightaway. "I didn't rightly mean to rush into this, Jack. But like I said, I aim to get Billy. I know he's got friends up the Ruidoso and I'm droppin' by sociable like to tell 'em when I get to be sheriff, I won't tolerate 'em giving Billy any kind of help."

"So this is really some kind of warning, isn't it?"

"Well, I'd rather call it fatherly advice."

Jethro pushed from his seat to turn meat and potatoes. But he was back in a minute. "I'm curious," he asked, "how did Doc and the Coe boys take to your fatherly advice?"

"They got a little hot, but they'll get over it."

Jethro set out dishes and tableware, then he thumped pans from the stove to the table. When he'd jerked his chair back around and taken his seat, Garrett said, "Jack, I hope you'll take my advice in the way it's intended. We've had word down below that Billy and his bunch have been seen up this way and some folks even say they get help here on the reservation."

The deputy held up his hand at Jethro's angry glare and said, "I ain't saying it's so. But if there's truth to any of it, I'm advising you to stop, because as sheriff I won't tolerate it."

Jethro started to eat, staring coldly at Garrett. When the men finished, he said, "Pat, a diplomat you're not."

"I'd rather be a good sheriff."

"You don't have any idea what you've done, have you?"

"I'm not sure what that's supposed to mean."

"You just pissed off half a dozen of the best and toughest men in Lincoln County, including me."

"Aw, you're getting it all wrong ..."

"The hell, you say! You're not even sheriff yet, and already you're riding over the county threatening Billy's friends. Have you got any goddamned idea how many people you'll have to brow-beat just to get around to 'em all?"

"Look, I ..."

"Do you know how close you must have come to getting your lights blowed out when you walked up to Doc Scurlock or George Coe and said to them the same thing you said to me?"

"Jack, listen ..."

"No, dammit, you listen! Scurlock and the Coes and Ab Sanders and me, we're all friends of Billy, you hear? But we don't hide him or supply him and he knows better than to ask. We don't help him—or we haven't, but that all might change now that an addle-brained, filled-with-his-own-importance sheriff threatened us with all kinds of bad things if we don't spill our guts when Billy the Kid and his boys next hit our part of the country."

Garrett knocked his chair over as he leaped to his feet. "I don't have to take that!" His hand hovered near his gunbutt.

Jethro's gray eyes were icy as he brought his hands slowly up from his lap. One of them held a forty-five. As Garrett watched spell-bound, Jethro eared the hammer back. "Sit down, Pat," he said. "I'm not done yet. Don't you know it's not polite to interrupt when a man is talking?"

"You want my gun?" Garrett asked. His voice was stilted and stiff with anger—but with a tinge of fright.

"What for? This is among friends. Right?"

Garrett retrieved the chair he'd knocked over. After he'd taken his seat and carefully placed his hands flat atop the table, Jethro said, "You go ahead and take Billy if you can, Pat. It's your duty. Besides, he's a mixed-up little mad dog who'll likely turn into something worse, given an even chance. But while you're doing it, you leave honest folk alone. That includes Scurlock and Sanders and the Coes.

"Now, that's damn good advice, sheriff, because while you were laying it out up at Fort Sumner, Doc and George and Ab and Frank were down here learning how to be crazy mean in an insane war against crooked and overbearing sheriffs. So did Billy. Billy says you're one tough hombre, and I believe him. But as tough as you are, you're not tough enough to match either wits or guns against a whole pack of those hot-head Ruidoso farmers."

When Jethro paused, Garrett asked, "You through?"

"No. I want to talk a little about Billy. I rode with him, fought with him, drank with him, and talked with him. He's tough and wild and squirrelly mean. But he's a man in which a lot of folks found something to love. He's got a heart of gold and one hell of a lot of friends. And every damned one of them he earned. Besides a heart of pure gold, he's got nerves of iron. He was trapped into a bad start because of the war and he got kicked down the outlaw trail by some damned funny court decisions he figured was all wrong."

"He's lily white?"

"No. I'm not making excuses, Pat. But I am telling you he's not all bad. If possible, he deserves to be taken for trial. If not, he deserves a chance to die like a man."

Garrett glared at the man he knew as Jack Winter. He said, "You know I could swear out a warrant on you for pulling that gun on a peace officer."

Jethro's tight face broke into a grin. "Anybody can swear a warrant on anything, Garrett. But you couldn't serve it."

"You might be surprised, Jack."

"No, you're the one who'd be surprised. This is *federal* land. You'd have to swear a *federal* warrant and get a *federal* officer to serve it. I can imagine a federal marshal out of Santa Fe giving a hell of a lot of sympathy to a filled-with-his-own-importance sheriff who had a gun pointed at him, just after he'd threatened the man holding the gun."

To his credit, Pat Garrett smiled sheepishly. "You're holding the aces, I guess."

Jethro dropped the hammer and slid his Colt back into its holster. "How about some tinned peaches to top off the meal?"

"Sounds fine." As Jethro took a can from a cupboard, Garrett said, "Look, Jack, I'm new to this job."

Jethro cut out the can's top with a knife and set it on the table. "I know that, Pat. And I'm willing to forget anything was said here ... if you are."

"Here's my hand on it."

Garrett's plans to capture William Bonney were undimmed. Reinforced by Panhandle cattlemen's agent Frank Steward and a posse of Texas cowboys, Garrett laid a trap near the old Indian hospital, northeast of Fort Sumner, where Charlie Bowdre's wife lived. Billy the Kid and five of his men blundered into it. Tom O'Folliard died in the first sudden volley, and Tom Pickett was unhorsed and captured. But Billy and three others escaped in a hail of gunfire, heading west on already jaded horses.

During the night of December 20, a seven-man posse under Garrett surrounded a stone house near Stinking Springs where Garrett believed the Kid would take refuge. A horse whinnied close to the hut, lending credence to Garrett's belief. At daylight, Charlie Bowdre slipped from the house to feed his horse and was cut down in a crossfire while three others of the outlaw's horses bolted away. Billy the Kid, as daring as ever, ran weaving from the hut in a mad attempt to pull Bowdre's horse inside the rock building. The horse was, however, killed in the attempt, blocking the doorway as it fell. The stone hut, built during the days when the Llano Estacado belonged to the Commanches, had only rifle slits for windows and the one doorway. The outlaws were effectively trapped.

The battle between the three remaining outlaws and the seven possemen lasted well into the afternoon. The December cold was intense and all ten men suffered from it. Finally, at four p.m., Billy the Kid shouted that they were surrendering.

"You're crazy!" Rudabaugh snarled.

"Nope, realistic," Billy said.

"They'll hang us all!"

"Not today, anyway, there ain't no trees around. Davy, boy, the way things are going here, we ain't got a chance."

"We can run for it tonight."

"Three against seven? When they know we can only leave by one half-blocked door? And with them mounted and us on foot? No thanks, I'll take a chance I can make it out of jail."

Garrett reached Las Vegas with Billy the Kid, Dave Rudabaugh, and Billie Wilson the day after Christmas. He turned them over to Deputy United States Marshal Charles Conklin in Santa Fe, on the evening of December 27. Garrett was now a certified hero.

———•◆•———

Billy Bonney languished in the Santa Fe jail for exactly three months before being taken from Santa Fe to Mesilla to stand trial. But before his departure from Santa Fe, Billy made two bold attempts to regain his freedom. The first was an attempt to dig his way out of the holding cell. The attempt was only discovered and foiled at the last moment.

The second attempt to regain freedom was via a direct appeal to the territorial governor.

Billy the Kid apparently ignored the fact that for two years he'd been engaged in a life of cattle stealing, interspersed with an occasional murder. His letter of March 2 even went so far as to engage in a mild threat to turn over letters to the governor's enemies. Those letters were relative to the governor's complicity in staging the Kid's surrender and testimony in exchange for the governor's pardon.

Governor Wallace's response was to release to the newspapers his own copies of the letters to which the Kid alluded. Bonney got the message: clemency from the territorial governor was a dead issue.

The spring term of the Dona Ana County Court began session April 6, with William H. Bonney standing federal court trials for the killing of Morris J. Bernstein and Andrew L. Roberts on federal reservation land. Inconclusive evidence quickly freed Billy of the Bernstein killing and a move to squash, based on Buckshot Robert's death actually occurring on Dr. Blazer's property—not federal land—was allowed by Judge Warren Bristol.

Bristol ordered Bonney turned over to territorial officials to stand trial for the Lincoln murder of Sheriff William Brady. That trial convened in territorial court, April 8, and lasted two days. William H. Bonney, alias Billy the Kid, was found guilty of murder in the first degree. On April 13, Judge Bristol formally sentenced the Kid to be hanged at Lincoln on May 13, "between nine and three o'clock, in conformity with a New Mexico law that put the execution date thirty days after the sentence."

Billy the Kid's transfer to Lincoln was accomplished April 22. A measure of respect the young outlaw was accorded, and a fear that was evoked, could be discerned by a glance at his guards during the transfer: three—John Kinney, Billy Matthews, and Bob Olinger—were enemies during the Lincoln County War. The *Semi-Weekly* reported:

> ... He was handcuffed and shackled and chained to the back seat of the ambulance. Kinney sat beside him. Olinger on the seat facing him. Matthews facing Kinney, Lockhart driving, and Reade, Woods, and Williams riding along on horseback on each side and behind. The whole party were armed to the teeth, and any one who knows the men of whom it was composed, will admit that a rescue would be a hazardous undertaking.

During Bonney's transfer to Lincoln, Governor Wallace had a caller. "Well, pon my soul, if it isn't Jack Winter.

Young man, you are indeed a sight for sore eyes."

"Good morning, Governor. Thank you for seeing me. You haven't changed a whole hell of a lot yourself."

"We've been hearing good things about you, down at the Mescalero Agency, Jack. You are making a name, so it seems."

"Thank you, sir."

"Well, sit down, for goodness sake. What brings you up to the capitol?"

"Several things, sir." Jethro moved to a chair.

Governor Wallace appraised the young grey-eyed man. He saw that he was better dressed and better groomed than at any time in the governor's memory. Obviously the agent had taken considerable care for this audience—a matter he'd never treated so seriously in any previous one. *He's soliciting,* the governor decided. *It must be an important petition for this man to be condescending.* "I'm sure you can tell me what they are?" the governor said.

"Yes, sir." Jethro laid his hat on the floor and pulled nervously at an ill-fitting broadcloth suit. "Are you aware of the Bureau of Indian Affairs order to cut expenditures on all Indian reservations by ten percent?"

"Yes. I've heard of it. It's causing considerable concern."

"Governor, my Mescalero rolls are continuing to grow."

"So I've heard. I'm sure such growth reflects the remarkable success you've had with pacification and actual Indian relations on your reservation."

"I can't cut expenses, Governor. Mine will be up by a third or more."

Wallace chuckled. "So you're running into the same kind of fiscal problems faced by all administrators sooner or later."

Jethro shook his head. "I hope you won't treat the problem lightly, sir. I can't come close to adequately providing for the Indians presently on my reservation with last year's full budget, let alone on ten percent less."

"Jack," the governor gently replied, "there is always fat

in any operation. The bureau knows that. They also know agents routinely pad reservation rolls in order to provide operational latitude in management...."

Jethro's mind turned to Susan McSween's attempt to get him to do what Wallace had just intimated was common elsewhere.

"...This ten percent thing is merely an attempt for better fiscal control."

"But I haven't padded my rolls, sir."

"No, I suppose you wouldn't. But, boy, that's naive."

Jethro ignored the governor's admonition and asked, "Do you also know they're not allowing us per capita budgeting? They've given us a lump budget based on ten percent less than last year's total."

"All right," Governor Wallace said, "how does that relate in hard figures?"

"We wound up last year with fourteen hundred and eighty on the rolls. Right now, we're over sixteen hundred. We probably ran an average of about twelve hundred over all of last year, and that's the per-capita dollars they've allocated me."

"Have you explained this to the bureau?"

"Yes," Jethro said, growing grim. "But they won't listen."

"And what is it you'd like from me?"

"I'm not sure, Governor. I guess I was wondering if you have any connection or influence with this new administration. I was hoping you might be able to help me out by working through channels not open to me."

"I'm just a territorial governor, you know."

"Yes, sir. And I'm just an agent responsible for a reservation full of tough, desperate, and deadly Indians that's smack in the middle of your territory. They're Mescalero Apaches who will soon be going hungry because of some stupid Washington order. I can see another war coming, Governor. Surely something can be done to head it off."

"Very well, Jack. I'll do what I can. Perhaps a letter to the Interior secretary will help. Can you supply me with a written report?"

Jethro nodded and reached into an inner pocket of his broadcloth coat. "I have a copy of my last letter to the bureau, sir. It puts it into solid figures."

Governor Wallace glanced briefly at the letter before laying it aside. "Well, now that's out of the way, perhaps we can discuss more pleasurable things."

"I do have another …"

"You've no doubt heard of Catron's store?"

"You mean that it's gone out of business."

Wallace smiled. "I understand Catron sold the building to the county for a pittance."

"Yes, sir. They've already turned it into a courthouse. Lincoln County needed it."

"Indeed they did. They also needed to shake the influence of Dolan and Catron. I must confess I'm taking considerable pleasure from that, even though neither are behind bars."

The governor looked pensive for a moment, then asked, "Tell me, Jack, Lincoln County seems peaceable enough now, doesn't it? I understand this new sheriff is very active and quite capable."

"Yes, sir. Pat Garrett has the makings, I think. And the general unrest seems to be a thing of the past. Dudley is quiet and working real hard to get along. Now, with Catron's closing, a good share of remembered bitterness is gone."

"And with Billy the Kid captured and his gang destroyed …"

"That's the other thing I want to talk with you about, sir."

The silence was deafening—had a cigar ash dropped, it would've thudded. Governor Wallace drew in a deep breath. "I do not wish to discuss Bonney, the outlaw."

"Then discuss Bonney, the man, Governor. Please!"

"I feel I've spent adequate time dragging my relationship with him through territorial newspapers without having to do so in private conversation with friends."

"Governor," Jethro pleaded, "you don't have to discuss your past relations with Billy with me—I already know all about that. What I want to talk about is the future."

Wallace leaned back in his chair, his face taut. "Believe me, young man, William Bonney has no future as far as I'm concerned."

"Sir, would you consider what I have to say?"

"No. I do not care to discuss it any further."

"Please sir. For old time's sake, for services rendered, for ..."

"No! Absolutely not—and that's final! I gave that young fool every chance and he ... did you know he actually had the impudence to threaten me."

"Threaten you?"

Wallace jerked open a desk drawer and threw a paper across his desk to Jethro. "Read that," he commanded.

Jethro read the letter that Billy had written the governor from his Santa Fe jail cell, threatening to expose their previous correspondence if Wallace did not free him. Jethro handed the letter back with a sinking heart.

"Well?" Wallace asked.

"Billy's guilty, sir. No argument about that. He should be punished. But I remain convinced there are circumstances involved that should be considered."

"I will not discuss it any further."

"Can't you commute his sentence from death to imprisonment?"

"*Mister Winter!*" the governor thundered. "*Will you shut up!*"

"Even life imprisonment would be better than ..."

Wallace leaped to his feet and Jethro did likewise. "Circumstances, sir," Jethro said, swallowing. "They ..."

"*Get out!*"

Jethro fell silent, turning to the door where Governor Wallace's index finger pointed.

⇒ CHAPTER TWENTY THREE ⇐

William Bonney, in a desperate bid for freedom, shot and killed J.W. Bell and Robert Olinger a little after noon, April 28, 1881. Billy coolly waited until Olinger escorted the county's other prisoners from the new Lincoln County Courthouse, across the street to a meal at Wortley's Hotel. Then he faked stomach cramps and asked Bell to escort him to the public courthouse privy behind the building. Once there, Billy found the .45-caliber revolver, concealed earlier by twelve-year-old Jose Aguayo in a stack of old newspapers. As the two men returned to Bonney's jail cell on the top floor of the courthouse, Billy, shuffling ahead in his leg irons, pulled his revolver from beneath his shirt and, at the top of the stairs, faced Bell. Bell made the fatal mistake of running. Billy the Kid shot him twice as he reached the lower landing. Billy hopped wildly with his leg irons to an east window. As he passed through the sheriff's office, he picked up Olinger's shotgun, loaded with double-ought buck. He'd just reached a window overlooking the street when Bob Olinger burst from Wortley's Hotel, sprinting to investigate the shots he'd heard. Bonney called from the upstairs window, "Hello, Bob!" Then he pulled the triggers on both barrels, cutting Olinger down in a swath of lead.

Godfrey Gauss, once cook for John Tunstall when William Bonney was a Tunstall cowboy, was now a courthouse handyman. Gauss was caught in the open during the sudden gunfire and he stopped and threw up his hands as Billy the Kid called his name. Bonney spoke reassuringly to the handyman, asking for some tool that he might use to free himself of the irons. Gauss threw a small prospecting pick through the window. Then he saddled Billy a horse, careful to tie food and a blanket behind the saddle.

Billy the Kid worked for over an hour with the pick, but managed to free only one leg shackle. During the hour, the townspeople of Lincoln—of two differing persuasions—carefully avoided the courthouse. His friends prayed Billy would make good his escape; his enemies prayed the slender youth wouldn't notice them. Finally, the youthful outlaw gave up the attempt to free his second leg and tied the loose shackle to his belt. Billy the Kid mounted his horse with some difficulty and rode from Lincoln.

Meanwhile, Sheriff Pat Garrett went about his tax-collecting duties in White Oaks, forty miles away, oblivious to events in Lincoln.

The *Santa Fe New Mexican*, leading organ of the ring and therefore always anti-McSween and disparaging to Billy the Kid, had this to say:

> The above is a record of as bad a deed as those versed in the annals of crime can recall. It surpasses anything of which the Kid has been guilty so far that his past offenses lose much of their heinousness in comparison with it, and it effectively settles the question whether the Kid is a cowardly cut-throat or a thoroughly reckless and fearless man. Never before has he run any great risk in the perpetration of his bloody deeds. Bob Olinger used to say that he was a

cur and that every man he killed had been murdered in cold blood without the slightest chance of defending himself. The Kid displayed no disposition to correct this until the last act of his when he taught Olinger by bitter experience that his theory was anything but correct.

As spring passed to summer, Jethro Spring grew more desperate as the plight of his Mescalero wards became more severe due to Bureau of Indian Affairs cutbacks. He kept up a barrage of official letters and telegrams detailing the situation in increasingly intemperate language. He tried appealing once again to Governor Wallace. In every instance his efforts brought only silence. Then one day a carriage rolled to a stop before agency headquarters and a pudgy little man wearing a checkered suit and bowler hat stepped down. Jethro went to meet him.

"You must be Winter?" the pudgy man asked, extending a limp hand. "I'm Terrill Phipps. I'm afraid I have news for you, sir."

"Afraid?"

"Yes. Could we go inside and talk. This July sun is too damned hot down in this godforsaken country."

"Come on in, Mr. Phipps."

Once inside, Phipps handed Jethro a sealed letter. Jethro took it with sinking heart.

This is to inform you that permanent appointment has gone to Mr. Terrill A. Phipps, the bearer of this letter, as Mescalero Indian agent, Territory of New Mexico. Upon receipt of this letter, your official duties will cease in capacity of temporary agent. The President of the United States and the Secretary of Interior join me in expressing gratitude for such service as you have rendered in the interim, and wish you success in such endeavors as you should choose in the future.

Most respectfully yours,
Abraham A. Arvid
Assis. Sec. Interior
Bureau of Indian Affairs

Jethro's eyes misted. He looked up from the letter and stretched out a hand. "Congratulations, Mr. Phipps."

"Why thank you, my good man. I'm sorry for you, of course. You seem to be taking it quite well, however."

"Not much choice is there?"

"None at all. May I ask how long it will take for you to tie up your ends here?"

"This letter says I'm done now. I don't see any reason to prolong it."

"You mean now?" the little man asked. "Right now?"

"Well no, not exactly. I'll have to saddle my horse and round up a bedroll. Say a half-hour?"

"Splendid. Yes, there really isn't much use in your staying around, is there?"

Jethro pointed the sorrel mare into the high mountains north of the Rio Tulerosa agency. Naiche Tana found him camped on a shoulder of Sierra Blanca.

"My heart is sad, my friend," the Mescalero war chief said.

"Mine, too, Naiche Tana."

Both men squatted by a small tumbling brook as their horses contentedly munched grass from a nearby meadow. Neither spoke for over an hour, preparing their hearts and minds for the necessary farewells. At last Jethro said, "I waited for you here, Naiche Tana. In this little place, I hoped you would come and we would speak together one last time."

"It is a good place, gray-eyed-one."

Jethro sighed. "Your people face difficult times, my friend."

The Apache chieftain nodded, his black eyes glistening. But he said nothing.

"You must be strong and of good heart. You must always bear in mind that the future of the Mescalero is most important."

Again, Naiche Tana nodded.

"One man. Two men. Ten. That is unimportant. For your people to survive, it will take much courage and perhaps much suffering. It may be this new agent will be a good man. Or it may be he is not. But when he is gone and the one after him is gone, and dozens more after those, there must be Mescaleros left. Those Mescaleros must grow in the white man's ways. They must learn all things, obey the white man's laws, keep the things that are good and ignore the things that are bad."

Naiche Tana stared through and beyond Jethro. "It will be so."

"I must go now," Jethro said, rising. "I have told all that I know."

Naiche Tana came to his feet, also, and gripped Jethro's arms, black deep-set eyes penetrating. "You have said everything anyone could say, my friend. Go with your God."

———◦◦◦———

Susan McSween opened the door at his first knock. "Well, well, if it isn't Mr. Winter. Out riding the grubline again?"

He smiled. "News travels fast."

"Don't just stand there, Jack. You'll let the bugs in."

He glided into the room, closing the door behind. And when she asked if he'd like a drink, he nodded and sprawled tiredly in an upholstered chair.

Susan also poured whiskey for herself, then sipped slowly, studying Jack all the while. "I'm curious," she said. "Did you learn anything?"

"Learn anything? About what?"

She grimaced. "Life. The way the world operates."

He raised his glass and sipped. "I don't follow you, Susan."

"Jack, you don't have a job because you didn't play the game."

"I don't have a job because I refused to stand idly by and watch my Mescaleros starve. Not without fighting for them, anyway."

"Yes indeed. And you are doing them a lot of good now, aren't you?"

"No. But my protests are a matter of record."

"I'm sure that is of enormous consolation to a hungry Apache."

"What's the purpose of this discussion?" he asked.

"You still don't feel you've made any errors, do you Jack?"

"Sure. Lots of them."

"You've alienated a governor and gotten yourself fired by the Indian Bureau and you don't see where you've done the least thing wrong, do you?"

"How do you know about my falling out with Governor Wallace?"

"Jack, I get around. J.H. Tunstall and Company has become an economic force in New Mexico. As its owner, my opinions are often solicited. I also make it my business to have inside knowledge of governmental actions affecting my business. I can assure you that a troublemaking Mescalero agent has been the recent subject of several internal debates in Santa Fe and Washington. This happened before the decision was made to pull the rug from beneath you."

He sipped his whiskey while digesting her words. "I tried to do my best," he finally said.

"And your best wasn't good enough," she replied. "You were in over your head and unable to learn as you went along."

"Again, what is the purpose of this."

"I'm trying to determine if I should offer you a job, or

send you packing."

He started to laugh, then looked more closely at her. "You're not joking, are you?"

She pulled a straight chair over in front of him and sat down to lean forward earnestly. "Jack, you are incredibly naive. You are so damnably clean, you squeak. Perhaps your biggest problem is you feel others are all as impeccably honest. In your efforts to do what you think is right, you often trample others who are also striving for what they think is right."

"I don't follow you, Susan."

"The Indian Bureau's effort to cut expenses is no doubt an honest effort to control escalating costs."

"And that justifies Indians going hungry?"

"Not at all. And certainly the bureau could have been made to see the light. But your abrasiveness alienated them to the degree they felt they couldn't back down.

"And what of Governor Wallace? Few people in the territory enjoyed the relationship you had with him. Yet what happened? You squandered it by attempting to force a territorial governor to reconsider a decision he'd already agonized over for weeks."

"He had? You mean he'd ..."

"Yes, Jack," she said. "He told me himself he'd already approached the Billy Bonney dilemma from every conceivable angle and concluded he had no other course to follow. But you, like Tennyson's poem, charged 'into the valley of Death', despite all the bloody cannons in the entire world."

"If he'd only told me ..."

"You wouldn't have listened! You had your mind made up going in. You squandered a valuable friendship with the territorial governor because of your obstinacy. And when you really needed his help with your Mescalero budget problem, you didn't have him."

Jethro tossed off the remaining whiskey and she took his glass to refill it. "No, no more for me, Susan."

"Oh yes," she replied. "I'm just warming up. You're

damned well going to hear more." When she handed him the re-filled glass and sat down to again face him, she said, "Then, as your problems mounted—problems brought on largely by your own precipitate actions—your letters and language grew increasingly strident. Despite your fine record, you made more and more enemies of your friends."

"Aren't you forgetting the Mescaleros? They're not pawns in a chess game. Or, they shouldn't be."

"No, you're the one who forgot. Again, you can hardly benefit them when you are no longer their agent."

"It sounds pretty clear the way you say it, but the hard facts are people are going hungry up there right now."

"And whose fault is that, Jack Winter?" she demanded. "I suggested a plan to you six or eight months ago where you could have developed a surplus for just this very situation. But no, you turned it down. Why? Because you are so damnably clean you're not practical."

"It wouldn't have been honest ..."

She tittered. "You take the cake. You really do. Every Indian agent worth his salt routinely stockpiles when he has the chance. That's hardly considered dishonest. The ones who then steal from their stockpiles—like Godfroy—are dishonest.

"Tell me, Jack, if you had it to do over again, would you take my suggestion and buy up grain surpluses."

"Yes," he said immediately. "But that's hindsight."

"It certainly is. And it points up the reason why I could no longer tolerate you as Mescalero agent."

The glass was halfway to his lips. He lowered it slowly.

"Is that a surprise to you, Jack? More of your naivete? Goodness knows, I tried to work with you. Despite the financial loss I took on the deal, I was willing to overlook your failure to take my surplus grain suggestion. But when you opted not to give J.H. Tunstall and Company an endorsement at bid-letting time, that hurt. And recently, when you so feverishly began burning your bridges, it seemed the most auspicious time to strive for an easier agent to work with."

"So you...." His voice trailed off.

"I certainly did. When Governor Wallace asked what I thought of your work as Indian agent, I ..."

He began to laugh. It started slowly, deep within his belly, and tumbled out uncontrolled. He spilled his whiskey, dropped the glass, and turned over a small end table as he twisted and rocked. Tears streamed down his face, and still he cackled.

"Well, I never!"

He picked up his empty glass and handed to her during a momentary pause, then began roaring again, holding his sides, laughing and crying at once, uncontrollably.

"Will you stop it!"

Abruptly, he quit, dabbing at his eyes with a fist and staring at her, eyes twinkling.

"I must say, I never expected that reaction!"

"Neither did I," he replied. "But what the hell? Might as well laugh since it don't help to cry."

"I'm sure everyone is better off now, Jack," she said. "The Indians will have a new agent who will be more effective in their behalf. The Bureau of Indian Affairs will have an agent who won't be so critical of their programs ..."

"And you'll have an agent you can bend to suit your will," he interrupted.

"And I'll have an easier agent to work with," she conceded.

"One thing. Have you thought about me?"

"Oh yes, you. That's what this discussion was all about, wasn't it? If I should hire you again."

"It's strange you'd even think of it," he said, "considering all my weaknesses."

"True. Except that you do have many fine strengths. One of the problems is that most of your strengths are no longer marketable. With the demise of Catron's store and the muzzling of Colonel Dudley, I no longer have powerful enemies. And with Sheriff Garrett's crusade for law and order, it's unlikely the outlaw element will rise to threaten again. At one time, Jack, your strong right arm and your influence among the peasants were needed by J.H. Tunstall and Company. But that is not so any longer. Right now, you appear to be excess baggage."

He pushed to his feet and struck a dramatic pose. "That I should come to such an end!"

She smiled fleetingly. "I suppose you could have some value," she mused, sliding her chair back to its former place. "You still have enormous respect from most of Lincoln County's residents. But in order for you to find a place in my company, you would have to demonstrate a willingness to conform; something you've never before shown."

He smiled down at her. "It's nice to know you'd think about providing a pension for me, Susan."

"Don't be boorish, Jack. Are you willing to conform?"

"You know," he said distantly, "I always thought you were using me. Fact is, in my head I knew you used everyone. But my heart kept telling me otherwise."

Susan McSween poured more whiskey into her own glass. "I don't want a scene, Jack."

"Susan, just answer me this one question, will you?"

"Ask it. Then I'll tell you if I'll answer it."

"What happened to the Fritz estate money?"

She laughed then, her own higher pitch ringing through the house. "Oh you fool!" she cried. "It is so hard for you to believe others aren't as honest as 'Mr. Goody Two-Shoes!' You fool, fool, fool. You want so desperately to believe the best of everyone. And the truth is, few will ever match your integrity."

"You haven't answered my question."

"No, Jack. And I never will."

He picked up his hat. "Goodby, Susan."

"Where are you going?"

"Out."

She moved to stand before the door. "If you leave, "I'll not let you come back."

"And you think that's going to make a damned bit of difference?"

"Jack, I want you. But I want you on my terms."

"Get the hell out of the way, Susan."

"Jack, I warn you!"

He actually chuckled as he shoved her aside.

"It doesn't have to end like this, Jack!" she screamed as he melted into the night.

⇒ CHAPTER TWENTY FOUR ⇐

Word of Jack Winter didn't end as Susan McSween feared when the man strode from her home in the wake of the woman's manipulative revelations. Instead, a week later, Susan heard he'd purchased three wagon loads of cracked corn at Dowlin's Mill, using the last of his salary as Mescalero Agent, ordering the wagons sent with his compliments to Terrill Phipps, the new agent. Then he vanished.

Pat Garrett slipped into Pete Maxwell's bedroom near midnight, July 13, 1881. Garrett had arrived in Fort Sumner after dark to investigate a report Billy the Kid was in the vicinity. Deputies John Poe and T.L. McKinney waited quietly nearby. Garrett had just awakened Maxwell and begun to question him when a barefoot man carrying a butcher knife padded past the two deputies. It was the beginning of a new moon and night was very dark. Billy was on his way to cut a steak from a side of beef Maxwell had hanging from a north-side porch rafter. None of the men identified the other, but after the Kid padded past, a subconscious alarm bell went off and he darted into Maxwell's open bedroom door.

"*Quien es?*" Bonney called to the outside men, supposing them, in the darkness, to be Mexican. "*Quien es?*" he cried again.

Pat Garrett shot Billy the Kid as he stood uncertainly in the open doorway, armed only with a butcher knife and looking the other direction. As Billy fell, Garrett shot again.

————◆·◆————

Jack Winter reined the sorrel mare to a halt in front of a Las Vegas livery and swung tiredly from the saddle. To the wizened old man who hobbled forward, he said, "Pony needs bed and board tonight, old timer. Hay and oats. Double on the oats, okay?"

"Si, senor. It will be done."

A few seconds later, Jack carried his saddlebags and Winchester into the hotel lobby. Just as he reached the registration desk, he heard someone call, "Jack? Jack Winter! Is it you, by God?"

Jethro turned and the first thing he saw was the star. Then he smiled, white teeth flashing. "Adolph Barrier. Say this is swell."

"What brings you to Las Vegas?" the deputy who'd held Alexander McSween in protective custody for several months asked.

"Just riding through," Jethro said. "Heading out."

"Out? You mean you've left Lincoln?"

Jethro nodded and the deputy was diplomat enough to ask no further questions on that subject. What he did ask, however, made Jethro's blood run cold. "You've heard about Billy the Kid, of course?"

"Billy? No. What about him?"

"Garrett got him. Shot him down in Pete Maxwell's bedroom, over in Sumner, a couple of days ago."

Jethro moved to a chair and Barrier followed. "What do you know about it?" Jethro asked.

"Nothing much. Garrett surprised him, I heard. Billy was barefoot and carrying a butcher knife. They say it was to cut some steaks off a fresh-killed carcass hanging on Maxwell's north porch. Garrett got him twice in the dark before Billy even knowed the war was on. Too bad. They say he wasn't wearing a gun. I know you and him was friends. I allus figured Billy could've been worth savin', what I knowed of him."

A tear trickled down Jethro Spring's face. He dabbed at it with a knuckle and murmured, "Me, too."

"Where you heading?" Barrier asked.

The younger man shrugged. "Out of New Mexico. Where, I don't know."

"You look like you should sleep for a week. But for friendship's sake, I don't want any trouble 'tween you and Riley."

"Riley?"

"John Riley." Barrier pointed off the lobby, to batwing doors, where sounds of merriment eminated. "He's in the bar, drunker'n a skunk. Says he's leaving the territory, too."

———•◦•———

"'Lo, John." The gray-eyed man pulled out a chair across from the lanky patron who sprawled at a table, face to forearms. "Came to see if you wanted to socialize."

John Riley lifted his head as if it was a great weight, then guffawed. "Well, I'll be double-damned! 'S the half-breed." The man's head started to sink, then snapped up. "If you followed me ..." his voice trailed off.

"I didn't follow you, John."

"Won't do any good if ... if you did." He focused only with great effort. "Dolan-Riley, tha' great ... great merchandising em ... emporium ... is finished. I am but a last, unlamented remnant. And not at all of any threat to your be ... beloved."

"How about some dinner, John? I've got a double eagle left from the years I spent in Lincoln County. What do you say?"

"Ha, ha. You offer me a bone. You, of all people, offer me a bone!" Riley made to rise, but a hand slipped from the table and he nearly fell.

"A cup of coffee, then?"

"Ahh. That would indeed be a godsend. If ... if I'm to match wits with my destroyer, I ... at least ... need to know when it's coming." He swallowed. "And where from."

Jethro murmured, "It's over, John. It's all over and it's like Buckshot Roberts told me with his dying breath: 'There are no winners in Lincoln County.' And you know what? He was right."

Riley seemed sobered for a moment. "No, indeed," he said at last. "Except for the woman."

Neither man spoke for a good half-hour as John Riley downed several cups of black coffee. At last, Jethro said, "Why'd you do it, John?"

"Do what?"

"Leave the black book and Rynerson's letter so McSween could find it; leave the note about Selman coming for Susan where I would find it?"

Riley focused on the gray-eyed man for the longest time. Then he whispered, "You were not the only one in Lincoln County with a conscience, my friend."

Watch For

Gunnar's Mine

Fourth in the exciting *Valediction For Revenge* series chronicling the life of Jethro Spring, a man born of two cultures who fails to comfortably bridge either. Riding at last from a violent and treacherous New Mexico landscape into an isolated region of southwest Colorado, the fugitive is befriended by a lonely miner with his own circling jackals.

From *Gunnar's Mine*

... probably the most important asset he and Gunnar possessed was his proficiency with a gun. He chuckled. Even Billy the Kid at the top of his game joked about his hesitation to test guns against Jethro, then known as Jack Winter.

At the time, that section of New Mexico had been filled with desperate gunslicks and outlaws as well as equally capable farmers and cowboys trained on Indian raids and rustler bands. There, Jethro Spring had been merely one gunhand among many. Here in this remote corner of Colorado mining country, however, his skills would be sufficiently notable to stand out.

An attack from ambush was another thing. The only way Jethro knew to respond to ambush was to respond to the threat of ambush, before it happened. And that was what he was doing right now....

A freight wagon from Telluride rolled past and Jethro waved at the driver.

It was said a railroad was headed out of Grand Junction,

destined for the San Miguel and Telluride. It was upon the rail line's reaching Placerville that whoever was behind the attempted control of the district would want to begin operations. That means with arrival of the rails they'd want all claims in the area in their hands.

How long did Gunnar have before striking a vein rich enough to hire armed guards and buy the kind of equipment necessary to take out gold? *Let's see,* he thought, *the line would have to come around the northwest end of the Uncompahgre to the Dolores River, then up it to the San Miguel. Telluride needs the line now, so they'll work hard at building it. Still, I hear they have yet to cross the Gunnison, so it's doubtful they'll get here before winter sets in. Maybe a year. At the outside, a year—if I can hold off the dogs until then.*

He threw away the last of his grass stem and rubbed his hands free of dust. A half-hour later, he pushed through the batwing doors of a dingy, low-ceilinged saloon with a high false-front grandiloquently painted, SAN MIGUELL EMPORIUM.

Jethro at first wondered if he'd not blundered into some sort of stage performance and the bartender was a vaudeville actor: coal black hair parted in the middle, black shaggy moustache, chewing on a dead cigar, sleeve garters, a grimy white cloth tied around a beer-barrel belly. The man waddled slowly from the far end of the bar, wiping at imaginary wet spots along the way.

Two cowboys who'd been jovially chatting with the bartender leaned indolently where they were. Three miners and what Jethro took as a townsman played poker at a corner table. He recognized none of them.

The bartender was in front of him now, saying nothing, staring steadily, unblinkingly over Jethro's shoulder. The newcomer said, "Anybody ever tell you you spelled Miguel wrong on your sign."

"Lots of people, once. Nobody ever said it twice." There was still no change of expression, no point to the off-the-shoulder stare.

Jethro grinned. "It's got two 'ells'. One is all it's supposed to have."

It took a full five seconds for the man's dark eyes to ratchet from beyond Jethro's shoulder to lock onto the gray ones across from him. Then it took an additional five seconds for the man to take the cigar from his mouth and ask, "You want something?"

"A beer." Then the newcomer grinned again, and said, "I'd also like to see you change that sign someday."

The bartender lifted a bung starter from beneath the bar and laid it on the polished surface, apparently as a warning. Then he drew a beer and slid it down the bar. At last he held out a hand, face up.

Jethro dropped a silver dollar in it. The bartender laid it on the back bar and turned to shuffle back to the cowboys.

"Change," Jethro said.

The bartender ignored him. Meanwhile the cowboys turned to face the newcomer, staring hard. As if on signal, they each pushed up the brim of his hat with a thumb.

Jethro walked down the bar, carrying the bung starter. The cowboys backed up a step at his approach, but the bartender put his hands below the bar. Jethro said, "I wouldn't. Fact is, if I was you, I'd lay my hands on top, in plain sight."

The card game stopped and a chair scraped. A glance from Jethro kept the players in their seats. Just to make sure, Jethro said, "Don't none of you play in a game where you don't know who holds the aces."

All laid their hands on the table top. Jethro's eyes swung back to the bartender. He handed the man the bung starter and said, you overlooked my change. I'm not overlooking your oversight."

The bartender started to put his hands under the counter again when Jethro snarled, "Left hand only." The lips puckered below the hairbrush moustache and the man bit his cigar in two. Still, the barman struggled with temptation. Then he shrugged, waddled down the counter, picked up Jethro's silver dollar and slid it toward him.

"Price is good," Jethro said, pocketing the dollar. Then he drained the mug, backed to the door and while easing through, said, "I really do think you need to change the spelling on that sign."

Other Books by Roland Cheek

Nonfiction

Chocolate Legs 320 pgs. 5½ x 8½ $19.95 (postpaid)
An investigative journey into the controversial life and death of the best-known bad-news bears in the world. by Roland Cheek

My Best Work is Done at the Office 320 pgs. 5½ x 8½ $19.95 (postpaid)
The perfect bathroom book of humorous light reading and inspiration to demonstrate that we should never take ourselves or our lives too seriously. by Roland Cheek

Dance on the Wild Side 352 pgs. 5½ x 8½ $19.95 (postpaid)
A memoir of two people in love who, against all odds, struggle to live the life they wish. A book for others who work and play and dream together.
by Roland and Jane Cheek

The Phantom Ghost of Harriet Lou 352 pgs. 5½ x 8½ $19.95 (postpaid)
Discovery techniques with insight into the habits and habitats of one of North America's most charismatic creatures; a guide to understanding that God made elk to lead humans into some of His finest places.   by Roland Cheek

Learning To Talk Bear 320 pgs. 5½ x 8½ $19.95 (postpaid)
An important book for anyone wishing to understand what makes bears tick. Humorous high adventure and spine-tingling suspense, seasoned with understanding through a lifetime of walking where bears walk. by Roland Cheek

Montana's Bob Marshall Wilderness 80 pgs. 9 x 12 (coffee table size) $15.95 hardcover, $10.95 softcover (postpaid)
97 full-color photos, over 10,000 words of where-to, how-to text about America's favorite wilderness. by Roland Cheek

Fiction

Echoes of Vengeance 256 pgs. 5½ x 8½ $14.95 (postpaid)
The first in a series of six historical novels tracing the life of Jethro Spring, a young mixed-blood fugitive fleeing for his life from revenge exacted upon his parents' murderer. by Roland Cheek

Bloody Merchants' War 288 pgs. 5½ x 8½ $14.95 (postpaid)
The second in a series of six historical novels tracing the life of Jethro Spring. This one takes place in Lincoln County, New Mexico Territory. It was no place for a young fugitive to be ambushed by events beyond his control. by Roland Cheek

Lincoln County Crucible 288 pgs. 5½ x 8½ $14.95 (postpaid)
Third in the Valediction For Revenge series chronicling the adventures of mixed-race fugitive Jethro Spring. Also set in Lincoln County, New Mexico Territory. by Roland Cheek

Order form in back of book

See order form on reverse side

Order form for Roland Cheek's Books

See list of books on page 278

See list of books on page 278

Telephone orders: 1-800-821-6784. *Visa, MasterCard or Discover only.*

Website orders: www.rolandcheek.com

Postal orders: Skyline Publishing
P.O. Box 1118 • Columbia Falls, MT 59912
Telephone: (406) 892-5560   Fax (406) 892-1922

Please send the following books:
(I understand I may return any Skyline Publishing book for a full refund—no questions asked.)

Title	Qty.	Cost Ea.	Total
_____	_____	$ _____	$ _____
_____	_____	$ _____	$ _____
_____	_____	$ _____	$ _____
		Total Order:	$ _____

We pay cost of shipping and handling inside U.S.

Ship to: Name _____

Address _____

City _____ State _____ Zip _____

Daytime phone number (_____) _____-_____

Payment: ☐ Check or Money Order

Credit card: ☐ Visa ☐ MasterCard ☐ Discover

Card number _____

Name on card _____ Exp. date ___/___

Signature: _____